DEAD RECKONING

Recent Titles by Claire Lorrimer from Severn House

DEAD RECKONING

Claire Lorrimer

This first world edition published 2009
in Great Britain and in the USA by
SEVERN HOUSE PUBLISHERS LTD of
9–15 High Street, Sutton, Surrey, England, SM1 1DF.
Trade paperback edition published
in Great Britain and the USA 2009 by
SEVERN HOUSE PUBLISHERS LTD

British Library Cataloguing in Publication Data

Lorrimer, Claire
   Dead Reckoning
   1. Female friendship – Fiction 2. Fortune-tellers – Fiction
   I. Title
   823.9'14[F]

ISBN-13: 978-0-7278-6774-2   (cased)
ISBN-13: 978-1-8475-1152-2   (trade paper)

For Arty, the future Sherlock Holmes,
with much love and high hopes for the future.

Except where actual historical events and characters are being
described for the storyline of this novel, all situations in this
publication are fictitious and any resemblance to living persons
is purely coincidental.

All Severn House titles are printed on acid-free paper.

Typeset by Palimpsest Book Production Ltd.,
Grangemouth, Stirlingshire, Scotland.
Printed and bound in Great Britain by
MPG Books Ltd., Bodmin, Cornwall.

PROLOGUE

'For Heaven's sake, Althea, get a move on. We're going to be late!'

Not only the words but also the tone of Geoffrey Lewis's voice betrayed his irritation. His reflection in his wife's dressing-table mirror as he stood in the doorway of their bedroom staring at her was exasperated.

'I'm sorry, darling! I'm having trouble with my hair!' Althea said as, for the third time, she pulled out the pins and let the silky coil of hair fall back over her shoulder. Although she was aware they should have left the house ten minutes ago and Geoff was understandably annoyed, it was his critical tone which upset her. There was a time not so many years ago when he wouldn't have dreamt of talking to her in such a manner. In fact, she thought wryly, he would have been the one to be late going out for dinner, as often as not telling her how seductive she looked in her evening get-up and promptly removing it in order to make love to her. From the doorway, she heard his voice.

'You should get it cut. Long hair doesn't suit women of your age!'

Only a few minutes ago, Althea had thought the same thing but hearing it from her husband was hurtful enough to bring sudden tears to her eyes. Geoff was seven years younger than her and when she was divorced from her first husband, Terence, and married Geoff, she had worried lest her girl friends called him her 'toy boy'! The age difference hadn't mattered then but now, almost overnight it seemed, she had reached the first big O – four oh – forty. Her two best friends, Cressida Cruse and Phoebe Denton, had wanted her to have a big celebratory party but Geoff had vetoed the idea. He was going to take her to Paris as a birthday treat and they would celebrate her birthday there, he'd said.

At the time, Althea had been pleased to think that he wanted to keep her all to himself.

There had been too many times these past two years, though, when she had experienced the painful certainty that he was falling out of love with her. She had also started to suspect that there were occasions, when he was on one of his prolonged business visits up north or to Europe or the States, when he was unfaithful to her. His attitude was always quite different when he returned. He would, of course, be armed with presents – her favourite perfume, a designer handbag, jewellery. But he was unable to conceal his veiled criticism. As if, she thought now, he was comparing some young girl with his middle-aged wife. Not that she expected the first years with their fierce sexual passions to continue on a level that dominated their lives. Her marriage to Terence, the father of her son, Daryl, had latterly been more one of companionship and friendship rather than passion, and Geoffrey, a devastatingly attractive twenty-six-year-old George Clooney lookalike, had pursued her relentlessly at a time when she was beginning to feel that life – real life – was passing her by.

Trying yet again to sweep her hair back into a French pleat, Althea avoided looking at her husband as he walked restlessly over to the window. She was not looking forward to tonight's dinner party. Geoff's close friend and golfing partner, Bob Pearson, was a bluff, middle-aged, overweight, loud-voiced stockbroker who handled a large part of Geoff's portfolio. He was openly admiring of Althea, and when his wife wasn't looking was invariably touchy-feely. She felt sorry for Jill, a plain nervous little woman whose one passion was her garden. She was a bad cook and went into a panic whenever her jovial husband invited guests to the house. Her nerves affected Althea, who seemed to spend her time saying: 'Don't worry, Jill, I thought it was delicious!' or: 'I really like my vegetables underdone!' Geoff, busy downing red wine in Bob's study with his chum, was indifferent to Jill's inadequacies and if he did refer to them on the way home it was to remark: 'Thank goodness you cope so well when we entertain. It's one of the reasons I married you – the perfect hostess.'

In the early days she had been pleased with his praise but now she often found herself thinking that Geoff had not been so much complimenting her as stating a truth. He'd married her for being such an effortlessly good hostess, and of course, her eager sexual responses.

Geoff's voice, cold, angry, cut across the room. 'If you don't come now, I'll go without you.'

Biting her lip, Althea put down her hairbrush and said quietly: 'Why don't you do that, Geoff? You can tell them I'm ill, if you want. I haven't the slightest wish to go, as well you know!'

He crossed the room and, standing behind her, put his hands on her shoulders. She looked up and met his reflection in her mirror. The look on his face had changed, softened.

'Come on, Al, you know we're both expected and the wretched Jill will have pushed the boat out for us.' He bent down and she felt the touch of his lips on her neck. She resisted the urge to respond, all too well aware that Geoff was using his usual physical effect on her to get his own way. In as calm a voice as she could manage, she said: 'Why don't you go downstairs and get the car out, darling?' She picked up her scent bottle, and spraying her wrists with J'Adore – a perfume she loved as much as its name – watched Geoff leaving the room. Alone once more, she found herself wondering whether the scent he had chosen for her years ago which had, he'd told her, reflected his feelings, still did so. Even more pertinently, she now questioned herself – did she still adore Geoff?

Pinning her hair into place with a diamanté butterfly clasp, she draped her pale blue pashmina round her bare shoulders. As she made her way downstairs, she knew she did not love the man Geoff had turned out to be.

PART ONE

ONE

'I had a phone call from Phoebe yesterday,' Cressida said as she took the cup of tea her friend Althea Lewis was holding out to her. The two women were sitting at the breakfast bar in Althea's state-of-the-art kitchen which, by unspoken agreement, they had chosen in preference to the large, beautifully furnished drawing room where Althea did most of her entertaining.

The two women, dressed alike in jeans and sun tops, looked surprisingly young for forty-year-olds; Althea fair-haired, blue-eyed and still remarkably attractive despite the mild thickening of her figure; Cressida dark-haired, hazel-eyed and big-boned. Where Althea's complexion was flawless, Cressida had a permanent frown forcing her eyebrows into a V over her aquiline nose.

The two women had been close friends since their boarding-school days, even after their lives had veered sharply in opposite directions. Cressida had been to art college and emerged a promising young artist who soon started to make a name for herself. Cressida Cruse's paintings, mainly of a botanical nature, turned out to be popular in the States, as a result of which she was entirely self-supporting.

She had lived at home in Northumberland, where her parents had converted their attic into a studio for her, but when Althea married the attractive Geoffrey Lewis and went to live with him in his mansion in Hurston Green, it had given Cressida the incentive to leave home, buy her own attractive little cottage in the same Sussex market town and resume their lapsed friendship. She herself had never married. 'Never wanted to!' she had told Althea. 'I need to be free to work when I want, which means I eat and sleep any old time, not when a husband or children need me to attend to them. I suppose it's selfish really. I don't need a man.'

She and Althea had delved deeper into modern women's lives, Althea finding it as difficult to understand Cressida's desire for solitude as Cressida found it difficult to understand her need for love. It wasn't a sexual need, she tried to explain, but a need to love and be loved. Terence Hutchins, her first husband, had been an ardent and devoted boyfriend in her youth, waiting patiently while she went through a series of brief affairs with young men she thought she loved and discovered she didn't. Finally, Terence's devotion had paid off and in her twenties, when she had become accidentally pregnant, and her choices had been having an abortion, being a single mum, or marrying the ever faithful and willing Terence, she had opted for the respectability of marriage.

In those early years she had done her best to settle down. She had tried to feel the proper maternal instinct towards her baby, to enjoy Terence's unimaginative love making, and not least, to accept the life of a farmer's wife. Terence came from the same background as herself, but was totally dedicated to his land and his animals. He would be up at dawn, snatch a quick breakfast and she would not see him again until nightfall, when he would return dirty and exhausted and unwilling to socialize.

It was into that void in Althea's life that Geoffrey Lewis appeared. New owner of the large mansion house Hurston Grange, he was a stunningly good-looking property dealer, with estate-agency businesses in Brighton and nearby Headingborough. A handsome bachelor in his twenties, he was inevitably invited to parties and had a large circle of acquaintances, mainly other well-to-do people such as Bob and Jill Pearson. It was at one of their Christmas drinks parties that Althea had met Geoff. Despite the differences in their ages, their attraction was instant and mutual and when Terence found out and divorced her eight years ago, Geoffrey had married her.

Cressida had come to know them both well and could not understand how her friend could fall in love with someone so entirely self-centred and avaricious as Geoffrey. Making money and his own personal pleasures were all

that seemed to matter to him. She was in no doubt that it
was sex which kept the marriage from floundering. Like
a jealous sibling, he resented Althea's love for her son,
Daryl, and she was unable to hide her distress when
Geoffrey was barely civil to the boy.

'What is Phoebe up to these days?' Althea asked, inter-
rupting Cressida's thoughts. 'We've not met up for ages! I
hope she's OK.'

In their schooldays, the three had been inseparable and
although they had gone their own ways, Phoebe to drama
school and Cressida to art college, they'd tried to meet up
in London at least twice a year. A year or two ago, she,
Geoffrey and Cressida had been down to Brighton to watch
Phoebe, who had a minor role in a revival of J.B. Priestley's
The Linden Tree. They had had supper together afterwards
and Geoff and Phoebe had seemed to get along well, but
when Althea had suggested to Geoff on the way home that
they should invite Phoebe for a weekend when the play's
run came to an end, he had announced that he'd found her
'quite pretty but boring. All she could talk about was the
theatre, acting, the plays she had been in. Besides,' he'd
added somewhat cruelly, 'it's obvious she's only a bit player.
If she'd ever been likely to get to the top, she'd have been
picked for stardom long since.'

At the time, Althea had informed him that she would
continue her friendship with Phoebe regardless of his
opinion of her, but although she had got as far as writing
to her to suggest a visit, Phoebe had written back to say
she was shortly to go up north as she had been offered a
good part in a pantomime; that she would get in touch when
she returned south. She never did. Cressida had tried to
make contact the following summer but this time her letter
was returned, *Unknown at this address*, so there was nothing
more she could do. Now she had suddenly reappeared.

'She's living in a flat in Worthing,' Cressida told Althea.
'She didn't give me her address but said she is going to be
in London on Wednesday next week, and wants either or
both of us to meet her for lunch. I told her I didn't think
you'd be able to make it because I knew you were going

to your Daryl's sports day at school. I said that I would go, and we're meeting at Selfridges.' Her face creased suddenly into a smile. 'Typical Phoebe – said she'd wear an orange beret so I would recognize her, as she had lost a lot of weight.' The smile left Cressida's face as she added, 'She sounded a bit depressed, poor old thing.'

Althea drew a deep sigh. 'Trouble is we are all getting older!' she said with a half laugh. 'Not that that affects you, Cressy. You've made a success of your life. By the sound of it, Geoff was right and Phoebe is still only a bit player and never will become a star. But you are becoming famous whereas I . . . well, with the fifties now in sight, I wonder what the hell I've done with my life.'

'Come off it, Al!' Cressida said, using the school nickname. 'You've got a really charming, clever young son – how old is Daryl now, sixteen? – and a gorgeous home and a madly attractive husband, not to mention enough money to buy, if not sink, a battleship! Not every woman has to have a career, you know. You're a wife and mother, which is more than I am! And a wonderful hostess. The parties you and Geoff give are legendary.'

The frown on Althea's face eased into a smile. 'I know I'm an ungrateful cow!' she said. 'I just hope poor old Phoebe isn't too destitute. Her parents died ages ago, didn't they? And she hasn't any brothers or sisters. At least I've still got Ma and Pa should I need a bolt-hole, albeit way up in Scotland! See if you can find out what Phoebe's circumstances are and maybe I can help. Give me a ring on Thursday, will you, Cressy, and tell me how she is?'

They were interrupted by Althea's son, who came into the room, his school bag slung over one shoulder. Although only sixteen, he was already six foot tall and towered over his mother as he walked across to the bar.

'Anything to eat, Mum? Afternoon, Aunt Cressida!'

'Hi, Daryl!' Cressida returned the boy's smile. 'And for the hundredth time, do please drop the "aunt". It makes me feel even older then I am!'

He was remarkably good-looking, she thought as he reached past her to the plate of biscuits neither she nor

Althea had touched. He had his mother's fair hair, large blue eyes and graceful body. It was not surprising the girls he was meeting in the sixth form of his grammar school fancied him. But according to Althea, he was only interested in one girl, Susie White, the daughter of a retired policeman and his wife who lived in a Victorian house in Hurston Green called the Poplars. A clever child, Susie had won a place at Headingborough Grammar sixth form where, like Daryl, she was studying for her A-levels.

'First love in all its intensity,' Althea had described her son's relationship with the sixteen-year-old. She liked the child, who was pretty and intelligent, and aiming for five good A-levels so she could get to veterinary college from which she would qualify and be associated in the same area as Daryl. His aim was to become a farmer like his father.

Cressida had never wanted a husband, let alone one like Geoffrey Lewis who she actively disliked, but she did envy Althea her handsome young son. Not only was he intelligent as well as good-looking, he had a delightful sense of humour. It did not surprise her that Althea doted on him. But for Daryl, Althea had once confided, she didn't think she could have stayed in the marriage, for all its huge financial advantages. But her son and his academic career came first, his happiness paramount. She was well aware that Daryl loved his father and would have lived with him had it been practical. She knew that for her sake he tried to disguise his dislike of his stepfather and he never failed to show his love for her. Now, as she had said to Cressida when Susie surfaced as a serious rival for his time and affection, she would force herself to take second place.

'You're home early, aren't you, darling?' she asked her son as he finished the last of the biscuits and took an apple from the bowl of fruit on the unit behind him.

The smile left his face and he scowled. 'He gave me a lift so I didn't have to wait for the bus!' he explained, refusing as always to call his stepfather by name. 'I wanted to wait for Susie but . . . well, he was in a hurry and insisted I went with him seeing as how he'd gone out of his way to pick me up. I didn't ask him to, and I wish he wouldn't.

He doesn't seem to understand I'd rather come back on the bus with Susie.'

Althea bit her lip. Daryl's dislike of his stepfather's interference in his life was nothing new. Right from the time of her divorce, when he had wanted to live with his father, he had deeply resented Geoffrey 'messing up all their lives', as he put it. But Logan Hill Farm, where his father was still living, was a considerable distance from the nearest bus stop whereas the school pick-up bus went from the bottom of Hurston Grange's front drive. Before her divorce Althea had always driven him to and from the village school, Terence being out somewhere on the farm at that early hour. Even Daryl couldn't fail to see that the obvious thing was for him to live with his mother, at least from Monday to Friday. On Friday nights, he had invariably gone back to the farm to spend the weekend with his father.

Recently, he had stayed overnight at the Grange on a Friday and Saturday so he could take Susie to a party or, on the few occasions her parents permitted, to the local Saturday night disco. But Geoffrey was always picking on him and Althea was well aware that her son still blamed Geoffrey for his parents' separation.

Cressida now eased herself off her stool and having kissed Althea on both cheeks she reached up and tapped Daryl affectionately on his cheek, saying: 'Bye bye, Big Boy! See you again soon.'

Daryl grinned. He had known Cressida all his life and even thought when he was much younger that it would be nice if she'd married his father after the divorce so there would be someone to cook and see to domestic things. That idea had been quashed when he was older and saw how dedicated she was to her painting and how domesticity was the last of her considerations. Nowadays she meant more to him than just his mother's favourite friend – she was his main confidante to whom he could express his acute dislike of his stepfather, and how he even hated him enough at times to wish he'd die! Only once had he expressed his feelings openly to his mother, calling Geoffrey boastful, selfish, vain, opinionated and, not least, rude and hateful towards her when he was in one of his nastier moods. These tantrums were nearly always as a result of his stepfather drinking too heavily, which invariably made him aggressive, argumentative and critical.

Althea tried to make excuses for her husband, explaining that his work as a property dealer was exacting; demanding time, concentration and special negotiating skills. It was what had made him at a very young age extremely successful as well as rich, and, she told Daryl, he should not forget that it was Geoffrey who paid for such things as his school skiing trip to Austria, his sports equipment, his mountain bike – to name but a few advantages he enjoyed. Geoffrey also paid for designer trainers, shirts, sweaters, golf clubs, a squash racket and last Christmas had bought the very expensive Nintendo Wii golf game. He'd even promised to buy Daryl a car once he was old enough to drive and had passed his test.

Daryl could not deny his stepfather's generosity although, as he said to Susie, it was a drop in the ocean of his wealth. He currently had two large housing developments on the go, which he had boasted would bring him in at least two million, as well as the estate agencies and the London branch. Whenever new friends were visiting, he liked to tell them how at the age of seventeen he had started work at Gibbs Estate Agents in the large affluent town of Headingborough as an inexperienced junior. Within three years he had bought out old Alfred Gibbs and added his own name, and within another had opened a second branch in Brighton. By the time he was twenty-four he had bought Hurston Grange, having already obtained planning permission to build a large housing estate in part of the grounds, and selling off four acres of the land beyond the immediate vicinity of the house to a developer, all of which had made him a small fortune.

Althea had not realized when she married Geoffrey how addicted he was to the financial games he played. In the days when she had still been married to Terence he had made himself totally available. No one could have been more attentive, more ardent or more persuasive and, neglected as she had been by her workaholic husband, she had swiftly given in to her ardent lover who, she found out, was seven years younger than herself.

She could understand Daryl's dislike of Geoffrey, who was responsible for the change of the lifestyle he had led at the farm. He and his father had got along very well in a silent, undemonstrative way, and he deeply resented the man who he thought was responsible for his parents' divorce, and with whom he must now share his mother's devotion. He had made no secret of the fact that he was deeply embarrassed when in those early years of the marriage Geoffrey displayed his sexual interest in his mother, standing behind her and pulling her against him, his arms encircling her waist, or crossing the room when he returned from work and, regardless of Daryl's presence, kissing her on her mouth – long, sensuous kisses – with undisguised passion. His mother had known how he felt and must have said something to Geoffrey, who made it clear that it was up to Daryl to make himself scarce when he arrived home.

Nowadays, things were different. His stepfather was often late home as he took on more and more work; and when he did show up, sometimes as late as nine or ten in the evening, he would eat the meal Althea had laid ready for him in the large dining room, and after a whisky or two, which he called his 'nightcap', he would retire to bed, quite often sleeping in his dressing room if he thought his restlessness would disturb her. He seemed to have a great many worries, which was perhaps not surprising as his property empire was growing ever larger. Daryl now saw him only rarely, usually when for some reason his mother could not take or collect him from a weekend with his father, and Geoffrey, albeit reluctantly, did so. He always picked him up and dropped him off at the farm entrance so, Daryl told Susie, he would not have to meet his father – the man whose wife he had stolen.

Susie was on Daryl's mind now. As Cressida was leaving the kitchen he hurried after her.

'Could you give me a lift into town, Aunt Cress?' he asked. 'I said I'd meet up with Susie at McDonald's at six.'

He turned to Althea adding: 'You don't mind, do you, Mum? I finished my homework at school.'

Althea managed to smile as she shook her head. In fact she treasured the time of day when her son returned from school and they could share a few hours' companionship before Geoffrey got back from work; but she had known ever since Daryl had talked about his first serious girlfriend that she would have to take second place. But she had no intention of letting Daryl see how lonely she was these days.

As he raced upstairs to change his clothes, she smiled brightly at Cressida, who was now patiently waiting for Daryl's return, knowing that her friend did not understand her feeling of isolation when she was alone.

Cressida spent most of her life in her studio perfectly happy with her canvases and paints. She didn't need people, friends, a loving, attentive husband such as Geoffrey had once been. Now Althea hardly ever saw him and this at a time when her beloved only child was beginning to leave the nest, and she needed him most. Of course, she did have friends – Cressy, who she adored, and Bob and Jill Pearson, whose house was only a mile away. But Bob commuted to London every day and Jill was a golf fanatic so it was only in extreme weather conditions that she was free to meet up with Althea. Then there was Daisy Roberts, who was her age and who Althea liked very much, but her husband was vicar of St Andrew's and Daisy spent a great deal of time visiting his parishioners and she also worked two days a week in the Oxfam shop in the High Street, sold poppies for Remembrance Day and raffle tickets for the Disabled Children Fund and collected second-hand clothes for European orphanages. Althea was well aware that she, too, could undertake such tasks but Geoffrey had always been adamant that she remained uncommitted. As he said, he never knew when he might want to invite a client for lunch or dinner, or a councillor or other such person with influence, who could be advantageous to whatever scheme he was currently involved in.

Daryl, now wearing his favourite T-shirt and jeans, his

hair damp from the shower and brushed up into spikes, apologized to Cressida for keeping her waiting, hugged his mother and hurried out of the house, a half-eaten banana in his hand.

No wonder Susie loved him, Althea thought as she watched Cressida's car disappear down the drive. Putting the tea things in the dishwasher, she looked round at the kitchen clock above the pine dresser and saw that it was only five thirty. Geoff had left that morning saying he would probably be home early. She should have been pleased and yet, standing alone in the large empty room, she knew suddenly that given the choice, she would rather spend the evening on her own. The fact was, she no longer loved her husband; still less did she want his love making. Where once he had been tender, sensitive, adoring when he wanted sex, now it was as if he resented her. She knew it was silly to think that way; to suspect that her still youthful husband had come to realize he had married an older woman. When she looked at herself in the mirror, naked after a shower, she could see all too clearly the signs of approaching age. Maybe, she thought, Geoff had a mistress! It would account for his late nights home.

But as Althea walked slowly out on to the York-stone terrace, feeling a welcome drop in the hot summer evening air, she pushed the thought away. Even if she found Geoff was unfaithful, she told herself, she would never agree to divorce him, to let him disrupt their family life when Daryl was at such a vulnerable stage. Nor would he ever be allowed to humiliate her by producing a mistress. For a moment, a surge of anger swept through her as she recalled how many promises of undying love he had already broken. As she walked back to the house, the piercingly sweet song of a thrush seemed to compound her fears.

I do believe I'd kill him first! she thought as she turned abruptly with tears stinging her eyes, and went back indoors.

TWO

It was several minutes before Cressida could see Phoebe among the people crowding Selfridges' busy balcony restaurant. She was seated at a small table overlooking the handbag and scarf displays below, and was waving frantically as she caught sight of Cressida.

'I was waiting to order,' she said as Cressida pulled out the empty chair, 'but I dared not leave the table in case somebody nabbed it. I'd no idea it would be so crowded when I suggested we meet here.'

With some difficulty, Cressida found her voice. The fact was she might not have recognized her school friend if Phoebe had not been wearing her orange beret. As she sat down opposite her, she tried not to stare at her thin, drawn face. Phoebe was only a few months younger than her and in the past had inadvertently put Cressida to shame, so perfectly was she always dressed and immaculate her make-up. Today, her fair hair cut short was topped by the dashing bright orange cotton beret. As a would-be star actress, she had once explained, she must always look her very best in case she ran into or was noticed by a director or producer, or even, less probably, a fan!

Cressida's surreptitious glance had not escaped Phoebe's notice. Her beautifully manicured hand reached up to finger the intricately carved pendant hanging from a black ribbon round her neck as she smiled tentatively at Cressida.

'I know I look an old hag, Cressy!' she said with a weak smile. 'I might as well tell you I haven't been awfully well – a heavy wallop of flu last Christmas which I was silly enough to ignore and paid the price with a stint in hospital with pneumonia.'

Cressida leaned forward. 'Why ever didn't you let us know you were ill, Phebes? I bet you were all alone in some dreary digs in the provinces when you got the flu.

You should have phoned me and you could have come down to Hurston Green and let me look after you in the cottage. Althea and I were both wondering what on earth had happened to you. Apart from the occasional postcards or email, and of course a Christmas card – do you realize, it's just on two whole years since you were properly in touch?'

Momentarily they were interrupted by a waitress asking if she could take their order. As the girl hurried away, Cressida saw to her dismay that there were tears in Phoebe's large grey-green, dark-lashed eyes. Quickly, she reached across the table to cover her friend's hand with her own.

'What's wrong, Phebes? Is it work? Last we heard from you, you were over the moon because you had landed that part in that panto.'

She chattered on for a few more minutes, giving Phoebe time to compose herself. When she looked up, Phoebe attempted a half smile.

'I didn't ask you to meet me for lunch in order to moan!' she said, her voice brittle. 'No, it's not work or lack of it. The producer was very good and when I was ill, he offered to keep the part open for me, but . . . well, I wasn't really up to it and I quit this time last year. I went down to Worthing and took a part-time job as a hotel receptionist – two to six, so it isn't very taxing and I only work weekdays!'

It was on the tip of Cressida's tongue to point out that Worthing was less than an hour's drive from Hurston Green – something Phoebe must have known very well.

'Why didn't you get in touch with us?' she asked, immediately wishing she had not as colour flared into Phoebe's pale cheeks. Obviously she had not wanted to disclose the reason or she would have already given it, although there had been a time long ago when the three of them had shared every secret. The arrival of their chosen salads and a bottle of chilled white wine gave Phoebe the chance to change the subject and she asked for news of Althea.

'You know Al!' Cressida replied. 'Living so close I usually see her once or twice a week. She hasn't changed – well a bit, perhaps, but then we're all growing older, aren't we?

She dotes on Daryl, who has grown into the most delightful kid – not that he'd thank me for calling him that. He's six foot tall, still growing, and he's a charmer. Here, I've got a photo in my bag.'

She put down her knife and fork and rummaged in the large black tote bag she always carried with her, and eventually produced a somewhat dog-eared print, which she handed to Phoebe.

'I took that on Daryl's birthday – sixteen, would you believe it. Al adores him but he isn't spoilt. She manages to keep herself busy – Geoff's away such a lot with all his business commitments. She doesn't have a job. But she does do lots of good works, hospital visiting, that sort of thing, and right now it's their annual Hurston Grange Garden Fête, so she's busy organizing that.'

As Phoebe handed back the photograph, she asked: 'So what's it in aid of this year? I know it's very popular but why does Al bother when with all Geoffrey's money they could simply write a cheque for a charity and save all the work?'

Cressida smiled. 'I think Al enjoys the challenge. She tries to think of new amusements every year to entice the crowds. This year, the proceeds are going to breast-cancer research. She's busy getting all their friends to donate objects for the raffles – that sort of thing.'

It was several minutes before Phoebe spoke. Then she said: 'If memory serves me right, they always have the fête on the first Saturday in July, don't they? I'll come and help, shall I? Maybe I can sell raffle tickets or cakes or something.'

Cressida beamed. 'That would be really great, Phoebe. Al will be over the moon when I tell her. She sent masses of love and made me promise not to go back without all your news and your address.'

Phoebe nodded as she allowed Cressida to pour her a second glass of wine.

'Will do!' she said, adding thoughtfully: 'Do you think Althea might like a . . . a medium, I suppose you'd call her – you know, "Let Gipsy Rose tell your fortune"; or should it be "future"?'

Cressida laughed. 'I'm sure she would. Do you know someone?'

Phoebe nodded. 'One of my friends introduced me to a clairvoyant in London. She has private clients but she also makes a bit extra telling fortunes at fêtes and parties. I only went to her once as she's quite expensive, but as Althea's fête this year is in aid of breast-cancer research, I'm sure she wouldn't charge much, if indeed anything, because it's such a good cause.'

Cressida reached across the table and clasped Phoebe's hand. 'What a wonderful idea, Phebes! It sounds great fun and Al will be thrilled when she knows you'll be there, too. As for your fortune-teller, I can pretty well promise you Althea will jump at the offer. What's her name?'

'Madame Clara Tokoly, I think it is, or maybe Kara,' Phoebe replied. 'She's actually half-Hungarian and quite old but still mobile. I don't believe in mediums and seances and that "over-the-other-side" spiel but I have to say this woman was quite remarkable. She told one actor I knew that he was going to another country in a month's time and blow me, he was suddenly offered a fairly important part in a film in Hollywood!'

She smiled at Cressida, her face looking younger as she elaborated: 'Just for fun, I went to see her. Out came those Tarot cards and next thing she foretold I was going to be ill, and it was shortly after that I caught flu!' Phoebe leaned forward, her voice suddenly wistful as she added: 'Remember how we used to tell fortunes when we were at school? That paper with the corners which had all the answers on them depending on how you turned them up – "*He loves me*", "*hates me*", "*adores me*", "*dislikes me*".'

Laughing, Cressida poured the last of the wine into their glasses.

'Yes! Rich, poor, millions, penniless. Colour of eyes – blue, brown, green, hazel. Tall, short, giant, dwarf . . . Oh, Phebes, I'd forgotten all that nonsense. I do remember how legless we got laughing when we worked out that Al was going to marry a dwarf with green eyes and no money and have eight children!'

After a few moments, both women ceased laughing and were silent, each recalling their teenage years; how romantic they'd been; how optimistic for the future; how trusting that life would only dole them out the good and never the bad things.

Suddenly Cressida's thoughts returned to the present and her concern for her friend's health. Phoebe had always been such an attractive girl – and woman. Today she was looking – well, almost haggard. The word shocked Althea when Cressida related it to her later. How was it Phoebe had never married, she wondered now. It was understandable when she was still hoping for stardom. Even at her thirtieth birthday party, which Althea had organized ten years ago in London, she had still believed that stardom awaited her round the corner. Phoebe had once mentioned in a letter a devoted army officer, who had proposed to her, but had added that there was still plenty of time for marriage and kids and she wasn't in love with the poor man anyway! Now time was running out. The devoted captain had married another girl and soon Phoebe would be forty and less likely to conceive a child even if she did find someone she wanted to marry.

Cressida gave a deep sigh as it struck her that she was the only one of the three friends who had achieved her goal; not that she was famous but her pictures were being bought by collectors, some even in America. Painting was what she liked doing above any other activity. As for Althea – well, her first marriage had failed and the second to Geoff was not by all accounts as happy as she had expected eight years on. Yes, she had her charming, loving son; a beautiful house, two cars, a tennis court, sauna, a superb garden and two men to tend it as well as a woman who came every day to do the domestic chores. She had enough money to buy whatever she wanted, holiday where she chose, and although it was not her money but Geoff's, he had always given her carte blanche. But at the end of the day, Cressida did not think Althea was a really happy woman; fulfilled, contented with her lot.

As they finished their salads and the waitress brought

them coffee, she sighed again, wishing that life could be perfect for everyone she loved; even those she merely liked such as Al's ex. Poor old Terence had adored Althea in his undemonstrative way and was now a very lonely man. There was some comfort for him in the ownership of his beloved farm and animals and he also enjoyed a good relationship with Daryl, if not a particularly intimate one, even though he saw him every weekend. But even those visits had been irregular since Susie White had turned up and claimed Daryl's attentions.

Glancing at her watch, Cressida saw that it was nearly three o'clock.

'I'll have to rush, Phoebe,' she said reluctantly. 'My train leaves in twenty minutes. I might just make it in a taxi. What about you?'

Phoebe shook her head. 'I've shopping to do. Tell Althea I'll ring and let her know if Madame Tokoly is free to go to the fête if she wants her.'

There was only time to pay the bill and give Phoebe a quick hug before she made her way hurriedly to the stairs. Phoebe sat down again and ordered herself a second cappuccino as she struggled to withhold the threatening tears. Cressida was such a warm, comfortable person; genuine, surprisingly maternal despite her childlessness. When they were all much younger, she had sometimes thought a little guiltily that she preferred Cressida to Althea, whose self-confidence could be quite daunting. Al always knew what she wanted and went straight out and got it! She'd even 'got' Geoffrey Lewis, all of seven years younger than her and the best-looking and most eligible bachelor all the girls fancied!

Phoebe gave herself a mental shake. No one knew better than she did how useless it was harping on the past, any more than it was for her to look to the future. She had very nearly told Cressida that there wasn't going to be a future for her; longing as she was to be able to admit her fears; her bitterness that her life was to be cut short; to feel Cressy's plump arms round her and shed all the tears locked inside her. Six months at worst, twelve at best, her oncologist had said. Had it been breast cancer then there would have been hope for a cure, but hers was inoperable.

Poor old Cress would have been horrified, Phoebe thought with a wry smile. What right had she to cast an ugly shadow on Cressy's happy life? Or on anyone else's for that matter. Her parents were dead; her mother when she was only five, her father not long after she had left school. As for the man she had once loved and who had professed to love her, the very week she told him she had terminal cancer he wrote to say he was very sorry but he couldn't cope with it.

When she had stopped crying, she had gone out and found a hospice, which would take her when she could no longer cope on her own. Then she had got rid of everything in her flat that she did not immediately need, torn up all but a few letters, photos, newspaper cuttings of her stage and television appearances and written to her theatrical agent saying she would only accept one more part provided she would not have to go on tour. When that was done, she had telephoned Cressida suggesting a reunion in town. They had been so very close at school and for a short while afterwards, before their lives took them in different directions.

Those early days had been the happiest of Phoebe's life and, if only for an hour or two, she had wanted to relive them. Meeting Cressida after so long a lapse of time, hearing her low, husky voice and seeing her smile, she realized just how much she'd missed her; missed Althea, too. Hiding herself away in Worthing had been a stupid and cowardly mistake, which was now too late to rectify. Those years were gone and even if some miracle cure suddenly surfaced, it would be too late to save her. Now it was not only regrets for the omissions of her life that consumed her, but bitterness for the unhappy cards Fate had dealt her.

As she stood up slowly and made her way down the stairs, she recalled Cressida's memories of their childish paper fortune-telling sessions. A tall, thin, grey-eyed millionaire pop star was to have been her lot, with six children, two lots of boy twins and two girls. She would be rich, not just rich but 'enormously' so; she would live in 'a bungalow'! How they had giggled over the likelihood of a hugely rich wife of a pop star living in a bungalow. They'd decided the bungalow must mean a beach house in the Caribbean. And then, finally, she would live to be a hundred.

So much for fortune-telling, she reflected as she went out of the cool air-conditioned store into the shimmering heat of Oxford Street on a June afternoon. A wave of dizziness overcame her and she was obliged to lean her forehead against a shop window until the faintness passed. Perhaps, she thought as she hailed a passing taxi, it had been silly of her to suggest meeting Cressida in London. Brighton would have been nearer for both of them but she had opted for the anonymity of the city, where she would not run into anyone she knew. There were two definites quite clear in her mind, the first being that she could not bear to be pitied; the second was that before the end of the year she would be dead. There was a third certainty now – that she still had one major undertaking to carry out before she died.

THREE

Geoffrey glanced at his watch and saw that it was nearly one o'clock – an hour to go before Simpson opened the big iron gates at the end of the drive and allowed the satisfyingly large number of waiting visitors to come in. Inevitably there would be the bargain-hunters hoping to be first at the bric-a-brac, toy or flower stalls. If this summer was like last year, they could expect at least six hundred visitors, perhaps even a thousand as it was such a perfect day, sunny but with a gentle breeze to cool the hot air.

From his vantage point on the terrace, he could see the whole length and breadth of the two-acre lawn, usually a clean sweep of beautifully mown grass leading down to the river that ran through the estate. But today it was covered by a dozen or more trestle tables, the refreshment tent, roped-off areas for bowling and other such games, and the inevitable Portaloos parked discreetly near the shrubbery.

Althea never misses a trick, he thought with grudging admiration, for whatever she organized, from a dinner party for sixteen, a birthday party for thirty kids, or this annual Garden Party – a name he preferred on the posters and advertisements to 'Fête'. After he bought Hurston Grange from old Laurence Ingram, he had agreed to the summer jamboree to win over the villagers who had had generations of Ingrams in the Grange and resented the new arrival. Laurence Ingram had been a particularly benevolent 'squire', paying good wages, never quibbling about the cost of repairs to his rented cottages, inconspicuously generous to the poor and needy. Geoffrey Lewis was an unknown and unwelcome interloper from the city, sentiments made clear to him when he first dropped into the Crown for a pint and was quietly ostracized. Althea had not seemed in the least surprised when he told her after they were married how not a single soul had spoken to him and the one man for whom he had offered to buy a drink had, albeit politely, refused it. She had set about doing whatever she could to reverse the local antipathy, and the fête was the beginning of their acceptance, Geoffrey thought now.

As she came through the French windows on to the terrace and walked over to him, he thought, far from the first time, that he had not misjudged her when he'd married her. She was a highly intelligent, capable and resourceful woman. This year's garden party was in aid of Breakthrough Breast Cancer, a charity very much in the news nowadays. Visitors could be expected to spend freely because it was a popular cause, and Geoff was well aware that the larger the sum they raised, the more enhanced was their reputation. As usual he'd let the reporter of the *Headingborough Weekly News* know that he would be matching the amount raised, as well as financing the expenses the day always incurred. Geoff was not concerned with the costs, which, being for a charity, he claimed as tax-deductible.

As Althea approached, he noted how elegant she looked in her brown-and-white spotted silk dress, which he had not seen before, and high-heeled sandals. Although she had put on quite a bit of weight since he'd married her, her figure was still good. She took care of herself, travelling up to London to an expensive hairdresser, buying designer clothes so she was always fashionable, playing tennis and going to the gym to keep herself fit. He might no longer be in love with her but he didn't regret marrying her. She had been every bit the asset he'd anticipated when he'd first met her.

'Aren't we lucky – perfect day!' she said now as she joined him. 'And you're looking very snazzy, Geoff!' She did up the button on one of the cuffs of his pink-striped shirt. Turning to stare across at the lawn, she smiled.

'I see Mr and Mrs Turner have picked a good stall for their flowers. Richards said the Misses Diehard have phoned to say they're on their way – they do the bric-a-brac, you remember. Oh, and by the way, I just had a phone call from Cressy: Phoebe rang her to say she's ill and can't come but the fortune-teller woman is coming by train and Cressy said she'll meet her.'

'What on earth are you talking about?' Geoff asked frowning. 'You didn't tell me Phoebe was coming. I thought you'd lost touch with her.'

Althea sighed. 'Yes, we did lose touch, but don't you remember, Geoff, Cressy met up with her in town a couple of weeks ago and Phoebe said she would come to the fête. Are you sure I didn't tell you about it? Maybe I forgot.'

It was on the tip of her tongue to add that she must be getting absent-minded in her old age, but bit back the words, conscious as she was of the fact that she was now forty and Geoff was still only in his thirties and looked even younger. So she merely shrugged off the oversight and continued:

'Maybe I also forgot to tell you about the fortune-telling woman she was bringing with her? I think Phoebe told Cressy the woman is Bavarian or Hungarian or something like that. She does a sort of Gipsy Lee fortune-telling thing at do's like ours. Cressy said she was sure we'd want her and it was arranged for Phoebe to give her a lift in her car. Now Phoebe is ill the woman is coming by train. I don't suppose you remember, Geoff, but Phoebe had pneumonia last winter and Cressy said she looked terribly thin and frail when she met her in town. It's such a shame! I was so looking forward to seeing her. It's been ages—'

'I can't stand here gossiping,' Geoff interrupted, not hiding a look of irritation. 'I'll have to go and arrange for a tent or a gazebo or some such for this woman to sit in. She can't very well tell fortunes on a chair on the lawn!' he added sarcastically. 'What's her name? I'll get someone to put up a sign.'

'Kara, Kara Tokoly!' Althea told him. 'Cressy and I thought something like "HUNGARIAN CLAIRVOYANT MADAME TOKOLY WILL TELL YOUR FUTURE". We thought five pounds would be a reasonable charge.'

'That'll hardly pay her train fare, let alone her fee,' Geoff commented wryly.

Althea smiled. 'That's why Cressy told Phoebe to book

her. She isn't going to charge anything at all because appar-
ently she's happy to help in any way she can when it's for
charity. It seems she's very clever at what she does.'

'Well, good for her!' Geoff said. 'I suppose she could be
quite an asset. I'd better get a chair and a table for her, too.
Will she bring her own crystal ball?'

Althea watched him as he took the steps leading down
to the lawn two at a time. She felt the old familiar physical reaction seeing his lithe, athletic male figure loping
across the grass in the direction of the huge marquee. Would
she ever stop this involuntary reaction, she asked herself.
It was because the sexual attraction he had aroused in her
when they first met had been so violent as well as un-
expected that she had finally left poor Terence. Geoff's love
making had been so evocative that she had been unable to
resist him.

In those early days their secret assignations had been few
and far between because Althea hated the knowledge that
she was cheating boring Terence, who still loved her in his
unimaginative way. But Geoff had no intention of compromis-
ing and had threatened to stop seeing her. 'Leave him and
marry me or I'm off!' he'd told her and had given her no
more than a week to make up her mind. The thought of
how a divorce would affect her young son, separating him
from the father he loved, had given her the strength to tell
Geoff she wouldn't leave Terence, and why she couldn't
do so. He had quickly dismissed her misgivings. They would
be living in Hurston Green so Daryl could spend as much
time as he wanted with either parent. Besides which, Althea
should remember that although Daryl was only eight years
old now, in another ten years or so, he would be leaving
home. What of her life then? It was certainly not his intention to wait that long to marry her.

Readily convinced she was doing the right thing, Althea
had agreed to leave Terence and marry Geoff despite the
disparity in their ages. When Cressida had asked why, she
confessed it was because of their intense sexual compati-
bility, which, she now realized, she had mistaken for love.

'It's as if he has given me back my youth,' she tried to

explain. 'I'm not like you, Cressy, I need a man in my life whereas I know you are perfectly happy without one. I'm in my thirties, remember, and I thought my sex life was pretty well over, Terence being the way he is. Geoff . . . well, he sets me on fire.'

In those early years she'd thought it didn't matter that she had no interest in the things that ruled Geoff's life – finance, business, property – which she soon found out were far more important to him than she was. They were his priorities, so much so that within weeks of their honeymoon he was spending days and nights away from home, involved in some business enterprise taking him to Scotland, Ireland, Wales. Often, he was too tired when he did return to make love to her and chose to sleep in his dressing room.

There is always one who kisses and one who turns the cheek, she thought now as she saw Geoff stop and talk to one of the workmen. Where had she read that very wise French saying, '*Il y a toujours un qui baise et un qui tourne la joue*'? Was it always true that in a partnership one loved more than the other? Certainly Terence loved her more than she had loved him.

With an effort, Althea turned her eyes away from her husband's distant figure and went indoors to telephone Cressy. If Phoebe was ill, she wanted to send flowers, go down to Worthing to see her, make sure she was getting adequate medical attention. Out-of-work actresses were not usually well off and maybe she could help financially. She would go and see her, if not tomorrow when there would be the detritus of the fête to be cleared away, but the day after. If Cressy wasn't in the middle of a painting, she would perhaps accompany her.

As Althea picked up the telephone, she remembered that Cressida was meeting the Hungarian woman at Hurston station and would be bringing Madame Tokoly to the Grange, so there would be time to discuss a visit to Phoebe then.

I've a good mind to have my fortune told! Althea thought wryly, going along to the kitchen where three of the village women were busy putting out scones and fairy cakes on platters for the set teas. Two pounds fifty was today's price. When they had had their first fête, teas had cost a mere fifty pence. Was five pounds too much for people to pay for Madame Tokoly's services? Which was she, a medium who went into trances, or who looked into a crystal ball? Or did she read palms? Hopefully there would be a reasonable demand for a fortune-teller; otherwise it would be quite embarrassing if, after travelling all the way from London, nobody wanted to be told their future!

She voiced her fears to Jill Pearson, who was in the hall with her husband, each of them loaded down with large black dustbin bags full of toys for their stall, but they laughed.

'Be queuing up!' said Bob. 'First thing the old girl does when her *Daily Mail* plops down on the doormat is reach for the horoscope page.' He chuckled as he put an affectionate free arm round his wife's shoulders. 'Don't get a squint at the sports pages till she's read my prediction as well as hers. Wouldn't put it past her if she reads the dogs', too!'

He broke off as Cressida came through the open front door into the hall. Beside her was a wizened, dark-skinned, foreign-looking woman wearing a loose embroidered white cotton shirt over a gathered Indian skirt of peacock blues and greens. A heavy gold chain dangled on her ample bosom and two gold loops hung from her ears, the tips of which showed beneath the brightly coloured scarf covering her grey hair. She was carrying a voluminous wooden-handled cloth bag, quite large enough, Althea thought nervously, to contain a crystal ball!

Cressida introduced Althea and the Pearsons and the woman gave a little bow to each in turn. Her voice when she spoke was heavily accented. Was she a true Romany Gypsy, Althea wondered as she led Cressida and the visitor across the drawing room and out through the French windows on to the terrace. Bob and Jill hurried off to add the additional bags of toys to their already laden toy stall, and Cressida suggested she might take Madame Tokoly down to the marquee for a cup of tea and, hopefully, a sandwich.

It was now one o'clock and with only an hour to go before the festivities began, it seemed a sensible idea for them all to have a snack. Almost as if he smelt food, Daryl came hurrying into the tent and sat down with them.

'Thought I find some food here. Afternoon, Aunt Cress! Mum!'

Althea introduced him to Madame Tokoly, who said: 'You have great likeness to your mama! Mrs Cruse has told me when we drived here that you have sixteen years. You are very much a grown boy!'

She then apologized for her poor English, adding: 'I haf been already one year in your country but I am too old to learn a foreign tongue more better than I do; but it is enough, I think, for my clients to understand.'

She smiled at Daryl adding: 'When we begin the party, I shall tell your fortune. I feel already you have many good things to come to you.'

Daryl's handsome young face took on a look of embarrassment when he realized everyone was staring at him. Then, as she refilled the old woman's teacup, Althea laughed.

'I think you will have a long queue of customers waiting to hear your prophecies if they are all as happy as the ones you promise for my son!' she said.

Madame Tokoly took the cup of tea and nodded to Althea.

'Good news is always welcome, is it not? But sometimes ...' The smile left her face. 'Sometimes I have only bad news, and that is not so good. I try not to permit such feelings come to me but it is not always possible to ignore them. I say bad things to the peoples only if they insist I tell them what I see.'

Cressida laughed. 'Then if you tell my future and it isn't a good one, I shall not insist on hearing it. Goodness me, time's getting on. I'm running the bookstall,' she explained, 'and I'm ashamed to say I have not yet put prices on some of them.'

Daryl turned back to Madame Tokoly. 'When you have finished your sandwich, I'll take you over to your tent. My stepfather has put one up near the sycamore so you won't bake in the sun. I've pinned a big arrow with a sign saying

THIS WAY TO HAVE YOUR HOROSCOPE FORETOLD BY MME TOKOLY. I hope I've spelt your name properly.'

The woman patted his hand, her own fingers heavily beringed.

'It is of no consequence. Persons will come when the early ones tell how it is I know so many true things about them. Then they believe I will also know true things about their futures, too.'

'Cool!' Daryl said admiringly. 'But how do you know "true things" about them in the first place?'

'That is my secret, but I will tell you one little thing . . . you come to see me. I know what is your age. I know also you must be at school. I can be sure you will be sitting for examination quite soon, so I can tell you, you will soon have excellent success with them. So you see, if you make study of it, you can tell many things about people just to see them.'

Daryl was intrigued. 'You mean you aren't a real fortune-teller? You just make it up?'

'Sometimes – but not all the time!' she replied. 'My mother is Hungarian Gypsy and she have gift to see the future like me. Sometimes I see good things but I see most strongly when it is bad. This I do not want, but cannot stop myself.'

Aware that time was passing and the first visitors were already appearing from the direction of the car park, Althea broke into the conversation.

'This is fascinating but we will have to continue later. Daryl will show you to your tent, madame!'

When he returned to the marquee, Daryl asked Cressida: 'Do you believe she really can foretell things, Aunt Cressy? I'm not sure if I'd want to know . . . not if it was some-thing nasty like being in a tsunami or an earthquake or something.'

Cressida shrugged. 'I suppose if she has Gypsy blood, she might be psychic. I wonder if she advertises herself on the Internet. You could look her up, Daryl, and see if she has a website. Maybe she has some recommendations. I think Phoebe told me she usually charges fifty pounds for a half-hour session, but she's not charging your mum anything as she supports Breakthrough Breast Cancer.'

She gathered up the empty plates and tea cups and putting them on a tray, handed it to Daryl.

'Be a dear and take these back to the kitchen,' she said. 'I've got to hurry down to my bookstall. You're doing the coconut shy, aren't you?'

Daryl scowled. 'Much against my will. I wanted to do the go-karts but my stepfather hogged them!'

As they parted company, Cressida reflected how difficult it must be for Althea that her son had always refused to refer to Geoff by name, always 'my stepfather'. For his mother's sake, he was never impolite and Althea had decided from the start that it would be wrong of her to insist upon Daryl's accepting the new man in her life. Quite early on in the marriage she had confessed to Cressida that much as she loved Geoff, Daryl's happiness and well-being came first.

As Cressida hurried towards her stall, she felt an un-expected sense of foreboding. Daryl's continued dislike of his stepfather had reminded her that Althea was far from happy in her marriage and there was nothing she could do to help. She was worried, too, about Phoebe, who was ill again and might have to go back into hospital. At least she could do something about that. It was such a shame she could not have been here today. They could have remi-nisced about their silly fortune-telling games and the fun the three of them had had getting up to mischief at school.

Through the mass of visitors now pouring in a steady stream from the direction of the car park, Cressida could just see Madame Tokoly's tent. Two teenage girls were standing outside, perhaps urging each other to be first to go in. Maybe she herself would see if the woman could tell her whether the painting of Ashdown Forest she had just shipped to America would find a buyer in the New York gallery which had commissioned it! On a more serious note, maybe Althea should see if her future was going to be happier. And Geoff could find out if the huge property deal he was hoping to bring off in Suffolk would be decided in his favour.

The flap of the fortune-teller's tent was now closed and seemingly both young girls had gone inside.

She's best at foreseeing the bad things, Cressida reminded herself with a smile, so maybe she wouldn't pay for a session after all.

FOUR

Despite the fact that the day's takings were far in excess of any amount they had raised in previous years, Geoffrey was in one of his difficult moods. When the last of the visitors, helpers and friends had gone home and Daryl had been given a lift into Hurston Green where he was meeting Susie, he had followed Althea into the drawing room for a much-needed drink. Far from ebullient at the success of the day and, indeed, the enthusiastic account the *Headingborough Weekly News* reporter had promised, he was tight-lipped as he handed Althea a gin and tonic.

'Bloody silly woman!' he swore as he sat down on the sofa beside her, a whisky and soda in his hand. 'Gave me back my fiver and refused to read her stupid cards; said it wasn't a suitable place to relate bad things!'

Althea looked up in surprise. 'You're saying the clairvoyant wouldn't tell your fortune? But—'

'She wouldn't tell me anything!' Geoff interrupted, his forehead creased in a frown. 'I asked her what she meant by "bad things" but she just shook her head and said nothing.'

'How very strange!' Althea commented. Nobody knew better than she did how Geoffrey hated to be thwarted even over the most insignificant of things. Nobody could be more charming and agreeable when he wished, but equally he could be most unpleasant when he didn't get his own way. She hoped she could talk him into a better mood or her evening was not going to be very enjoyable.

'I dare say Madame Tokoly was just trying to sound more psychic than she is. Cressy and I think she probably makes things up so her clients are pleased with her readings. She told Cressy her paintings would be hung in the Royal Academy, which Cressy says is amazing.'

Geoffrey was clearly not listening. He had downed his drink and gone over to the table to pour himself a second one. Althea's heart sank even lower. Geoff in a foul mood was bad enough; drunk, he was painfully rude, jeering at her shortcomings; calling her old and 'past it', saying he couldn't think how he had ever fancied her. Once she had answered back and their rows had intensified, ending with her in tears and Geoff so drunk he passed out. The following morning, he could not remember a thing – or pretended he couldn't.

On one dreadful occasion, Daryl had returned home from a disco unexpectedly early and heard them rowing. He'd flown at Geoff, punching him in the chest as hard as he could; but Geoff, both taller and a good deal stronger, had merely slapped the boy's face and hustled him out of the room. She'd rushed up to her son's bedroom to comfort him, but Daryl had refused to allow her to put her arms round him; tears pouring down his cheeks as he'd shouted, 'I hate him! I hate him! Why did you marry him? If he ever talks to you like that again, I'll kill him. I'll get one of Dad's guns and shoot him.'

Since then, Althea had bitten her tongue and refused to let Geoffrey's jibes get to her. She ignored the humiliation, the bitterness; she had made up her mind to leave him one day – but not until Daryl had flown the nest and was independent of her. There was still a year to go before his A-levels, then a gap year before he went to university. His was to be spent getting work experience in a horticultural college so he'd be knowledgeable enough to help his father modernize the farm. It would be at least a couple of years before she could put an end to a marriage she had grown to hate.

She watched Geoffrey top up his glass and walk with it to the window, where he stared down across the deserted lawn. She could almost feel his restlessness. Surely his encounter with the Gypsy woman could not be the cause?

'What on earth made you decide to have your fortune told?' she asked, her tone casual. 'Doesn't sound like you!'

He swung round to stare angrily at her. 'How do you know ʼhat I want!' he said rudely. 'Anyway, I didn't want my ʼne told, as you put it. The old fool was standing outside ʼt and rattled her cash box at me saying something all being in a good cause and surely I would want to support it. Anyway, I put a fiver in to shut her up and she caught hold of my arm and literally dragged me inside.'

Picturing the scene, Althea had a job to conceal a smile. She could just imagine Geoff looking thoroughly sheepish, disappearing into Madame Tokoly's twilit den!

Sensing rather than seeing the smile on Althea's face, he said truculently: 'It wasn't in the least funny. She got out her stupid Tarot cards, asked me to shuffle them and then spread them out on the table. Next thing, while I'm doing that, she goes into a sort of trance, I suppose you'd call it; moaned a bit and then started jabbering in a foreign language, Hungarian I imagine. Next thing she sits up, looks me straight in the face and says she won't tell me anything.'

Geoff's accusatory voice took on a different tone. It was almost tremulous as he said quietly: 'Told me she only imparts good forecasts on occasions like this. She gives full readings when clients go to her privately. Well, of course I told her I didn't give an effing toss what she told other people but I wanted to know what disaster she thought was awaiting me. Her answer to that was I wouldn't have asked that if I'd known what my future was!'

Despite herself, Althea smiled. 'Honestly, Geoff, you can't be taking that seriously. I mean, you don't really believe she knows something nasty that you don't?'

Geoff's face, which had coloured when his blood pressure had risen, now paled.

'Of course I don't believe that mumbo-jumbo. All the same I can't get my head round *why*. I mean why not simply make something up like she did for Cressida, and send me away happy? It's irritating, that's all.'

But it wasn't all, Althea thought as he followed her into the dining room, where a cold meal had been laid out for them. Clearly it was niggling at him and he was unable simply to write the whole thing off as ridiculous and forget about it. He returned to the subject later when they were back in the drawing room and the TV *News at Ten* had finished.

He switched off the set without asking her whether there was a programme she wanted to watch and went once more to stare out of the bay window. The sun had gone down but there was still enough light to make out the shapes of the tents, the marquee, the posts encircling the go-cart circuit. Only the ugly Portaloo van had disappeared into the deepening shadows of the shrubbery.

Tomorrow morning, the men would be coming to clear everything away and the grass, which had been kept quite long so the number of people walking on it did not damage it, would be mown and in a few days would be more or less back to its usual velvety green. He could see the Gypsy fortune-teller's tent quite clearly under the sycamore, lit by the solar lamps put down to protect people from falling over the guy ropes in the dark. The tent flap had been left open and was moving slightly in the gentle breeze that had been so welcome during the day.

Just for a moment, he thought he saw someone going into the tent but realized at once that it was only the shadow of the flap. He turned abruptly to look at Althea, who was glancing through the daily paper.

'Can't think why you ever hired that woman,' he muttered. 'She's obviously a crank.' He went across to the side table to pour himself a nightcap. When he returned to seat himself beside her, his mood had changed.

'So what's the matter with your chum Phoebe? Come to think of it, she hasn't been here for years. Have you and dear old Cressida ganged up on her?'

Althea tried to conceal her irritation as she replied: 'I told you, she's been ill, Geoffrey. Last winter it was pneumonia and neither Cressy nor I knew it. When we hadn't heard from her other than a card at Christmas, we both assumed she must have joined a repertory company and was on tour or something. In fact she was in hospital and, silly girl, didn't tell us.'

Geoffrey's expression was sardonic as he commented: 'Well, you're all grown up now, for God's sake. The way ʉu and Cressida hobnob is beyond me.' He gave a short ⸱ᵗ of amusement. 'I'm surprised people don't suspect you ⸱ǵ a pair of lesbians!'

᷄ stood up, aware that if she stayed they would have

yet another row. The sort of remark he'd just made had been in order to rile her, as nobody knew better than Geoff that her sexual inclinations were entirely conventional.

'I'm exhausted!' she said. 'Been a busy day. Think I'll go up.' She realized that she did not want him to go up to bed with her. As a rule, even after a row, she would want to make it up; feel that all was well between them; and after their love making, Geoff's mood was always benign. A long time ago, when she had first met and married him, he had been wildly passionate and adoring but Althea had had to accept that in time familiarity had cooled his ardour. Whereas she had continued, until recently, to want him, it still shocked her to realize that she didn't love him; that the truth was she didn't even like him.

He got to his feet saying he would stay and have another brandy.

'Don't wait for me,' he said. 'I'll sleep in my dressing room tonight so I don't disturb you.'

By the time Althea had had her bath and was about to fall into bed, she heard Daryl's taxi pull up outside her bedroom window. She gave a sigh of relief, for she still worried about him. Geoff said she was raving mad with her fears of muggings, drunk drivers, knife-carrying yobs, spiked drinks, drug addicts. 'Next thing you'll tell me your precious son might be kidnapped!' he'd jeered. 'Like that child in Portugal. For pity's sake, Al, he's bloody nearly grown up!'

'And so what!' had been her reply. 'You're grown up and I worry about you if you're late home, car accident, over the limit and—'

'Shagging another woman!' he'd interrupted, grinning. 'Maybe I will one of these days. What would you do if you found out? Kill me?

'Probably! Anyway, quite apart from the fact that you've got me waiting at home for you, with the amount of work you do, I doubt you have much time to be unfaithful to me!'

'Nor any desire to be so!' he'd replied and dropped the subject.

Was he still faithful, Althea wondered now as she pulled a single sheet over her body. The night was airless and despite the fact that she had opened the curtains, which she had closed earlier against the heat of the day, the room was still warm. The night sky visible from her bed was littered with stars and a new moon was rising. She was reminded suddenly of the day's activities, which had been a huge success not least due to her planning. The go-karts had contributed quite a large amount of money, and of course the home-made cake and jams stall was, as always, sold out. Even Madame Tokoly's fortune-telling had contributed a handsome sum – far more than expected. It was kind of the woman not to charge anything for her services. Althea had had almost no time to talk to her as she'd left with Cressida to catch her train back to London before there had been a chance to thank her. She would get her address from Cressy and drop her a line.

On the brink of sleep, Althea's thoughts turned to the Gypsy's strange behaviour with Geoffrey – and his even stranger reaction. Had Madame Tokoly really foreseen some major disaster in his future? Something horrible like a car accident, maybe? He spent a huge amount of time haring up and down the motorways in his Mercedes and every time she heard on the news there had been another pile-up she worried about him, whether he'd been involved, and tried to remember which motorway he would have been on that day.

Were some people really psychic? she wondered. As far as Geoff had related, the woman had gone into a kind of trance, but there'd been no spirit voice, or any such thing! He had paid his fiver, so in a way she'd been obliged to tell him something. Why hadn't she simply made up a nice surprise – a luxury holiday, maybe – or simply warned him not to walk under a ladder?

There was a smile on Althea's face as she drifted into sleep. She had as much belief in lucky black cats as in unlucky ladders. They were silly superstitions, that was all.

Downstairs in the drawing room, a third brandy clasped 'ween his hands, Geoffrey Lewis was telling himself exactly 'me thing. Thousands of people believed their horo- 'n newspapers and magazines but anyone with a grain would know that, as there were only twelve star signs, the forecast of a definite occurrence such as a pending financial disaster for billions of people was statistically totally unrealistic. Not every single Aquarian, for example, was going to be knocked down by a bus! Forecasts were, therefore, nearly always worded ambiguously, applying to anyone.

So why was he feeling so . . . so what? Uncomfortable? Concerned? Uneasy? And all because the silly Gypsy woman had refused to tell his future because, according to her, some hidden horror was hovering over his head. He had not a single financial worry. On the contrary, all his projects were going extremely well, and only yesterday he'd been able to buy a beautiful Georgian house in Headingborough for a ridiculously low figure because of its old-fashioned and neglected interior. One thing had been certain in his life, that where there was an obvious opportunity to make money, he would never ignore it on a matter of principle. Growing up as he had with parents who were always scraping pennies together, he'd known from boyhood that it was not a way of life for him.

There was no business crisis pending; no personal one. Althea ran his home faultlessly and she wasn't about to give him trouble. As for his health, only a week ago he'd had what he called his yearly MOT and passed with flying colours. Short of tornados, tsunamis or earthquakes, none very likely in the south of England in the beautiful sunny month of July, the worst disaster the Gypsy had implied might befall him was the advent of a tropical downpour during the fête!

The tension left his body. He need not give the Gypsy another thought. He might even call her bluff – if such it was – and find out where she operated, pay the fifty pounds Cressida said the woman charged for a full, private reading, and see what she could come up with. If there was nothing, he'd damn well make her give him his money back and threaten to expose her as a charlatan!

With a shrug, Geoffrey put down his empty glass and yawning, went upstairs to bed.

FIVE

The elderly gentleman seated in the waiting room of his local NHS surgery in Brighton was holding a copy of *Country Life* magazine; but he was not reading it. Laurence Ingram's mind was on the coming interview with his doctor, a pleasant enough, fresh-faced young man but, he feared, too young to understand what was wrong with him. For one thing, he had no symptoms to relate. Sleeplessness and depression did not give one a temperature or a swelling or a broken bone. Granted he had lost a great deal of weight but there were a hundred and one reasons for that.

The hint of a smile crossed the old man's gaunt but aristocratic features. The hair on his head was still quite thick despite its snowy whiteness. His shoulders were only very slightly stooped and only the deeply etched lines on his face portrayed his eighty-one years.

They had been good years, he thought now. He'd married a wonderful woman and they'd been happy together for fifty years despite her multiple sclerosis and their ever-increasing poverty. On the advice of a friend he had taken his pension as a lump sum and invested it, with the bulk of his savings, in the stock market, which at the time was booming. When his investments failed he lost everything. Only the beautiful house he had inherited remained, the last of their treasured possessions. He kept the knowledge from his wife, knowing he could not bear to see Moira's dear face pale with worry, but then the smartly dressed property dealer had, in front of Moira, spelt out his knowledge of their financial situation and offered to buy the Grange.

Even now, the memory of the consequences of that after-was clear enough to fill his eyes with stinging tears; ause a week later, just after their golden wedding ry, a totally unforeseen heart attack robbed him overnight of the woman he had never stopped loving in all the years they had been together. Although Moira had never said so when the would-be buyer had left after his curt refusal to sell, he'd always known that it was the shock of hearing she could lose her home that had killed her.

After that, he'd stopped caring about life; let day-to-day affairs slip by, leaving bills unpaid and the house to become ever more dilapidated. It was then, six months later, that the prospective buyer, Geoffrey Lewis, had returned. He seemed to have got hold of every detail of Ingram's debts and made it painfully clear that he knew he was on the point of bankruptcy; that were his house sold by the receivers, he would not only lose it but in all probability see none of the proceeds, which would be used to meet his many debts.

The fellow had then made him an offer for the house, which yet again he refused. If he had to sell, he said, it would not be to the man who had brought an end to Moira's life. Lewis had appeared – or chosen – not to understand why he held him responsible for his wife's death. Nor had he understood the other reason why Ingram would not sell the Grange. Since Moira had died, his only consolation, indeed, his raison d'être, had been Barker. The dog was fourteen years old and almost blind. He had tried to point out to Lewis that Barker would not be able to find his way around if he moved to new surroundings.

As it happened, there was a third reason why he fought against the proposal, though he did not impart it; namely that he could not bear the thought of living in the tiny one-bedroomed bungalow in Hurston village that Lewis suggested would be within his means.

His thoughts were now cut short when the doctor opened his surgery door to allow his present patient to depart, and beckoned Laurence inside. He was a locum who had replaced the regular doctor, who was on two weeks' holiday.

Looking young enough to be Laurence Ingram's grandson, he guided the elderly man into a chair and sat down on the other side of his desk. For a moment he was silent while he looked at his notes.

'Mr Ingram, isn't it?'

His patient looked down at his hands – thin, gnarled hands, he noted; unused to manual work. An author, teacher, musician? He must look more closely at his back history, the doctor thought.

'My wife died, you know!' Laurence said. 'Ten years ago today.' His voice hardened suddenly. 'So it isn't a happy day. But I'm not ill. It's just . . . well, I'm not sleeping too well. Thought you might be able to give me something . . .'

The doctor observed his patient more closely. He had not met him before but something in his tone of voice told him this was a question of depression. A brief examination confirmed his opinion that the old chap was in reasonably good health for his age, but was clearly still grieving for his wife.

'When you do manage to sleep, do you dream – you know, of happier times, perhaps?' he suggested hoping the old fellow would open up.

Ingram's face was suddenly suffused with colour. 'Happier times!' he said in a hard, bitter voice. 'No, I don't dream. I have nightmares. I relive that terrible day my wife died, the day I left our house . . .'

His voice broke and suddenly he was weeping silently as in broken sentences, he told the young doctor how he had come to live alone in the bland meaningless security of his empty flat. When he had quietened and sat dejectedly wiping his eyes with a silk handkerchief, the doctor suggested he might try and get out and about, make a few friends, go to the day centre at the hospital, perhaps. But even as he put forward these ideas, he knew he was wasting his breath. This reserved old gentleman was not going to enjoy bingo or pass the parcel!

He was looking at the physician now with a wry smile.

'It's not that I'm lonely, you know. I'm just angry! I can't get over the man's dishonesty; made out he was doing me a favour getting me out of financial trouble.'

'You mean the buyer welched on the deal?' Despite himself, the doctor was interested although he knew he should not be wasting time when there was a queue of patients waiting to see him.

Laurence Ingram's voice hardened as suddenly he said: 'Oh, he paid up all right – in full. In fact it was a very good price, for what I was selling, and he couldn't wait to get the deal done. He'd made it his business to get to know Phil Jenkins, influential chap on the planning committee. Not that I knew what was going on. A year after Lewis bought my estate, he sold off a ten-acre field bordering the road leading to Hurston Grange. Next thing he had an architect draw up plans for sixteen private houses to be built on it. Somehow, he managed to get planning permission. I'd tried, of course, was turned down flat. He had no neighbours so the only person who might have raised objections was the owner – i.e. himself! Must have made himself a millionaire several times over . . .'

He had suddenly become breathless and the doctor decided it would be better to leave this unhappy story where it was, since relating it was causing his patient further distress.

'Look, Mr Ingram, I'm going to prescribe an anti-depressant. It will cheer you up and should help you to sleep better. If it doesn't do the trick, we'll think about sleeping pills. I expect you know they are addictive so it's best not to start taking them if you don't have to!'

Am I depressed? Laurence asked himself as he left the surgery and walked slowly back along the seafront to the large building which had once been a hotel before conversion into flats above a branch of Lewis & Gibbs. The sea was dead calm, small waves creeping up the beach, which was crowded on this hot July day – mostly mothers with very young children, the older ones not having broken up for the holidays, he supposed. Once he was jostled by two fat girls in bulging sun tops and white shorts as they made their way chattering loudly towards the shops.

By very contrast, the women made him think of Moira, slim, always elegant in pretty coloured summer dresses and her favourite straw hat with the white daisies on it. She should be here with him now, enjoying the sun, the sea, and the holiday atmosphere. He wouldn't have minded so much leaving his family home and coming to live in his present cramped accommodation if Moira had been alive to come with him. No matter how bad things were, and she had suffered quite badly from multiple sclerosis, she never grumbled, never accused him of incompetence, of naivety. Unlike his son, who had written to him from New Zealand, where he lived with his wife and children, admonishing him for not knowing better than to accept Lewis's offer for the house and estate without first consulting at least one if not two other estate agents as to its value.

James's blunt criticism was, he'd told himself, no more than he'd deserved. When his son had flown home for his mother's funeral, he should have confessed how precarious his financial position was; had he done so, James would in all probability have taken matters into his own hands and organized a far better sale. With outline planning permission, he might have trebled the selling price. But he hadn't felt able to admit to his son how financially naive he had been. For one thing, he had not quite reached the point of bankruptcy; for another, his relationship with James was a difficult one.

Moira had always doted on their only child and Laurence had found it hard to forgive him when he had opted to go and live on the other side of the world and all but broken his mother's heart. Granted, James had suggested they join him out there but he'd known very well that she couldn't with MS undertake such a move. They were both too frail to leave home. Laurence had been born at Hurston Grange and the lovely old house and estate had been in the Ingram family for eight generations. He had been the last custodian.

Although he had managed to hang on for another six months, he had finally given up the fight. Lewis had been very persuasive as well as persistent and when poor old Barker had to be put down, the day came when he didn't care about anything very much. Lewis's offer was a quick and easy way out of all his financial problems, and he'd taken it. It was only when he learned about the housing estate that was being built on his former land that he started to appreciate how gullible he had been and how viciously Lewis had taken advantage of him. When news filtered back to him from former Hurston Green neighbours of bulldozers felling the birch coppice to make way for yet another dozen houses, anger had replaced despair and his insomnia had started. One of his former shooting friends told him of a huge crane and piles of building materials on the meadow where the young partridges used to feed on the kale, and a row of garages now stood where Moira's treasured herb garden had been.

So unwelcome was the news of the desecration of his old home that Laurence let the friendships lapse, not telling them when he moved on his doctor's advice to a manageable flat by the sea.

As he turned into the entrance to Templeton House, he drew a deep sigh. He had been silly, he told himself as he pressed the security bell to be let indoors, to expect the young locum to understand that he was not suffering so much from depression as from a growing bitterness and hatred for the man who had knowingly twisted him out of several million pounds. Simpkins, his accountant friend, had agreed that the planning officer might have been 'got at' in some way. These days, there was very little honesty left in business. But Laurence had not had the energy or the heart – or indeed the money – to pursue the matter. He had reached the conclusion that he no longer cared what was done to his land. Since Moira was no longer there to enjoy their home with him, he didn't much care about anything. What he needed, far more than pills for depression, was pills to subdue the bitterness which was eating away inside him. He would lie awake at night knowing that when he closed his eyes he would see Geoffrey Lewis's smug, satisfied face as he had signed away the family home.

Maybe he wouldn't bother to take the pills the locum had prescribed for him. Lewis, that clever swindler, had his whole life in front of him – his wife, stepson, holidays, fun; and all the money he could ever spend and not least, Hurston Grange to live in; whereas *his* future was like a blank sheet of paper. The bitterest pill of all to swallow was the knowledge that if he'd done what he'd known Moira wanted and gone to live in New Zealand as their son had suggested, Moira might still be alive and he could have given her her heart's desire, the means for them to start a new life in New Zealand with James and be enjoying the company of their three grandchildren.

It was several minutes before Laurence could fit his key into the lock of his door. Not only were his hands shaking too much, but his eyes were once more filled with tears, tears not of sadness but of rage.

A few days after the fête, Althea received a letter from Phoebe. She opened it at the breakfast table as Geoffrey was about to leave the room and called out to him.

'Geoff, there's a message for you from Phoebe. Apparently Cressy told her about your session with the fortune-teller – or rather lack of it!' Seeing her husband's expression, she controlled the smile. 'I'll read it to you:

> Tell Geoff he shouldn't ignore Madame Tokoly's warning. However silly it might have seemed, she has a fantastic reputation for accuracy. I can get her telephone number in London for him if he wants a private reading. She charges a lot but people seem to think she's worth it. She foretold my pending pneumonia at a time when I thought it was just flu . . .'

Althea stopped reading as she recognized the angry irritation on Geoffrey's face. His voice was brittle as he rejoined, 'Of all the bloody silly nonsense you women get up to! Just because the wretched female hit one nail on the head accidentally, you're all gullible enough to take her seriously. Besides, despite what Cressida may think, I didn't want to have my bloody fortune told! I gave her five quid for her charity box and then she practically dragged me into the wretched tent. You can write and tell your precious Phoebe I don't want the woman's telephone number and I strongly advise her not to visit her again . . . Throwing good money after bad . . .' he added.

Althea laughed, surprised at Geoffrey's emphasis. 'Calm down! I can't think why you're getting so upset. Sounds like you're scared of what she might tell you. Anyway, Phoebe must have found the telephone number because she has scribbled it down in a PS. Here!'

Geoffrey's face turned a dark red. 'I don't want the bloody thing!' he swore adding rudely: 'Don't you ever listen to a word I say?' Seeing the look on his wife's face, he drew a deep breath and apologized. 'Sorry! Didn't mean to bark at you. Had a bad night . . . in fact, I might go and see Dr Hughes; get him to give me some pills. I haven't been sleeping too well lately.' He turned towards the dining room door and as he opened it, he said: 'Isn't it about time that son of yours was up? It's nearly half-past nine!'

Althea curbed the angry retort that had risen to her lips as always happened when Geoffrey criticized Daryl.

'Not a school day!' she muttered. 'Something to do with the school inspectors' visit. Whatever, the kids have a day off. Daryl will be up soon. He's going into Headingborough with Susie to the leisure-centre swimming pool.'

'Lucky devils!' was Geoff's parting remark. 'I,' he emphasized, 'am off to work.'

'And I,' Althea said to herself, 'am going to do the flowers.' One of her great pleasures was arranging the freshly gathered blooms in vases to place round the house. She would pick some of the beautiful roses and gladioli, and a big bunch of gorgeous-smelling sweet peas. The garden was filled with lovely mature trees, colourful shrubs and swathes of wild flowers as well as cultivated ones. They had two gardeners, one who had been employed for many years by the Ingram family, the other a young man who did the heavier digging.

As she left the dining room, she felt a sudden rush of pity for the elderly man who had been forced to leave such a beautiful home and garden. The new housing estate Geoff had had built was hidden by the big sycamore trees which stretched across the garden at the far end of the lawn. But for the occasional noise of car engines, grass mowers and hedge cutters from the estate, one would not know the houses were there. Cressy had promised to paint a picture of the front lawn and flower beds for her but so far she had been kept too busy with waiting commissions.

As Althea went upstairs to find her sun hat, she decided to ask Cressida if she would go down to Worthing tomorrow to visit Phoebe with her. It was only when she saw Phoebe's letter lying on her dressing table that she realized that her friend must now have been well enough to leave the previous day for Manchester, where unexpectedly she had landed a good part in a play.

So much for my plans to see her, Althea told herself wryly. Remembering Geoff's rude reaction to Cressy's well-intentioned letter, the depression she so often felt these days began to settle over her like a dark cloud. She didn't want to think of the causes for it. She didn't want to face the fact that her marriage was no longer a happy one. Least of all did she want to admit to herself that not only did she not love her husband any more, but that she had come actively to dislike him.

SIX

It happened ten days after the fête: he was on the M25
heading towards the Dartford Tunnel when a silver car
being driven in the opposite direction in the fast lane
almost killed him. More than two hours later, when the
police had finished taking witness statements, and the traffic
had started to move again, Geoffrey reached into the glove
compartment and drew out a packet of cigarettes.

Keeping his eyes well and truly on the car in front of
him – the whole single line of traffic was only moving at
little over five miles an hour – he lit the cigarette and drew
the nicotine deep into his lungs.

'Bloody hell!' he muttered as he exhaled and drew once
again on the cigarette. He'd been incredibly lucky. All
the people in the Renault in front had been killed.
According to the policeman who had taken his statement,
the Vauxhall which had caused the accident had burst a
tyre and the car, which was being driven at over eighty
miles an hour, had simply catapulted over the central
reservation and hit the oncoming Renault head on. Both
cars' occupants had died instantly. When Geoffrey, who
had been behind the Renault, had screeched to a halt, he
had ended with his front bumper within an inch of the
pile of mangled metal.

'Lucky you were able to stop in time, sir,' the traffic cop
had commented. 'If you'd been driving a bit faster . . .'

The next hour had been horrific. Ambulances had come
screaming down the hard shoulder and a fire engine had
arrived, its occupants doing what they could to extract the
crushed bodies. He'd felt sick and thought he might vomit
but the policeman had told him and the drivers behind him
to remain in their vehicles. Like a prisoner in a horror
movie, he'd had to sit and watch what was left of the corpses
being removed. By that time the firemen had sprayed foam

in huge quantities over the wreckage, some of which covered the bonnet of his Mercedes.

His thoughts went back to the moment when he had come up behind the Renault. The driver had put on his left indicator and he'd presumed the man was going to come off the motorway as he had swung across to his left. But a minute later he had swung right again, narrowly missing a lorry in the centre lane, and pulled out in front of him.

Filled with justified anger at this appalling bit of driving, Geoffrey had put his foot down and accelerated. His intention was to pass the Renault and, with a shake of his fist and a blast on his horn, show his disgust. At the last minute, he drew back. He already had six points on his licence for speeding and there were too many police cars around for his liking. This was not the time to take a chance. Now, recalling all too vividly the mangled remains of the Renault, he realized that had he and not the Renault been the car in front, it would have been his car the Vauxhall struck when it vaulted the crash barrier.

As he drove carefully into the semi-darkness of the Dartford Tunnel, a horrible thought shot through his mind. Was this near-death accident what the Gypsy woman had seen in the cards? Was there anything real behind all that mumbo-jumbo? Not only Althea but Cressida, and indeed Phoebe, seemed to think so. But they were gullible females with the usual feminine fantasies. On the other hand, he could remember there had been someone famous who believed in a spirit world and before he died thought to prove it by promising to return to talk to his fellow believers; but never did so!

Coming out into the daylight, Geoff negotiated his way carefully into the fast lane, reckoning that he had still over three hours to reach Manchester by lunch time. He should do the trip easily, unless there was another pile-up, he thought irritably. It was almost impossible to drive anywhere without being held up by something these days – road works usually, although accidents, too, were all too frequent.

His thoughts returned to the one he'd been unfortunate enough to witness. The victims' remains being dragged from the wreckage filled his mind once more and he felt a return of the nausea which had afflicted him earlier. This time, it was not just the memory which troubled him but a return of the realization that it could have been his remains on the way to the morgue. No doubt Althea and the rest of their friends would be telling each other that Madame Tokoly, or whatever she called herself, had foreseen it.

If by some freak of nature the Gypsy did have second sight, she might at least have warned him of the danger, he told himself angrily. All she had done was refuse point blank to impart bad news. If he did as Phoebe had suggested and paid for a proper reading, would she tell him the 'bad news' was past? She would have no way of knowing that he had been at risk in today's accident so her bluff would be called – unless she foretold some other major disaster looming over him. It would cost him fifty quid to find out how genuine she was; not that he minded the money. Fifty pounds was peanuts to him these days.

The miles slipped past him and the density of traffic eased a little now that he had turned off the M25 and joined the M1. His inclination to put the fortune-teller to the test diminished a fraction as he realized that appearing to give any credulity to all that airy-fairy nonsense about second sight was tantamount to an admission that he actually believed in it. He could just imagine the look on Tim Middleton's face were he to admit to such nonsense to that particularly forthright, entrepreneurial friend. Next thing his general manager would be asking him was if he believed in fairies!

No, he would definitely not go and see the clairvoyant, he decided. Coincidences occurred every second of the day and the fact that he had nearly been killed so soon after her prediction of danger was no more than that – a simple coincidence.

Feeling a lot calmer as he put distance between himself and the accident, Geoff relaxed into the driving seat and, resisting the impulse to have another cigarette, turned his thoughts to the meeting ahead. He was hoping to do a deal with a farmer called Alistair McAde, a Scotsman who, with

considerable foresight, had purchased a number of fields
that had been part of an RAF airfield. Most of them had
road frontage and Geoff had seen at once that they were
prime building land; or would be were they not in the green
belt. The man was undoubtedly asking far too much for
what was currently farmland – almost ten times what he
had paid for it. But it was not Geoff's intention to quibble
over such a paltry sum when he knew, as McAde did not,
that it would escalate into hundreds of thousands if planning permission for residential or commercial development
was forthcoming.

Geoff's business instinct told him that as the airfield was
neither a site of Outstanding Natural Beauty, nor ever likely
to be used as an airfield again, it might not be long before
it was released for much needed building land. Wasting no
time, he got his architect to draw up plans for a number of
attractive houses, shops and a small industrial site to spawn
employment as well. He had no doubt it would be a very
profitable investment if he could get the planning officer to
see the advantages – financial advantages in which he would
ensure the man would partake.

McAde had promised two months ago to make up his
mind whether he wished to conclude the sale or withdraw
his interest, and Geoff had used the time very profitably.
For a moderate sum of money, he had hired a private
detective to shadow Fellows, who was known to be the
most influential man on the planning committee. Within
a fortnight, his investigator had come up with some very
interesting information; namely that Fellows had on two
occasions accepted what could only be called bribes from
others such as Geoff who wanted the rules bent a little in
their favour. A three-week holiday at a five-star hotel in
Barbados for Fellows and his family of five had been one
such 'thank you'; another, a year-old Volvo family estate
worth over twenty thousand pounds. To pull off the deal,
Geoff told himself jubilantly, it would be worth an even
bigger backhander; and if Fellows wouldn't play, he had
enough on him to force his hand.

His thoughts raced ahead as he drove towards the White

Stag, where he and McAde were to meet. Apart from the purchase price for the airfield, there would be other expenses. He would have to improve road access, put in mains drainage, electricity, gas and so forth to add to his architect's fees, the investigator's bill and not least, the actual development itself, which he would sell on. At the end of the day, he could count on a significant profit. It was, however, not the foreseeable large addition to his already very sizeable wealth that excited him. It was pitting his wits against what appeared to be difficult odds and coming out on top that gave him the kick he needed. He was impelled always to prove himself better than the other man whether by fair means or foul. There had been one or two transactions, which he himself called 'dicey deals', in the past, but he had never yet been obliged to resort to blackmail. But if that was what he had to do to Fellows, it would be the man's own fault when he could perfectly well accept Geoff's bribe.

Thinking about what lay ahead, Geoff's mood lightened and a brief smile flitted across his handsome face. He was staying the night at his favourite five-star hotel in Manchester, where he had struck up a friendship with the very attractive girl who ran the hotel boutique. She closed the shop at six o'clock after which time, she'd told him, she could do as she pleased. When Geoffrey suggested on their second meeting that she did as *he* pleased, she was more than willing to do so. Twenty-five years old, blonde, dark-eyed with a slim eye-stopping figure, Scarlett reminded him of Althea when he had first met her. The fact that she had a steady boyfriend, who she referred to for some reason as Squid, did not deter her from responding enthusiastically to Geoff's suggestion that he took her out to dinner, after which she spent the night with him in his hotel room.

On the first occasion, Scarlett had been concerned that if the manager saw her fraternizing with one of the guests she might lose her very lucrative boutique in the hotel. That problem had been quickly settled when Geoff opted for a man-to-man talk with the manager on which occasion several banknotes of large denominations changed hands.

It was not Geoff's policy to delve into the backgrounds
of the girls he picked up and slept with. That they were
attractive to look at, more than happy to be treated so
lavishly by him, and were totally indifferent to the fact
that he was a married man, was all that concerned him.
Scarlett, with her model figure and eagerness to please,
was his favourite stopover. 'Bet you have a girl in every
city you go to!' she had teased him. He had not denied
it, merely shrugged and told her that if it was true, she
was by far the most desirable.

It had come as a slight shock on his last visit when she
had told him that Squid was jealous, and had forbidden
her to meet him again. Not, she'd added quickly, that she had
told Squid that she'd had sex with Geoff. She was not going
to take any notice of Squid's complaints but they *would*
have to be more careful. Maybe the hotel was too public a
place for their assignations. Maybe, if Geoff could afford
it, they should rent a small flat somewhere. She could tell
Squid that one of her girlfriends owned it and that would
mean she could get away to visit 'her friend' whenever
Geoff came up north and wanted to see her.

It amused Geoff that she never referred to him wanting
to have sex with her. It was one of the facets of her provin-
cial background that what she called 'the niceties' were
observed. They didn't 'fuck'; they 'made love', according
to her, and a condom was called 'one of those things'. Her
prudishness amused him at the same time as he wondered
whether such behaviour was natural or whether she put on
this pseudo-ingénue persona to attract him. He was not
sufficiently fond of her to care either way and as long as
she was prepared to enjoy their sexual encounters as much
as he did he would go on seeing her. Scarlett, she'd told
him on his last visit, was not her real name; it was Tracey,
which she thought common. Scarlett was after her favourite
actress, Scarlett Johansson.

His meeting with McAde was a singularly congenial one.
The Scot, now in his mid-sixties, had decided to give up
farming altogether and return to his roots in Scotland. There
was only one moment when Geoff had felt a trifle uneasy.

McAde had enquired what possible reason there was for Geoff to want the farmland. Geoff muttered something about a friend wanting to produce organic food and keep free-range chickens as he suspected battery hens and intensive farming would soon be banned. McAde did not question him further and after a brandy they shook hands on the deal and went their separate ways.

Half an hour later, Geoff parked his car, checked into the hotel and after a quick wash, went down to the ground floor where he knew he would find Scarlett in her boutique. She was serving a customer as he approached. For a moment, he stood looking in at her as he had done the first time they'd met. A petite version of Catherine Zeta Jones, she was wearing white leather knee-high boots, a white miniskirt and a black top which barely covered her surprisingly volup-tuous breasts. Her blonde hair, carefully highlighted, framed a small heart-shaped face dominated by dark, heavily shad-owed eyes. Somehow, despite her eye-catching clothes and heavy make-up, she still managed to look not elegant, but classy. Most of all, she looked incredibly sexy. He glanced at his watch and saw that there was still another half-hour to go before she would close the boutique and he could take her up to bed. If she was in one of her contrary moods, she might insist on going to the bar for drinks first.

'What's the hurry, doll?' she'd ask, pouting. 'We've got all night! Let's have a drink first. My tongue's hanging out. See?' And she would stick it out to show him her gold stud, her eyes dancing.

Today Geoffrey was in no mood for provocation and momentarily he felt like telling her he had changed his mind and she should go off home to the sulky boyfriend. He posi-tively hated it when she called him 'doll'! At such moments she would lean right over as he lit her cigarette and leave her shapely breasts so exposed as to send his pulses racing. That would be when he would decide to send her packing after they had made love rather than before.

She looked up suddenly as another customer came in to collect a purchase. The woman followed Scarlett to the desk to pay for the designer handbag, which Scarlett was tucking neatly into one of her very expensive boutique carrier bags. As she did so she shot Geoffrey a cheeky smile, grinning like a naughty child. His mood changing yet again, he smiled back, raised six fingers to indicate the time and pointed in the direction of the bar. Catching his meaning, she nodded vigorously and turned her attention back to the customer. Geoff made his way through one of the several lounges until he came to the Blue Bar, a dark, intimate corner of a larger room. Chrome stools circled the counter above which were soft blue lights. Scarlett complained they did nothing for a girl's complexion but nevertheless the bar was popular, perhaps because of its intimate seclusion.

Ordering a gin and tonic, Geoff ignored the barman's friendly overtures and gave himself up to reflection on the day's events. With the meeting with McAde going so well, he had entirely forgotten the horrific car accident he had witnessed that morning. Presumably, the wreckage had long since been removed, but he did not intend to think about it and his all too near brush with death. He preferred to think about Scarlett and the pleasures to come.

The thought suddenly came into his mind that in a strange way she looked very like Daryl's girl, Susie White. Strange it had never occurred to him before; same colouring, same height, same sexy little figure and large breasts. Of course, Scarlett was nine or ten years older; Susie was only a kid, a schoolgirl, he reminded himself. Not that girls her age didn't look every bit as tarty as the rest of the youthful female population. His mother, a strict Methodist, would have called them Temptresses!

Geoff was smiling at the thought of his long-deceased mother looking down from the heavens to see Scarlett, barely able to walk for the tightness of her minuscule skirt, waving a scarlet-tipped hand to him as she came up to the bar. Having already had one large gin and tonic, he would have much preferred taking Scarlett straight up to bed rather than remaining at the bar so she could have her usual two vodka and Red Bulls, a highly toxic combination which seemed to have little effect upon her. There had been occasions, he recalled, when she had remained quite sober when he had been too drunk to find the bed.

Scarlett climbed on to the bar stool beside him and kissed his cheek. As soon as the barman had placed her drink in front of her she bent her head to sip it at the same time as she twined one leg in a strangely intimate manner round his. His pulse quickened, as she had known it would. Even in the early days when he had first met and fallen for Althea, he'd never felt quite this same sexual urgency. However, he knew better than to speak of it to Scarlett, who often seemed to know exactly what he was feeling and always took advantage of it. Her apparent disinclination for love making could change in a matter of minutes if she thought he was losing interest in her. He had only to admire another woman, talk of his love for his wife, or indicate that he would have to cut short their meeting for her to start making passionate overtures.

While Geoff sat watching her flirting with the barman as she cradled her glass between her small white hands, his jealous irritation changed to amusement. He was too old and experienced not to know that she was deliberately trying to incite him. He also realized that for all she claimed to be totally faithful to her boyfriend with the exception of his irresistible self, she was in fact a call girl. He didn't doubt that his very lavish gifts to her (he never gave her money), his top-of-the-range Mercedes, his expensive cuff-links and Rolex watch were all proof of his wealth, and it was that which attracted her to him.

He wondered suddenly whether there really was a faithful boyfriend in the background. Maybe it would be worthwhile suggesting to her that he bought her a flat in London rather than in Manchester, where he could visit her a great deal more often than he could drive up to the Midlands. A business engagement in town would be much more plausible to Althea, who must sometimes wonder what kind of business could keep him away from home for three or four days on end.

If Scarlett were to become bored in such a set-up, he had no doubt with her looks she could get a job in one of the trendy boutiques in Chelsea. If the arrangement went well, he might even get her her own boutique.

As Scarlett started on her second vodka and Red Bull, because his thoughts had been elsewhere and not on her she turned her attention to him. Fingering his tie, she said admiringly, 'Love the colour. Wicked!' and kissed him on the lips. Her scent renewed his desire for her. This time he did not have to suggest they leave the bar; Scarlett was now whispering in his ear: 'Shall we go up, Georgie?'

It was a nickname she had used from the time of their first meeting. 'Because you look just like George Clooney,' she had said, 'and like all the girls, I really fancy him!'

She did not need to make the suggestion again.

SEVEN

Terence Hutchins placed his gun carefully against the scullery door to await cleaning after he had given his neighbour a drink. The new month had begun with a minor heatwave and both men were looking forward to a cold beer as they sat down in the kitchen at Logan Hill Farm. Terence had been rough-shooting with his long-time friend Nathan Swift, who owned the land adjoining his. Both farms were overrun with rabbits, which they were determined to cull with the aid of Barry, Nathan's foreman, and his two ferrets.

'Barry said to tell you he'd counted the bag and we've nabbed two hundred of the little blighters,' Nathan said cheerfully as he lowered his large frame on to one of the kitchen chairs. On the table was a home-made walnut-topped cake, produced by his wife, Evelyn, who now came into the room bearing a large plate of scones, and another of shortbread which she placed on the table.

'Honestly, Evelyn, there was no need for you to go to all this trouble,' Terence said as he sat down. He was as thin and angular as his friend was short and tubby. Evelyn, too, was tubby – ample-bosomed, wide-hipped and with a plump, rosy-cheeked face. She was a picture-book apple-cheeked farmer's wife, as young Daryl had once described her. 'Mrs Swift would make two of you, Dad!' the boy had said, but his tone was affectionate rather than critical.

Ever since his divorce, Evelyn had quietly and tactfully done her best to act as a substitute mother to Daryl. When he returned home at weekends, there was always a plentiful supply of tasty things for him and his father to eat. Not that she ever intruded on their privacy. Only once had she come over uninvited and stayed overnight, when Daryl had caught a nasty bout of flu. His temperature was so high his dad had felt unable to cope. That was a long time ago and by now her visits to Logan Hill Farm were a matter of course. The good-natured Nathan seemed perfectly happy for his wife to take on a second household and there was no hint of jealousy, knowing as he did that Terence still carried a torch for his former wife.

He would get over her loss one of these days, Nathan had remarked to his wife, but Evelyn, more intuitive, disagreed. If the divorce had not been so devastating for the poor man, she maintained, he would be able to talk about it by now. By some strange silent agreement, no one ever mentioned Althea's name, not even Daryl, in his presence. Maybe if Terence was a less reserved man, able to express his feelings, Evelyn suggested to her husband, he would be far happier. As it was, he only ever opened up a little when Nathan was around. With Daryl and herself he was polite, attentive, considerate, but never, ever intimate.

'It's a wonder Daryl gets on so well with his dad seeing how different their lives are,' she had remarked to Nathan. All father and son really had in common was their love of animals, and she would find them working side by side in silence tending a sick or orphaned lamb or a cow in labour.

'Is Daryl coming home this weekend, Terence?' she asked as she joined him and her husband at the table. Terence nodded and a brief smile flitted across his face.

'Bringing his girlfriend – if I didn't object,' he said. 'First one that's serious, I believe. Susie White – ex-policeman's daughter.'

Evelyn's round face creased into a big grin. 'First love! None to match it. Pity you were number six,' she added mischievously as she looked at her husband.

Certain of her enduring love for himself, he laughed. 'Don't you believe it, Kitten!' This pet name was so totally inappropriate that no one but he ever used it. 'Remember the old song? Ends with: *"But it's when you meet your last love that you loved her as you never loved before!"* Something to do with *"If you were the only girl in the world . . ."'*

Listening to their banter, Terence Hutchins felt a familiar pang of envy. The old question of why Althea had had to leave him was, as always, immediately followed by the answer: because he was a dull, unimaginative, silent man who had never been able to express his deep, lasting love for the woman he had married. In the early years, before they were married and Daryl was born, they had seemed to get along very well despite the fact that Althea was a bright, popular, outgoing, adventurous young woman with a mass of friends of both sexes – and the fact that she had several brief, unsuccessful affairs with unsuitable men. He could never have imagined in a hundred years that the beautiful, popular, laughing girl would like him. But she had . . . because, she maintained, he was different from the other fellows she knew; he took love seriously and, moreover, he hadn't tried to get her into bed, so she knew he loved her for herself rather than for her body.

Eventually the inevitable happened. They grew closer, Althea fell in love with him, and within a few months was pregnant. They married, the baby was born and for the next few years, when she was fully occupied looking after their son, she had not had time to be restless. That had begun after Daryl started school, a cataclysm compounded by the unexpected death of her horse from colic. Her depression coincided with the serious financial problems farmers were having with all the new complications evolving from the endless EU dictates and Terence having to work overtime to stay viable. Long hours doing hard physical jobs left him exhausted when he finally went home and soon after supper he was in bed and fast asleep.

No wonder Althea was bored out of her mind! he'd told himself when the first shock of her departure had worn off, and he had tried to rationalize her desertion. No wonder she preferred to live with a man who not only wanted to make love to her but had the time! Maybe their marriage wouldn't have lasted in any event, but it might have done if Althea had only told him how unhappy she was: *if* he had employed a foreman like Nathan had done, so he could have spent more time with her: *if* they had had another child . . .

'I've a chap coming to see me about the barn roof,' Nathan said, into the silence that was so characteristic of Terence, 'so I'm going to push off now. You coming, Kitten?' he asked as he stood up from the table.

Evelyn shook her head. 'I'll stay a while longer, if Terence doesn't mind. I haven't seen the boy for ages and besides, I'm curious to meet his girlfriend. I'll walk back in an hour or so.'

When her husband had left, Evelyn cleared the table and when she had washed the dishes and put them away, she sat down once more and looked at Terence's face as he studied the local paper. Tiredness had added to the lines round his eyes and he looked far older than the forty-six years she knew him to be.

'You're not worried about Daryl, are you, Terence?' she enquired. 'Unless he has changed a great deal in the last ten weeks, I don't think you need be concerned. He's a thoroughly nice, well-mannered, decent lad despite—' She broke off, realizing too late where her sentence was leading her. But Terence met her anxious gaze with a wry smile:

'Despite having to live in two camps!' he finished for her. 'In some ways, I wish he could live here with me all the time but . . . well, he's doing all right as he is. Anyway, I expect it's more convenient for him living at the Grange where he can meet up with Susie when he wants – they've a nice tennis court there and Daryl says they are going to put in an Olympic-size swimming pool ready for next summer!'

It was a long speech for Terence and, encouraged by it, Evelyn risked another personal question.

'Won't it be a bit lonely for you here when Daryl goes off to college? He's a bright boy, isn't he, and sure to get offered a place.'

For a moment, Terence did not answer. Then he said in a hard, bitter voice: 'Yes, he'll be going to college all right, but I have been informed by his mother that Geoffrey Lewis has arranged a trust fund to see him through.' He looked up into Evelyn's face, his own sharpened by bitterness as he added: 'Of course, I'm delighted for Daryl that he won't have any money worries, but I'm bloody annoyed I wasn't asked first if I intended to fund my son. Sorry about the language, Evelyn, but this isn't the first time that effing man has managed to pip me at the post. Last Christmas I bought Daryl a .22 shotgun so he could come shooting with me and dammit if Lewis didn't come up with a 12-bore Chiswick costing twice as much.'

He drew in his breath and exhaled slowly as if trying to calm himself.

'Of course Daryl wanted the 12-bore not because of the value but because it's a man's gun. I consider the kickback too strong for a youngster; but Daryl didn't want to upset me, so he suggested he ask Lewis to return it and get a refund. As you can believe, I wouldn't let him do that and we compromised; he'd keep the 12-bore here for when he was older and meanwhile, he'd use mine.' He looked up and met Evelyn's sympathetic gaze, his eyes dark with misery.

'Am I wrong to get so het up about this sort of thing?' he asked wretchedly. 'It wasn't even as if it was a coincidence; Daryl had told him I was giving him a shotgun for Christmas. Are all divorced fathers sidelined by the new man in their mother's lives? Bloody hell, Evelyn, I know I shouldn't but I really hate that man! He took my wife and now it looks as if he's trying to bribe my son, giving him all the things he knows I can't afford. He has even promised to pay for Daryl to have driving lessons – which I was going to do anyway – and buy him his own runabout, as he called it, for the boy when he passes his driving test. As it happens, I don't think it's a good idea to give a kid a high-powered sports car so soon. To do so after a few years' driving experience, maybe. But to put a novice behind the seat of a souped-up MG – no! Now, if I put my foot down and refuse to let him have it, Daryl will resent me. He's all I've got, Evelyn. I can't stand aside and let that bastard turn me into a spoilsport father.'

Had it been anyone else that Evelyn was listening to, she would have got up, gone round the table and put a comforting arm round their shoulders. But she knew Terence would only be highly embarrassed if she did so. He was in all likelihood already embarrassed at having revealed his feelings so freely. She leaned across the table and laid a hand gently over his clenched fists.

'You are misjudging your son, Terence! Daryl loves you. He may not have told you but he has told me on many occasions he thinks the world of you. And what's more, he doesn't like his stepfather. No, Terence, believe me, money won't ever buy Daryl's love, that I can assure you.'

As if on cue, the kitchen door opened and Daryl came in. Seeing Evelyn, he crossed the room and gave her a hug.

'I wasn't expecting to see you, Aunty Eve!' he said.

She patted his cheek affectionately. 'I stayed on to see your young lady!' she said. 'I know her mother, by the way. We were at school together, would you believe.'

Daryl beamed. 'I like her, too. I'm afraid Susie couldn't come. She forgot she had a piano lesson at five.' He glanced over at the table and his grin broadened. 'Walnut cake – cool! And scones. Hi, Dad, can we eat? I biked over and I'm absolutely starving.'

'And hot, too, by the look of you. Stick your head under the old pump in the yard – that'll cool you off!'

Nothing loath, Daryl did as his father suggested and was back within minutes rubbing his wet hair dry with a kitchen towel.

'Beats me how that well water stays so cold even in this weather!' he said as he sat down and started to butter one of Evelyn's home-made scones. 'Dad, Mum got a phone call from Aunt Phoebe this morning to say she's starting rehearsals at the Theatre Royal in Brighton next week. She said she can get us all tickets for the opening night on the sixteenth, and wants us to go and see her.'

It was several minutes before Terence spoke, then he said: 'Good for Phoebe! Last I heard she wasn't well enough to go to the fête. I'd like to see her performance, but . . .'

As if anticipating his father's question, Daryl said quickly: 'Mum and co. can't go. They are giving a dinner party that evening for some business friends. Mum badly wanted to go but . . . well, when she told my stepfather when he got back from London at teatime, he said he'd invited people to dinner that night and Mum couldn't go because they were important clients and she had to be hostess. She's dreadfully disappointed. But, Dad, Susie and I can go and if you want to go, too, then you could drive us.'

He stopped talking and looked up from his plate on which now lay a generous helping of cake as Terence said: 'I see, I'm to be chauffeur, am I?' But there was a twinkle in his eye as he added: 'What play is it? I'm not a theatregoer, as you well know!'

'But, Dad, Aunt Phoebe's in it! Anyway, Mum says you would like it because it's an Oscar Wilde play and she said to tell you Aunt Cressy might come with us if you'll be driving as she doesn't like driving alone at night and—'

'Enough!' Terence interrupted. 'I'll strike a bargain with you, Daryl. You take the tractor and turn that hay I cut yesterday – it should be well dried this weather – and I'll chauffeur the three of you to Brighton.' He stood up and nodded to Evelyn. 'Thanks for the tea,' he said. 'I'm off to shut up the hens.'

As he disappeared through the doorway, Daryl looked at Evelyn and smiled.

'Dad knew perfectly well I was going to turn the hay tomorrow anyway. He just wants to make out I'm not to take him for granted.'

Surprised at the boy's understanding of his father, Evelyn rose from the table and went round to his chair.

'Your dad's a good man, Daryl and you mean a great deal to him,' she said.

'I know!' Daryl replied, adding thoughtfully: 'I wish I could get to like my stepfather. I mean, for Mum's sake. She's always telling me he likes me but I know he doesn't and anyway I simply can't. He's so . . . I don't know how to describe it – sneaky. Whatever he says I don't seem able to believe it. Even when he's being all lovey-dovey with Mum I get the feeling he's just pretending he cares.' He broke off and then in a barely audible voice, added: 'Sometimes I hate him so much I want to hit him; times when he treats me like . . . like a ten-year-old and makes me feel . . . Oh, I can't explain it. Probably I'm not being fair to him. I dunno!'

He drew a tremulous sigh before saying in a resigned voice: 'I do try and like him for Mum's sake but I don't and I never will. Do you think I ought to try harder, Aunt Evelyn?'

Resting a hand on Daryl's shoulder, she was frowning as she replied hesitantly: 'I'm not sure if it's possible to make yourself like another person. I suppose you can try and think about their good points rather than their bad ones. From all you've told me – and indeed what I've seen – your step-father is a very generous man. I know you can't buy love, but I'm sure he means to please you, for your mother's sake if not for his own. After all, he doesn't have any children of his own, does he! But, Daryl,' she added in a brighter tone, 'you aren't going to be spending the rest of your life under his roof. Can't you just accept that all you have to do is to put up with him for a year or two more, and then you'll be off! Best thing you can do is try to ignore him; don't lose your temper or give him reason to rile you, if that's what he is doing. Now I must go, Barry will be chafing for his tea. I'll meet your Susie another time.'

'Sure thing!' Daryl said. 'And thanks again for the cake, Aunt Evelyn. I'll tell Susie you made it specially for her, shall I?'

'You do that – although I have to admit I knew it was your father's favourite, too.' As she reached the doorway she paused and looked back at the boy she all but thought of as her own. 'Any time you feel like a chat, Daryl, you know where to find me. And I don't have to tell you that I would never repeat what we say to each other to another soul, not even to Nathan.'

Daryl's handsome young face was suddenly thoughtful. 'Suppose I told you I'd been shoplifting? Taking drugs? You mean you wouldn't tell Dad? What if I told you I had committed a crime? Murdered someone?'

'You know perfectly well what I mean,' Evelyn said. But as she walked away from the farmhouse in the direction of her own home, she recalled his parting words and was not so sure she knew what Daryl had in mind.

EIGHT

Geoff sat in the VIP departure lounge at Gatwick Airport and, furious about his plane's prolonged delay, started on his second whisky. Although there were a dozen or more plates to which he could help himself, he was in no mood to eat. The passenger who had been sitting next to him in the first-class compartment was, by contrast, returning with a tray laden with food. To Geoff's irritation, he seated himself in an adjoining chair.

'Good thing we were upgraded, eh?' He laughed through a mouthful of smoked salmon. 'I doubt the economy class is getting much of a meal on their free lunch ticket.'

David Williams now raised his glass of beer to Geoff and his round, fat face wrinkled even further in a large grin.

'Cheers, boyo!' he said swallowing over half of the contents, his accent sufficiently Welsh for there to be no mistaking his origins. 'Reckon it's our lucky day, eh?'

The last thing Geoff wanted to do was to get into a long drawn-out discussion with this fellow passenger but he could see he was not going to be left in peace.

'Depends how you look at it!' he said. 'I shall most certainly miss a very important lunch date with clients in Manhattan. I've postponed the meeting till tomorrow but the people I'm hoping to do business with aren't any too pleased. If there's one thing I hate, it's a bad start!'

Through another half-eaten mouthful of food, his companion said: 'Take your point, but the way I see it, we could have been killed. Good God, man, if we weren't smashed to a pulp when we landed, we could have been burnt alive!'

Which was undoubtedly true, Geoff told himself, and he was well aware of it without the reminder. The aircraft had taken off on time just after eight o'clock, but an hour into the flight, the captain had come on the intercom and informed them there was an electrical fault and they would be turning back to Gatwick; he was very sorry but they would all agree, better safe than sorry!

That was an excuse for Geoff's neighbour to tug on his arm and get his attention away from the newspaper behind which he was hiding. The man was noisily cheerful, telling not only Geoff but all those near enough to hear him that this turnaround was nothing to worry about; no need for anyone to panic; it wasn't as if something like the under-carriage being stuck which could, of course, be potentially dangerous.

Those who heard his announcement wished he had kept his mouth firmly shut when, two hours later, having circled the airport to burn fuel, the captain came on the intercom again.

'We shall be circling for a little while before landing as we have a slight problem with the landing gear; we are speaking to engineers on the ground who are advising us the best way to rectify the problem. In the meanwhile, as a precaution, the cabin staff will repeat the emergency drill in case we are obliged to make an emergency landing. Please remain seated and keep your safety belts fastened.'

Next to Geoff, for the first time since he'd boarded the plane, the Welshman remained silent. Momentarily Geoff enjoyed the irony as he recalled how very inappropriate the man's earlier statement was. But then it began to register that they really were in considerable danger; that landing so huge an aircraft without wheels could easily result in a fire.

He looked out of his window as the plane began to lose height. With a spine-chilling shock, he realized suddenly that he might be about to die a horrifying death. The fortune-teller's prediction shot into his mind and he felt physically sick with a fear he could not control that she'd actually foreseen this disaster and had not wanted to tell him he was going to die!

Although at the last minute the wheels came down and the captain effected a near-perfect landing, not even the two stiff drinks Geoff had now poured down his throat had entirely subdued the vestiges of that fear. No matter how often he told himself that no sensible human being would pay the slightest attention to the airy nonsense of mediums, fortune-tellers, clairvoyants and such like, the Gypsy's strange behaviour that day at the fête still haunted him.

As if to negate such lingering doubts, he said suddenly to the man opposite him: 'Do you want to hear a useful little piece of advice, Williams? I've heard you Welsh people can be a bit airy-fairy – you know, Celtic – believe in ghosts, second sight – that sort of thing . . .'

For once, David Williams did not interrupt him as he continued to tell him how he'd been warned about a horrible disaster awaiting him in the near future; and how now, for the second time, he had been close to death.

'So you see, these charlatans can make up a vague prediction like that and sooner or later something nasty will happen coincidentally to all of us,' Geoff concluded. 'It's the same as if they told you you were going to get a nice surprise; we all get surprises sooner or later, too. See what I mean? One shouldn't believe a word they say.'

For a moment, his companion remained silent. He had even stopped eating as he looked thoughtfully back at Geoff.

'But who's to say your Gypsy woman might not really have seen death close to you? If you'd gone back to her for a second sitting, she might have told you that neither brush with death would be fatal.' His face suddenly creased in a broad smile as he added: 'Glad you didn't tell me that before we took off!' he said. 'I wouldn't have sat next to you! Despite what you say, I don't write off that sort of thing – ESP and ghosts and second sight. I mean, look at dogs. Dogs can actually tell when someone is dying or having a fit ages before we can. And they hear things we don't.' He paused before giving another laugh, although there was an underlying note of seriousness in his voice as he added: 'If I were you, I'd take things pretty easy for a while. I mean keep away from anything dangerous. You know, just in case!'

The man's response was very far from what Geoff wanted to hear. He had hoped for the whole fortune-teller episode to be ridiculed. He had not had the reassurance he wanted from Althea when, after a few drinks one night, he'd confessed he had wondered whether his near-death in the motorway accident had really been foreseen by Madame Tokoly. Far from rubbishing it, she didn't decry the possibility of a spirit world; that there could be some truth in the belief that people did exist who had second sight.

He had drawn little reassurance from the fact that she had no feelings one way or the other about Madame Tokoly herself as she had barely exchanged two words with her. She'd not had time to have her fortune told and Cressy had driven the woman back to the station before there'd been a chance to thank her.

'Don't tell me *you* believe what she told you, Geoff?' Al had asked incredulously. 'Or should I say what she didn't tell you because it was too awful?'

'Of course I don't take any of that nonsense seriously,' he'd replied and now repeated it to the Welshman. 'I was only curious to know your reaction to the coincidences.'

But it was a lie, he realized, as after a long, tedious wait, the repaired aeroplane took off shortly after three o'clock and flew him very belatedly to New York. Two of the seats in the first-class cabin which had been occupied on the morning flight were, significantly, empty. Williams, who seemed to make it his business to know everything, informed him that the two women had thought the flight was jinxed and were too frightened to board the plane. He would have been less surprised, he added, if Geoff had not turned up seeing what his clairvoyant had predicted.

The man's laugh irritated Geoff profoundly; the more so since even after a few more stiff drinks inside him courtesy of the airline he was unable to quell the underlying fear that haunted him. It had even crossed his mind that he should after all cancel the trip and go home. But to do so would mean he was giving credence to the whole stupid business and he certainly didn't intend to do that. Nevertheless, throughout the six-and-a-half-hour flight, his nerves were on edge lest something went wrong again.

Settled into his air-conditioned room in the St Regis

Hotel, Geoff debated whether to organize himself a girl for the evening, as was his custom if he did not have a dinner date. There was the secretary who came to his room on occasions to take dictation and a young woman he'd picked up in a bar, both of whom were prepared to drop whatever plans they had, to enjoy his company and his bed. However, having had a shower and a quick shave, he opted instead to go down to the bar for a drink and afterwards have a leisurely meal in the Astor Court dining room.

As he went down in the lift, he found himself wondering whether Althea had heard anything about the morning's debacle. It might have been on the BBC's six o'clock news, which she always watched if she was at home. Would she be worried? A few years ago, the answer would have been yes, without a doubt. She'd been madly in love with him then. Since those days . . . well, perhaps she knew about his unfaithfulness, or at any rate, some of the times he'd slept around. He didn't think so, and he was certain she had no knowledge of Scarlett.

Nor for the first time, Geoff pondered on the state of his marriage. Althea had begun to show her age and their sex life was devoid of novelty. He infinitely preferred to bed Scarlett. There was something about that girl which kept him going back to her despite the casual way she behaved with him. The first time he had sensed her indifference to their assignations he had left the hotel determined to drop her. Her expectation of expensive gifts and lavish lifestyle he took for granted, coming as it did from a young woman, so it was not that he objected to her avariciousness. It was her dispassionate manner when they were not actually having sex. He wanted her to be crazy about him; treat him with the same veneration other women did; to adore him. He was the one who was having to do the adoring, or at least appear to do so, if he was certain she would be eager to see him when he came up to Manchester. It irritated him to compare her casual indifference with his past mistresses, who had been madly in love with him; irritatingly so. Scarlett, who had aspirations far beyond running a boutique, did not even try to hide her lack of commitment to him.

What irritated Geoff even more than her feelings, or lack of them, for him, was his own obsession with her. It had got so that he even had difficulty getting an erection with other women; with Althea. Scarlett's very indifference drove him wild. Because of her, he no longer wanted the usual call girl the porter sent up to him when he stayed at the hotel. He wanted Scarlett, and hated the fact that he needed her – he who had never yet in his life been rejected by a woman.

As he walked into the restaurant for a solitary meal, he told himself he would take matters in hand when he got home. He would get Scarlett to move down to London, where he could see her as often as he wanted. He'd offer her whatever it took to get her there, a car, designer clothes, a beauty salon – whatever she wanted. He could afford her extravagances. He could promise holidays in the Caribbean, at a ski resort, a fortnight on their own private yacht on the Mediterranean . . . anything she damn well wanted. And all she had to do was be there for him . . .

His thoughts were interrupted by the arrival of one of the hotel bellboys.

'Excuse me, sir, are you Mr Geoffrey Lewis? There's an urgent telephone call for you, sir. The caller said she'd failed to get you on your cell and I was to tell you it was urgent. May I take you to the phone, sir?'

As Geoff rose to follow the boy to the telephone room, he hoped it was not Al wanting to know if he was safe; but realized she would have found out from the passenger list that he'd been flown out on the repaired plane. Somewhere along the line he had lost his mobile phone – probably in the first-class departure lounge after the aborted flight where he had last used it. But if not Al, who else might have known his movements? And why the urgency?

The call was from the middle-aged manageress of his Brighton estate agency. Sounding quite flustered, she apologized for disturbing him; she had not forgotten that he had told her he did not want to be bothered with any business matters while he was in New York, but in this instance . . .

'What instance, for heaven's sake, Mrs Smythe?' Geoff

broke in impatiently. He was feeling vaguely uneasy at the way misfortune seemed to be dogging him lately.

'The fire, sir. There was a fire in the reception room at lunchtime . . . that is to say, one thirty our time, sir. The fire brigade seemed to think it might have been caused by faulty wiring—'

'How bad was it?' Geoff broke in.

'The front desk, sir, and most of the files; and the visitors' chairs and most of the carpet. And I'm afraid the computers were all burnt and—'

'Have you been in touch with the insurance company? I take it we are adequately insured.'

Mrs Smythe's affirmative was voiced in a tone of relief. She had already telephoned them, she told him, and been assured they were fully covered for any losses.

Geoff felt a sudden wave of tiredness. It had been a long day which had started singularly badly and was now ending badly.

'Thank you for letting me know, Mrs Smythe, but there's nothing I can do here. I'll be back on Thursday. Meanwhile, call in a computer expert and see what can be retrieved. And keep in touch with the insurers. I take it you have had to close the agency?'

'Yes, Mr Lewis, but I've put a notice on the door saying any information or outstanding business can be dealt with by our Preston Park branch, and I've given the telephone number. It'll be several weeks before we can open up here again. We have a firm installing dehumidifiers and they are taking up the wet carpets and furniture this afternoon. I'm afraid the firemen were a little overgenerous with their water!'

She gave a tentative little laugh but when there was no response from Geoff, she deemed it best to wish him a very good night and rang off.

His appetite for dinner had by now completely disappeared. In a far from happy state of mind, Geoff stuck his hands in his pockets and with a scowl on his face returned sullenly to the comfort of the hotel's King Cole bar.

NINE

'You were marvellous, Aunt Phoebe!' Daryl said with genuine admiration. 'I liked the bit where you produce the famous handbag!'

Terence elbowed a way for the five of them through the jostling crowd still lingering outside the Theatre Royal stage door at the end of the evening's performance. Having waited the best part of half an hour for Phoebe to emerge, he was more than ready for a long cold pint of beer.

'Keep the compliments for later,' he interrupted his son, 'and don't let young Susie out of your sight. Far to go, Phoebe?' he enquired.

Phoebe shook her head. 'Just round to the front. It's right next door to the theatre – only a couple of minutes. It will be pretty crowded I'm afraid, but at least we'll get a drink.'

There had been no room in her dressing room so it was not until she had appeared through the stage door that she had been able to suggest a drink at the Colonnade Bar. The first-night performance of *The Importance of Being Earnest* – and her part in it as Miss Prism – had gone extremely well. She was on a high so the last thing she wanted was to return to her dingy room in the dingy digs she had rented for the duration of the play, her flat in Worthing being just too far from the theatre for convenience.

Nobody – other than her oncologist and her GP – knew that she needed to conserve every little bit of energy she could if she was to fulfil this one last stage appearance. As her agent had said, she'd been so lucky to get the part after an absence of nearly a year – a year spent not on holiday as the agent thought, but enduring weeks of chemotherapy followed by radiation and a slow convalescence alone in her flat. Tired though she had been, it was almost a relief when she was able to don a wig and take a part-time job as a receptionist in order to pay off some of the debts she had incurred while she had been so ill.

Because she had chosen not to tell her friends she was going to die, the treatment had bought her time, time she desperately wanted to play just one more part. When her agent had telephoned to say they were auditioning for Miss Prism she had jumped at the chance. Her sympathetic doctor, after a consultation with her oncologist, had agreed to give her far stronger painkillers to take before each perform-ance. The fact that the drug was addictive was of little consequence they had agreed since she was going to die anyway.

Now, as Terence tucked his arm through hers, she was suddenly aware of his strong masculinity. Memories raced through her mind as he shepherded them into New Road, skirting the groups of people sitting in the hot summer evening drinking at the tables outside the various pubs and restaurants on the approach to the theatre. They had met when she and Althea had gone with a group of students to a pub and had on impulse picked him up. Terence was far too shy to approach them and urged on by her, Althea had gone up to the bar to stand next to him and suggested he join their party. They had grown to be good friends; Terence had become very fond of Althea even though she had several very minor flings with other young men, during which time Phoebe grew close to him. Althea, however, suddenly decided Terence was the boyfriend she desired and set out to seduce him.

There'd been no thought of marriage at that time and Phoebe had decided to wait and pick up what she guessed would be the inevitable pieces. What none of them antici-pated, Althea became pregnant. Terence immediately proposed and since, as Althea confessed, she not only disliked the idea of an abortion but was finding Terence a very desirable partner, she went ahead and married him. Daryl was born six months later.

Now, sitting at a small table in one corner of the area outside, Phoebe watched Terence returning with their drinks and realized suddenly how he had aged. Although still a

handsome man, there were deep lines grooved in his cheeks
and frown lines crossing his forehead. His untidy wavy hair
was thinning on top and he looked as tired as she felt.

'Cressida has found a corner seat for Daryl, Susie and
herself inside,' he said. 'She has suggested when we finish
our drinks we all go home and you come back with us and
stay at her place tonight. It would give you a chance to see
Althea tomorrow. Or you can stay at the farm with me if
you like.'

Phoebe did not reply immediately. Cressy's welcome
invitation had been unexpected. Tomorrow was Sunday so
there were no performances and if she was to go back to
Worthing she would have nothing whatever to do other than
washing and ironing and cooking herself a solitary meal.
It would be really nice to see more of young Daryl, who
reminded her so strongly of the young Terence of bygone
days. She and Cressy had been especially close as girls but
– and it was a very big but – would she be able to cope
without anyone noticing how ill she was? Would they remark
how much weight she had lost? How tired she got at night?
She might have to forgo the stronger medication. Whatever
happened, she did not want someone else to jeopardize the
next week; to take her part on the last night. After that, she
didn't care what happened.

Her doubts about her health were followed by a decision
to enjoy this one last opportunity, come what may, for her
and Cressy to be together. If the pain became too much,
she could always pretend a gastric upset.

'I think that's a lovely idea!' she replied to Terence. 'I'd
love to stay overnight with Cressy. I can pick up my night
things from my digs – it's only a few minutes from here.
The only thing is, someone would have to bring me back
on Sunday night or early Monday morning.'

Terence's face lost its troubled look as he said in his
clipped manner of speaking: 'Can't manage mornings –
milking, chickens, jobs. But I'll be happy to drive you back
Sunday evening, if that's OK?'

Phoebe put a hand on his arm. 'You're a dear, kind man
and I love you!' she said with a smile, adding: 'You know

there was a time when I was madly in love with you, Terence
. . . before you married Al, I mean.'

A slight blush spread over Terence's face. 'I never knew
that! You were joking, Phoebe?'

'Well, no, I wasn't actually!' she replied. 'Mind you, I
thought when you and Al got together, although I was heart-
broken, I decided it was probably all for the best . . . you
know, with my ambitions to become England's finest
actress? In those days, we couldn't know the future.' Her
voice trailed into silence, which Terence immediately filled.

'You mean that my wife would run off with that . . . that
man!' He spoke the last word so forcefully that it barely
concealed his contempt for Geoffrey Lewis. 'Sorry, you
probably like him. Most women seem to.' He drew a deep
sigh adding: 'According to Daryl, even young Susie thinks
he's really cool!'

'Wicked might be more appropriate,' Phoebe said dryly.
'Pinching another man's wife the way he did!' For a moment,
neither spoke as they drained their glasses and then she said
thoughtfully: 'Would you have Al back, Terence? If she
wanted to come?'

He returned her gaze uneasily. 'I don't know. For Daryl's
sake, perhaps. He has always hated us living in different
houses and he doesn't . . . well, he doesn't get on too well
with Lewis. None of us are allowed to refer to the man as
his stepfather!'

Cressy, with the two youngsters in tow, interrupted their
talk. She looked affectionately at Phoebe and pointed to
Daryl.

'Your fan here has a hundred and one questions he wants
to ask you, and Al would be thrilled to death to see you
tomorrow.'

Phoebe stood and turned to Terence, who had already
risen to his feet. 'Will we all get into your Range Rover,
Terence? Because if you're sure it's OK, I think we ought
to be on our way.'

'Sure thing!' Terence replied almost jovially. 'That is, if
you don't mind the smell of pigs. I took half a dozen weaners
over to Nathan yesterday morning. His sow had farrowed

and lain on all but two of her little 'uns. Bessie, my old sow, had fourteen so she won't miss six of them.'

Three-quarters of an hour later, as they approached the outskirts of Hurston Green, Susie whispered in the circle of Daryl's arm: 'I really like your dad. He isn't a bit like other farmers. Do you think if I asked him he'd teach me to drive on the farm roads? Dad said driving lessons are dreadfully expensive.'

Daryl was aware that Susie's parents had told her they couldn't possibly afford driving lessons, let alone a car if she did pass her test. His father had said he would teach him but then Geoff had given him a voucher for the local driving school for a dozen lessons as his seventeenth-birthday present, and it had seemed churlish to refuse.

Susie said suddenly: 'Your stepfather said if I got a provisional licence, he might take me out for some practice if he had time.'

'Stone the crows!' Daryl exclaimed, using one of Nathan Swift's old-fashioned sayings. 'Doesn't sound a bit like him. When did he say that?'

'Yesterday when we'd been playing tennis and you'd gone to get a drink. He said you'd be pleased if he did something nice for me. I think he wants to get in your good books, Daryl. He kinda knows you don't like him.'

'Hate him, you mean!' Daryl retorted, but there was no time for further discussion as Terence stopped the Range Rover outside Susie's house. A few minutes later, although Cressida had invited them into her cottage for a nightcap, Terence drove Daryl and himself back to the farm and Phoebe was alone with Cressida, who was regarding her anxiously.

'You're looking terribly pale, Phebes!' she said. 'Being on stage like that must take it out of you. Why don't you go on up to bed and I'll bring you a hot drink. You're in the Blue room, where you stayed last time you visited – God only knows how long ago that was!'

The effect of the medication was indeed wearing off and Phoebe needed no second invitation to retire to bed. Above all, she needed rest; time to regenerate some of her waning strength for the following day when she wanted so much to be at her best. They would go up to the Grange at around eleven o'clock, Cressida suggested when she arrived in the little guest room with a steaming mug of Ovaltine. That would give Althea time to tidy up after the party. They wouldn't tell her they were coming, as it would be fun to surprise her. Meanwhile, Phoebe was to have a nice lie-in.

'You're much too thin, Phoebe darling!' she said as she drew back the curtains to open the window. The night was balmy, the summer sky bright with stars and a full moon, casting patches of silver on the lawn and flower-beds. Because it was so warm, Phoebe had only a sheet covering her and Cressida's sharp artist's eye had noticed the angular outline of Phoebe's bones. 'I'll bet you don't eat enough,' she said.

'Oh, but I do, Cressy!' Phoebe replied quickly. 'At least I do when I'm not working. Believe me, I'll put it all on again once the play comes off and I'm sitting around on my backside doing nothing more energetic than answering the telephone and sending emails!'

Cressida was about to ask her for further details about her temporary job as a receptionist, but noting the dark shadows under Phoebe's eyes she decided it could wait until tomorrow. There was a lot of catching up to do.

As she went downstairs to lock the front and back door before she followed Phoebe to bed, she decided there was a strange indefinable aura about her friend. She thought suddenly that if it were possible, she would like to paint Phoebe. As a rule, she only painted landscapes, botanical subjects, but very occasionally she had this strange urge to reproduce a face. She had painted Daryl as a little curly-haired three-year-old holding a red toy tractor with a beatific expression as if he had been given his heart's desire. Althea had insisting on buying it and it hung in her bedroom.

Now, as suddenly as she had needed to paint the child, she wanted to paint Phoebe; to catch that unusual trans-parency of her skin, the sea-water colour of her eyes, the strange texture of her short, curly hair. She couldn't remember Phoebe even as a girl at school ever having hair like that. She always wore it long and straight. What was presumably a perm did, in a strange way, suit her. It made her look even more elfin than she had as a young girl.

As she made her way up to bed, Cressida's thoughts returned to the play. Phoebe had been faultless – bringing Miss Prism perfectly to life and holding the audience's close attention every time she spoke in her rather governessy, prosaic but self-important way. Of course Lady Bracknell got the loudest ovation from the audience but Phoebe had looked absolutely radiant when they had given the cast five curtain calls. Cressida knew she had been ill with pneumonia the previous winter but this was a wonderful comeback. Perhaps Phoebe had been unsure whether she would make the grade again after so long a bout of illness and that was why they had seen so little of her. The few letters, phone calls and texts were always brief and in a way impersonal. She asked questions rather than relating how she was enjoying life.

When Cressida finally climbed into bed and lay back sleepily on her pillow, her thoughts turned to the other woman she had been close to nearly all her life. Although Althea rarely discussed her relationship with Geoff, Cressida knew she was no longer happy in her marriage; that she was lonely much of the time with Geoff so busy building his empire away from home. And Daryl was growing up, needing her less and less as, indeed, it was right he should do so. In a couple of years' time he would be off to college and what then could Al do to fill her days? An only child with well-off parents, Al had never had a job; never needed one. Nor had she been blessed with any particular talent. Once, half jokingly, she had said that when Daryl left home she might try her hand at journalism; travel to a remote jungle, climb the Himalayas, visit remote tribes in South America, and then write about her experiences. On another occasion, she had said she might become an interior decorator; do up old houses, new penthouse apartments! The truth was, she was unqualified for any such occupation and knew it. But never once had she suggested she might accompany Geoff on his many trips abroad.

Close to sleep, Cressida's thoughts turned to Althea's

husband. Still only thirty-three years of age and, thanks to a lot of outdoor activities and regular visits to a gym, in near-perfect physical condition. With his closely cut black hair, Grecian nose and chin and dark brown twinkling eyes, Geoff never failed to turn women's heads. No matter what age, they fell over themselves to carry out his wishes in the hope that he would turn his attentions to them. Althea never had trouble employing female staff, all of whom became Geoff's willing slaves. She even had the benefit of his sexual dynamism at second hand, her hairdresser giving her last-minute appointments and asking hopefully if her glamorous husband would be coming to collect her; in pubs barmaids rushed to serve him out of turn; waitresses vied with each other to attend his table for no better reward than his smile, a smile which on principle he never failed to give.

She had always understood how Geoff had managed to sweep Althea out of Terence's bed and into his. When he wanted to exert it, his personality was magnetic. Not that she had ever been attracted to him, while the artist in her fully appreciated his physical beauty. At the end of the day, she knew Al was not happy. There was little she could do to brighten her friend's life but tomorrow she would be able to do so. Al had always been devoted to Phoebe – if anything, she was closer to her than to herself – and she would be thrilled to have her company for the whole day. It would be good for Phoebe, too, to sit in the sun in Al's lovely garden in one of the large cushioned basket chairs and relax. She herself might take her sketch pad and some water-colours and do one or two drawings of them both in Hurston Grange's beautiful setting. The big rose-bed would be ablaze with colour and the herbaceous border brilliant with blue delphiniums, lupins, red-hot pokers, dahlias . . .

Cressida fell asleep still positioning the subjects for her painting in her dreams.

TEN

Daryl was, as usual, weekending at the farm with his father, so only Cressida and Phoebe were in Cressida's somewhat elderly Polo as she turned into the long drive leading to Hurston Grange. She was wearing an old-fashioned flowered short-sleeved cotton dress, but despite the hot August day, Phoebe wore loose-fitting linen trousers and a long-sleeved collar and cuffed shirt which, as she intended, helped to disguise her anorexic-looking figure. She had used a tan make-up and rouged her cheeks, employing her stage experience of make-up to ensure she looked as healthy as possible.

'I wonder if we ought to have phoned Al to say we were on our way?' Cressida remarked as the manor house came into view. 'It's only eleven o'clock and they might be having a lie-in with the Sunday papers.'

Phoebe shook her head. 'I doubt it. Anyway, much more fun to surprise them. Don't let's ring the front-door bell. The French windows will almost certainly be open on a day like this so we can go in that way. Or they may be out in the garden.'

Cressida parked the car, and taking her carpet-bag containing her sketch pad and painting gear off the back seat, she linked her other arm through Phoebe's.

'It's donkey's ages since you last saw Al and Geoff, Phebes; more than a year, surely. I know Al's going to be over the moon when she sees you. We often talk about you, you know, and wonder what you are up to.'

Before Phoebe had time to comment, they had rounded the east wing of the house and were approaching the York-stone terrace on which was a large swing seat and a number of cushioned lounge chairs. All the furniture had matching heavy white canvas covers with dark-brown piping, as were the two sun umbrellas shading the occupants of the chairs beneath them. Both were reading Sunday newspapers and it was not until Cressida called out hullo, they realized they had visitors. Althea jumped to her feet, her face lighting up with pleasure.

'Cressy! What a nice surprise. I didn't—' She broke off as Phoebe removed her large straw sun hat. For a brief moment, Althea stood staring at her and then cried out: 'Phoebe, how utterly wonderful to see you. I was quite devastated missing your show last night and—' She broke off once more as she put her arms round Phoebe and hugged her. 'You're too thin!' she exclaimed as she released her. 'You've been working too hard. And—'

'I had pneumonia last winter,' Phoebe interrupted. 'Didn't I write and tell you? Anyway, I'm fine now and you look just exactly the same.'

'Plus a few more wrinkles – and I've put on weight. I'm forty years old, for heaven's sake! Wait till you hit four oh!' As she turned to call out to Geoff, she missed the flicker of Phoebe's eyelids. Although almost the same age as Althea, she was never going to reach four oh.

Putting down his newspaper, Geoff now stood up and, staring at the group of women, only just managed to conceal an expression of angry irritation. Sundays were sacrosanct unless he had previously invited special guests, and although he didn't dislike Cressida, she and Althea were thick as thieves and he saw too much of her to want to give up his Sunday leisure. As for Phoebe . . .

'Hi, Geoff! How are you? Long time no see!'

Phoebe stepped forward and kissed him French fashion on each cheek. With an almost visible effort, Geoff managed a smile.

'This is a surprise,' he commented, adding for his wife's benefit: 'You didn't tell me they were coming!'

Althea linked her arms through her friends' and led them towards the chairs, her eyes dancing with pleasure.

'I didn't tell you, Geoff, because, my lord and master, I didn't know!' Despite the jocular words, her tone was almost derisive.

Al should never have left Terence, Phoebe thought, as she

seated herself in the shade of one of the big umbrellas; she should have thought twice before marrying a man not only younger than herself, but so physically attractive that women inevitably fell for him. Men like him were seldom faithful. Had Al realized his true nature?

Geoff disappeared indoors to make a jug of Pimm's. Laughing, Althea said the three of them could now go back to the good old days and get happily drunk together. Phoebe had to explain that regretfully she couldn't have alcohol for the time being; she was still on antibiotics, she lied, because her doctor said there was still a trace of fluid on her lungs since she'd had the infection, which had kept her from attending the fête.

'I was so sorry to miss it!' she said. 'Cressy told me the clairvoyant raised quite a bit of money but somehow or other, she upset Geoff!'

Althea laughed. 'Well, it wasn't deliberate. She was actually trying to warn him about something nasty in his future. You'd have thought Geoff of all people would have called it rubbish and forgotten it, but you know how these things happen, a whole load of nasties including a near plane crash happened one after another and he's really tetchy. Best not to mention your Gypsy friend, although Cressy quite liked her, didn't you, Cressy?'

Cressida nodded. 'Not that I saw much of her as we only spoke when I drove her to and from the station. I have to say I am not in the least superstitious.'

'Nor I!' Phoebe added, 'Although I do read my horoscope in magazines when I'm at the hairdresser. Are you saying Geoff is into that sort of thing? I should have thought he was the very last person to believe in anything supernatural.'

'I don't think he does, but with two quite major dices with death, he has become very tetchy even though he calls them coincidences. He gets into a foul mood if I talk about them, so keep off the subject or we won't be able to enjoy our Pimm's!'

Despite the several glasses he, Althea and Cressida drank, Geoff remained unusually quiet and withdrawn. He finally

excused himself with the caustic remark that if Althea was
not going to do anything about getting some lunch for their
guests, he had better do so. When Cressida struggled off
her lounge chair saying she would go with him, he refused
her help.

'Thanks but no thanks! I may be a male but I am perfectly
capable of rustling up a meal without assistance.'

Althea tried not to look surprised. In all the years of their
marriage, she had never known Geoff produce anything
more worthy of the name meal than bread and a platter of
cheese.

'There's plenty of beef left from last night's dinner,' she
informed him, 'and tomatoes, lettuce and cucumber in the
fridge. There may be some—'

'For goodness' sake, Althea, I'm not blind. Carry on with
your girlish chatter and leave me to carry on getting a meal!'

As he disappeared into the house, Althea refilled Phoebe's
glass of apple juice and poured the last of the Pimm's into
her own and Cressida's glasses.

'Don't look so concerned, you two!' she said, her voice
almost jocular. 'Geoff loves putting me in my place but it
doesn't mean anything. You'll see. He'll be his usual gregar-
ious self once he has proved what a master chef he is!'

But although Geoff's mood did improve slightly during
the adequate cold meal he provided, he did not remain with
them after they had eaten it but retired to his study to do
some work, taking with him the coffee Althea had made.

'You mustn't think he's trying to avoid your company,'
Althea said. 'Geoff's a workaholic! He's often like this,
isn't he, Cressy? He'll end up with a heart attack if he
doesn't ease up a bit. The only time he ever relaxes is when
he manages to get home for a day or two. Even then, he
lives on his computer or his mobile!'

For a while, they discussed Phoebe's occupation when
she wasn't in a play or touring, then Phoebe shrugged her
thin shoulders and said: 'Sometime ago, I had a lover – a
theatrical producer who I only saw occasionally as we were
seldom in the same place at the same time.'

She was silent for a moment as were her two friends

each with the same thought. It was Althea who asked: 'But why didn't you tell us before? Surely you didn't think Cressy or I would be shocked? We'd have wanted to meet him and—'

Phoebe interrupted her. 'I wasn't able to introduce you to him; he wouldn't let me tell anyone. He was married, you see, and didn't want to leave his wife, so he always insisted on the utmost secrecy.'

Althea swung her long shapely brown legs over the side of the lounge chair and sat up, her brows drawn together in a frown as she regarded Phoebe.

'Are you making all this up, Phebes?' she asked. 'If it's true, what's he doing now? I mean, do you still see him?'

Phoebe's expression became cynical. 'He exists all right, Al, but we aren't an item any longer. When I had to go into hospital, I was ill enough to be put into intensive care for almost a week. Lover-boy thought I was going to die and that I might leave a clue to his identity. He got cold feet and when I returned to my digs, I found a letter saying he was out of it! Affair over! So that was that!'

For a moment, neither Althea nor Cressida spoke. Althea was first to do so. She asked tentatively: 'Did you . . . care for him . . . very much? Were you in love with him?'

'Desperately!' Phoebe replied quietly. 'Stupidly! I knew all along he didn't love me. I knew he was never going to leave his wife. As a matter of fact, I don't think he loved *her* very much either!'

'Oh, Phebes, I'm so sorry!' Cressida broke in. 'I suppose he is why you never got married. You must feel very bitter.'

Phoebe drew in her breath and then exhaled slowly. 'I don't think I'm bitter so much as angry . . . angry with myself for letting the affair go on for so long when I knew in my heart of hearts he was an egotistical bastard who didn't really care about anyone other than himself. If I'm bitter at anything or anyone, it's at myself for being so weak.'

As if anxious to change the spotlight from herself, she turned to Althea and said: 'You must know what it's like, Al – being so madly attracted to someone that you blind yourself to their shortcomings. I know you have Daryl and a wonderful home and holidays and things, but can you put your hand on your heart and say you are blissfully happy? I bet Cressy can, can't you?' she asked turning to her.

Cressida put down the paintbrush she was holding and smiled at Phoebe.

'You know me, I only love art. It can never be anything but beautiful and totally rewarding. And I'm not referring to my pictures – they are just daubs. I mean the work of the great artists, which fill one with inspiration and are tirelessly beautiful. Those aren't adjectives you can use to describe a man!'

They all laughed and Phoebe, suddenly exhausted, lay back against the cushions and closed her eyes.

'You two talk and I'll listen!' she said. 'I think I was overexcited last night – too full of adrenalin – to sleep very well in Cressy's lovely soft guest bed, so I may doze off. If I do, don't worry. I never nap for long.'

She knew this to be true because the pain woke her, alerting her to the fact that it was time for her medication. She had taken two pills when she had been to Althea's loo directly after lunch and the sedative was beginning to kick in.

Fortunately, her two friends seemed to take her behaviour completely for granted, believing her stage appearance had sapped her strength. In fact, she invariably felt much better when she was performing. It was as if she had psyched herself into the persona of the character she was adopting. Phoebe Denton and her cruel cancer for a few hours no longer existed, as she became Miss Prism in *The Importance of Being Earnest*. Even now she could not believe her luck in getting such a large part in the Oscar Wilde revival. The money she earned would come in handy to pay for her funeral, she had told herself cynically. As for her savings, they would just about see her out!

She could hear Al and Cressy talking to each other as she drifted into sleep thinking not only how different they were from each other but also how diverse their lives had been. Her last conscious thought was that they would both be terribly sad when her end came.

An hour later, Geoff emerged from the house and joined them on the terrace. His mood had changed and he apologized to Phoebe for absenting himself for so long.

'No need for Cressy to take you to the station,' he said. 'I'll run you back to Brighton.'

'Thanks, but Terence is taking me home after tea,' Phoebe told him. Geoff looked momentarily put out.

'I was going anyway,' he said. 'I want to have a look at the painting job they've done on the facade of my premises. I suppose I could go tomorrow. Did you know there was a fire?'

Phoebe nodded. 'I read about it in the *Argus*. Have they found out how it happened? The article said it was a mystery!'

'God knows!' Geoff replied as he sat down on one of the empty garden chairs. 'I've just had to accept I'm having a run of bad luck – forecast by your chum, Madame Tokoly or Kotoly or whatever her name is.'

Phoebe smiled. 'No chum of mine, Geoff. I only saw the woman once. As a matter of fact, she gave me bad news, too; said I'd be very ill and sure enough, I got pneumonia. So, I do believe she sees things we can't. You ought to go and have a proper reading, and hopefully she'll tell you the bad things are behind you.'

Althea now joined in the conversation. 'I think Phoebe's right. You know how that day at the fête has preyed on your mind,' She turned to Phoebe, adding: 'He has even had nightmares about it, haven't you, Geoff?'

Geoff looked uncomfortable as he said: 'My grandfather would have used the word "poppycock" to describe any form of clairvoyance and I totally agree with him. As for the nightmares, they were obviously a result of the plane incident we've been discussing. Association of ideas. No, I shall certainly not waste my time or my money seeing our Gipsy Lee again!'

None of the three women who were now hugging each other as they said their goodbyes was aware that he had made a mental note of the telephone number of Madame Tokoly which Cressida had mentioned at the fête; still less would he ever reveal that he intended to make an appointment to visit her in a fortnight's time when she returned from a visit to her home town in Hungary. Quite simply, he had to find out if the sword of Damocles was still suspended over his head. The Gypsy's warning was like a flea in a dog's ear and would not stop irritating him until it was well and truly dead.

ELEVEN

It was the first week in September and the new term at Headingborough Grammar School had begun. Daryl found that he had been promoted from the rugger 2nd XV to the 1st. It meant that on away-day matches he could not go back to Hurston Green with Susie after school.

'I don't like you biking all that way on your own!' Daryl said paternally as they discussed the new arrangements at lunch. 'Suppose you had a puncture!'

Susie laughed, her aquamarine eyes sparkling. 'Then I'd mend it, stupid!' she said. In a softer tone, she added: 'At least three other kids bike to Hurston, so don't fuss!'

In point of fact she wasn't certain she liked him worrying about her. Ever since she could remember she had been cosseted by her father and now that she was in her teens his constant vigilance irritated her. She was an only child, and he was far too overprotective. They owned a few acres of land adjoining their bungalow and grew fruit and vegetables, which they sold once a week in Hurston Green Farmers' Market.

Her father, Peter White, a retired policeman, was a quiet, hard-working man of Presbyterian faith devoted to his small family and inordinately proud of his pretty teenage daughter. A non-drinker himself, he never went to the local pub and until Susie was sixteen had forbidden her even to go inside one. Like any other town in England, he maintained, the usual bunch of hoodies and yobbos, if they weren't actually in the pubs, were gathered outside them, and he wasn't going to have his Suky dragged into their lawless, drunken net!

Pauline silently sympathized with her daughter. Although she herself wanted at all costs to keep Susie from harm, she understood how hard it was for the child not having the freedom enjoy by her schoolfriends. Sleepovers, fo example, were out of the question, just as were parties lasting until after midnight.

It had been a great relief to her when Daryl Hutchins had suddenly entered Susie's orbit. First and foremost, Peter approved of him because he liked the boy's father, and admired the way he ran his farm. He didn't approve of Daryl's mother, who had run off and married her lover, the toff who, in his view, had cheated poor old Mr Ingram when he'd purchased his family home, Hurston Grange. But none of that was young Daryl's fault, he told Pauline, and even a blind man could see that the boy not only doted on Susie but was very caring and respectful of her.

Susie was Daryl's first love, Pauline said, and first love was always awesome, to use the children's current jargon. Peter was not quite so pleased to be told by Pauline that his beloved child was equally infatuated with the boy. Until Daryl's arrival on the scene he had been the most important man in her life, his wife reminded him, and he was simply jealous! Although she spoke jocularly, there was some truth in her remark. When Susie was little, on Peter's off-duty days she had dogged his footsteps up and down the rows of vegetables in her little pink anorak and Wellingtons, or helped him in the greenhouses, her face as serious as her father's as she poured water from her tiny watering can on to his tomatoes. As Susie grew up, she had spent less time with him but there was always a hug and a kiss when she came back from school, and if he wasn't in the house, she would go off and find him. All that had changed since the day when, shyly, she had first brought Daryl home to tea!

Fortunately Peter liked the boy and when Susie begged to be allowed to bike to and from school with Daryl and one of her girlfriends, he was persuaded to agree when Daryl promised to see she came to no harm. Although Susie was only sixteen, she was mature for her age and he trusted her but when he learned Daryl would not always be riding home with her he was concerned.

'Nights are drawing in,' he commented as the three of them sat down at the kitchen table for their high tea, 'and as like as not this time of year there'll be fog, rain, storms and such.'

Susie squeezed his hand, smiling as she told him he was a proper old fusspot.

'As bad as Daryl, you are, Dad, and that's saying something. And we get out of school at four o'clock so it won't be dark for ages yet. And don't forget, Clare and Kate will probably be with me and I've got my mobile so if I got into trouble, I'd only have to phone you.'

Peter's face relaxed a little as he reminded her that he might well be down the bottom of the field at the end of a row of raspberry canes and wouldn't hear the phone ringing.

'So Mum might be standing right next to the phone shelling peas!' she pointed out. 'Don't be such a pessimist, Dad. You're always dreaming up bad things happening to me whereas something really, really good happened at school today. I'm going to be in the Christmas play, *Pickwick Papers*. I'm to be Mrs Bardell. Mrs Mathews – she's our drama teacher – is making the play a bit shorter and the cast list bigger so more people can be in it.'

'Well, now,' her father said, his voice as proud as it was affectionate, 'you'll have a lot of learning to do, won't you? And what about your young man; is he Mr Pickwick?'

'Not him!' Susie said laughing. 'He's much too self-conscious. He's got into the 1st XV, though, so he's happy. I wonder if Daryl's mum would take me to visit her actress friend, Phoebe Denton? She's the one we went to see in Brighton. She was Miss Prism, which was quite an important part and I know she could give me lots of useful tips. I really want to do well.'

Not unaccustomed to his young daughter's abrupt subject changes, he simply nodded. For the first thirty years of his working life, he had been pounding the city streets or doing paperwork at the police station. Then, on his fiftieth birthday, he had been given the opportunity to take early retirement and that was when he and his wife and daughter had moved to the countryside, to Hurston Green. Now, even though it was sometimes difficult to make ends meet, there was not a dark cloud in the sky other than a whisper of a shadow on the horizon whenever it crossed his mind how few were the years left to him before his little princess was old enough to leave home.

For the half-hour after tea, Peter returned to the harvesting of his autumn raspberries and filling the punnets with the ripe fruit. They had done exceptionally well this year and Pauline had managed to put several pounds of fruit away in the freezer. Although they didn't defrost well, they nevertheless made delicious ice cream and she had sold last year's freezing this past hot summer and added quite a large sum to her fund to buy a new cooker.

When he returned to the house, he stacked the punnets on the larder floor where they would remain until tomorrow's market day. Back in the sitting room, Susie and Daryl were seated on the floor playing poker. Vast sums of paper money were changing hands. Their laughter was mingled with childish taunts, which did nothing to lessen the loving looks they gave each other from time to time.

Pauline was in the kitchen baking bread. He sat down to watch her. Although she'd put on quite a lot of weight since they were married, she was still a very pretty woman, at least in his eyes. He enjoyed the sight of her bare arms kneading the dough and her rounded figure in its pretty floral apron as she moved around the room.

Pauline looked at him when he seated himself at the table. She was aware of his continuing concerns for their daughter and said reassuringly: 'I'm sure Daryl is right when he says Susie will be perfectly safe riding home without him. Lots of the sixth-formers started using bikes when all that Keep Fit carry-on was in the newspapers – "British Children Fattest in the World" or something like that – and all the medics were saying to the kids, don't diet, exercise. I don't think any of the children took a blind bit of notice until that pop star, whatshername, did a "You too can have a body like mine!" campaign.'

Albeit reluctantly Peter agreed that Susie could bike home without Daryl provided there were other girls or boys with her. But it was neither a hit-and-run driver nor a kidnapper who, not more than a month after the new term had started, caused an incident with very serious consequences; and Susie's assailant was someone she knew.

With Daryl back at school, Althea saw even less of him than she had throughout the summer holidays. Time often hung heavily on her hands, and ever more frequently, she stopped off at Cressida's cottage where she sat drinking coffee while Cressida painted. Not long after term had started, she confided in her friend.

'Geoff is becoming impossible to live with! He is driving me up the proverbial wall.'

Cressida looked from her easel at Althea's white, drawn face and said: 'I guessed something was wrong, Al. You may not be aware of it but you've lost a huge amount of weight. You'll be as thin as Phoebe soon. You can talk away to your heart's content because I don't mind being your agony aunt! And of course, Al, you know I'd never, ever betray a confidence.'

Althea gave a weak smile. 'He's so unfair!' she said. 'Things go badly for him at work and when he does come home, he takes it out on me. He's particularly rude when Daryl's around because he knows I won't bite back if Daryl is there.'

Cressida's look of sympathy deepened. 'Surely Geoff doesn't have to worry too much if some of his projects go badly? I mean, putting it bluntly, everyone knows the pair of you are . . . well, extremely well off, so I don't see why when they do go wrong he has to make life so unpleasant for you. He's not exactly facing poverty, is he?'

Althea sighed. 'It isn't lack of money or fear of losing it; it's Geoff's nature. He can't stand being wrong, making mistakes, having his wishes thwarted. Everything always has to be the way he wants and quite often, it isn't even particularly important.' She gave another deep sigh: 'This time it's all about the flat he wanted in town – a pied-à-terre for when he's too late to get home. He said he lost it because he left it too long to sign the lease. I suppose I should have been more sympathetic whereas, stupidly, I told him I thought it was a bloody good thing it had fallen through and I would have said so before if he'd told me what he was planning. That's when he really lost his rag!'

'He didn't . . . hit you?' Cressida asked anxiously.

'Goodness me, no!' Althea told her. 'Geoff's abuse is all verbal. Sometimes I wish he would hit me and then I could hit him back! Am I shocking you, Cressy?'

They both laughed and the conversation changed to Daryl's progress in the rugger team and then to Phoebe. Cressida showed Althea the postcard she had received from Bath.

'She's coming to stay for two whole weeks when the tour finishes!' she told Althea. 'See on the card, it says hopefully a week with me and a week with you.'

Althea nodded. 'Be really nice for the three of us to be together again. Seems ages and ages since we used to meet up regularly whenever Phebes was between plays. Her being so ill broke our routine, didn't it?'

Geoff was forgotten as they started to reminisce, which they so often did when they were alone together, about their schooldays and how lax discipline was in schools these days.

Althea was a lot more relaxed, even happier, as she left Cressida to return to her painting while she drove herself into Headingborough to keep her appointment at the gym.

Geoff, meanwhile, was driving south on the M23, his mind and body still tense with the irritation that had affected Althea the previous night. He had told her he'd intended renting the flat in town for himself whereas it was to have been for Scarlett. As he had promised her, it was ideally situated over a vacant shop, so she could have her own boutique which she could stock at his expense – something she had professed to want so ardently.

Finding suitable premises had not been easy. He was after all an extremely busy man and could not always get to London to view the properties when they became available. Finally, two weeks ago, he'd discovered the perfect place. He'd driven up to Manchester to tell Scarlett the exciting news and to his acute irritation, she had informed him she was no longer sure she wanted to go to London. Squid had threatened to leave her if she moved south, and there'd been veiled threats of violence if she walked out on him.

Geoffrey had been furious. What did it matter if her boyfriend did dump her? She wasn't in love with the guy. She spoke vaguely of 'security' but she wouldn't need him once she had his protection. Within reason, she could have as much money as she needed and the boutique would be in her name.

When he had Scarlett in bed with him, she had promised to break off the relationship with her boyfriend without further prevarication, and come down to London. Now, at the critical moment, she told him she had changed her mind.

He was very angry, not least because he had agreed to pay the deposit on the flat the previous week, and common sense told him that there was no way he could be sure she wouldn't change her mind again. Consequently he had postponed the signing and two days later, the agent phoned him to say it had gone. His frustration was paramount. He was not used to being thwarted on one count, let alone two.

He'd been so completely confident that Scarlett would jump at his offer to set her up in London. Finding the right place had proved more difficult than he had expected, and then, when he did find it, it was only to be thwarted a second time.

He would pack Scarlett in, he told himself as he drove home. It wasn't as if he was in love with her. On the other hand, there was something about her which aroused him sexually more than any other female he'd known. Even when he was physically exhausted after a long day's work or travel and wanted nothing more than a good night's sleep, the sight of Scarlett's voluptuous little figure, her surprisingly husky voice, breasts spilling out of the tight sequinned tops she always wore, was sufficient to arouse a fierce surge of desire.

He had finally faced the fact that Scarlett was different from the other women with whom he'd had affairs. Invariably, they had wanted more than sex, professing if not at first then later in the relationship to have fallen in love with him. At that point his interest in them would begin to pall. In the past, he'd never had any difficulty seducing women, society women, married women, girls. It was doubly galling that Scarlett should be rejecting him in favour of the boyfriend she had described as an 'ignorant Italian' – not only demeaning but also intensely exacerbating to say the very least. What he wanted to do was to tell Scarlett she and her boyfriend could go jump in a lake for all he cared; but he couldn't bring himself to do so. He guessed she might now be playing hard to get but that left him still unsure of his next move.

Such was Geoff's tormented frame of mind as he turned off the main road and took the B road to Headingborough. As he neared the big brick-built grammar school he passed groups of pupils. One boy, however, was standing on his own by the school gates and, for a brief moment, Geoff thought he was Daryl. He slowed the car, deciding that he might as well give the kid a lift home, especially if he was now waiting for the approaching pretty girlfriend with whom doubtless he was having it off.

These days, he thought bitterly, even fifteen- and sixteen-year-olds were hard at it. He himself had been cursed with a sergeant major for a father, a regular, old-fashioned disciplinarian who had dictated every aspect of his life before he had finally escaped when he came of age. The one time his father had caught him having sex with a girl he had beaten him with a leather belt so brutally that it was a week before he could get out of bed. It was over three years after he'd left home before he was able to rid himself of his fear of his autocratic parent.

Belatedly, he discovered there was no shortage of girls vying for his attentions, and it was not long before he realized that quite suddenly he had become the piper who played the tune. He had only to charm a girl into falling in love with him and she became putty in his hands. One girl had tried to kill herself because he'd broken off their relationship. There had subsequently been a number of further doting females with whom he soon became bored. Althea had been different. For a start, she was older, a married woman and therefore not readily available. Her inaccessibility was a challenge and for a while after he met her, winning the struggle to make her leave her husband had kept him obsessed. But after they had finally married, the deeper in love she became, the less enchanted he was. There was no further challenge to captivate him and it was only a year before he was unfaithful to her, two years before he took a mistress.

Realizing his thoughts were wandering, Geoff looked again at the boy by the school gates and saw that it was not Daryl. The engine of his Mercedes was still running when a Volvo estate drew up in front of him and the driver beckoned to the boy. Only then did he remember that Daryl had told them that this term he would often be staying late for training now that he had been elevated to the 1st XV.

Irritated by the fact that he had stopped at the school for no good reason, Geoff slammed the car into gear. He had only driven a few yards when Susie White waved to him from where she was standing by the bike shed. He pulled up sharply. Not only did he enjoy young Susie's company, but he knew she had a crush on him as she always blushed when he paid her a compliment. If she was up at the Grange when he was home she would eagerly run errands for him, much to Daryl's irritation! Althea accused him of encouraging the child by laying on the charm for no better reason than to upset Daryl. But that wasn't true. He liked knowing that he could still attract girls no matter what their age. Sometimes he didn't get any response and the more indifferent they were, the harder he strove to attract them.

He got out of the car and walked over to where Susie was looking ruefully at her flat tyre. She gave him a shy smile.

'I feel such a fool,' she said. 'In the past I always kept a puncture-repair outfit in my saddlebag, but one day when Daryl had a puncture, I lent it to him and he forgot to give it back. It didn't matter 'cos we always used to ride home together.'

She pointed to the now almost deserted school grounds and added: 'If Daryl isn't out of school early, I usually bike home with two of my friends but stupidly I told them not to wait for me as I could easily fix the tyre by myself. It wasn't until they'd gone, I realized my repair tin was missing.'

Geoff put a comforting arm on her shoulder. 'Seems I came along at the right time, eh?' he said, enjoying the rush of colour that now stained her cheeks. Sixth-formers wore their own clothes, not school uniform, and in her skin-tight jeans and T-shirt she really was a very pretty little thing. She stared back at him shyly from beneath her long eyelashes. No wonder Daryl fancies her, he told himself.

'What say I drive you home?' he suggested. 'We could stash your bike in the boot and we could stop at Hurston Green garage and buy you a new repair kit. Then you could mend the tyre when you get home.'

Susie's look of delight was mixed with relief. 'That's really kind of you, Mr Lewis, if you're sure it won't be too much trouble.'

'No trouble at all! I'm glad I stopped by in time to help out.'

'That's wicked!' Susie said, her smile returning. 'It's really very kind of you, Mr Lewis,' she repeated.

With the bike safely secured in the boot, Geoff helped her into the car and shutting the door, settled himself in the driver's seat.

'I'm ever so grateful,' Susie repeated as Geoff drove off. 'I would have had to wait ages for Daryl to come out after rugger practice, or walk, and then my dad would have had fifty fits. He's bad enough worrying about me even biking back with friends.' She gave a little giggle. 'You'd think I was six, not sixteen, the way he goes on. Do you think all parents are like that, Mr Lewis?'

'I wish you'd stop calling me Mr Lewis,' he said. 'My name is Geoff and unlike your father, I see you as very grown up and mature for your age.'

'Do you really?' Susie asked. 'Most of my friends are older than me. They think Daryl and me are stupid because we don't—'

She broke off, blushing furiously as she realized she had forgotten to whom she was now revealing her private life.

Geoff, however, reached out a hand and put it on her knee, patting it paternally.

'No need to be guarded with me, young lady! I pride myself on being pretty with it and, frankly, I admire you very much for not following your friends' example. Takes courage to stand up to peer pressure. Besides, although you act much older, you are only young and it's often better to wait until someone with a bit of experience comes along rather than give your virginity to the first boy who takes your fancy.'

Susie now stared uneasily at her clasped hands. Mr Lewis – Geoff – now had his left hand on her shoulder while steering with the right one. She had not expected an older man to be quite so explicit about sex. His reference to virginity – often enough openly discussed by her and her girlfriends – seemed somehow wrong coming from Daryl's stepfather. She knew Daryl disliked him but he would never say why, and as he was always polite, charming and attentive to her, she had not understood Daryl's attitude.

As if divining her thoughts, Geoff removed his hand from her shoulder and placed it casually on her knee again.

'Both Daryl's mother and I were delighted when he introduced you last term, Susie. He's a thoroughly decent, likeable young fellow. Young, of course, being the operative word. I suppose that's because his mother has always babied him. At a guess, if I didn't know better, I'd take you to be a good two years older. My wife refers to you as being a schoolgirl but I think of you as a young woman – and a very pretty one at that!'

Susie was blushing once more. For some reason, his compliments were embarrassing her, as was his left hand which was now gently stroking her leg while he continued to steer the car with his right. She felt uneasy but she couldn't think how best to remove it. He suddenly did so himself, saying:

'Tell you what, young lady. If you aren't in too much of a hurry to get home, why don't we stop off at the Forester's Arms and have a quick drink. We can sit by the window and watch for Daryl when he comes past. I expect he'll see your bike sticking out of the boot of my car and come in and find us. Good idea?'

Flattered that Mr Lewis considered her mature enough to be drinking in a pub at four thirty in the afternoon, Susie nevertheless remembered her father's warning – *never get into a strange car with a strange man whatever temptation he puts in your way.* But Mr Lewis wasn't a stranger and everyone knew his beautiful cream Mercedes. Daryl would be surprised and perhaps think a little more kindly about his stepfather if he did stop by and Mr Lewis offered him a drink, too.

The Forester's Arms, a small country pub tucked halfway between Hurston Green and Headingborough, was surprisingly busy. A group of walkers were sitting outside on the wooden benches with large glasses of cold drinks in their hands. They were talking noisily and waved in a friendly way as Geoff drew up outside and turned off the engine.

He turned to look at the girl beside him. 'OK, Susie-Q?' he asked. 'Not worried, are you?'

'Only about my parents,' she replied hoping she didn't sound childish. 'My father gets worried if I'm late home. I expect you think it's silly but he—'

'Nonsense!' Geoff broke in as he tucked his arm through hers and led her through the open front door. 'I think he's perfectly justified these days when every day young girls are kidnapped and raped or even murdered. Now what's it going to be, Susie? If you haven't tried it before, I suggest a Red Bull. I think you'll like it although I suppose it is a bit potent for a girl of your age. Maybe—'

'I'd like to try it!' Susie broke in as he led her towards the bar. 'Even if it is potent, I don't have to have more than one, do I?'

'Certainly not!' Geoff replied, beckoning to the barman, but even as the words left his lips, he decided the young girl beside him would have as many drinks as he could persuade her to imbibe. Then she would be the one to beg him to stop the car and kiss her before he took her home.

TWELVE

Althea was cutting chrysanthemums for the house when Daryl arrived back from school and, flinging his bike down on the grass, came storming across the lawn to her side.

'Hi, darling, you're home a bit late!' she greeted him.

'Mum, I need to talk to you!' Daryl replied unsmiling.

His voice was gruff which, together with the look on his face, alerted Althea to the fact that this was serious. She put down her secateurs and lifted the basket of cut blooms.

'We'll go indoors and get you a Coke, shall we? And then we can chat in the study.'

'No!' Daryl's voice rose and he was almost shouting. 'I want to talk to you here, now.'

Althea regarded her son's flushed cheeks and felt the first stab of concern. Whatever Daryl wanted to talk about, it was very important to him. Almost seventeen, he was already six foot and stood looking down at her. She waited for him to speak, which, from the number of times he cleared his throat, he was finding difficult. An explanation for his unusual behaviour sprang to mind.

'You haven't quarrelled with Susie, have you, darling?'

Daryl exploded into speech. 'Of course not! Mum, you've got to divorce him . . . He's a perv— Susie's told me what he's done. She didn't want to but she daren't tell her parents as her father would go looking for him and beat him up.' His voice broke as he added: 'I hate him; I've always hated him and you will too when you hear what he did!'

Althea's heart had doubled its beat as she tried to quell the sudden fear Daryl's words had evoked. She didn't want to hear any more. Playing for time she said: 'By "him" I take it you are referring to Geoff. I know you've never liked him, Daryl, but—'

'He nearly raped Susie!' Daryl broke in. 'He's a stinking

rotten pervert. If you weren't married to him, I'd shoot him, and so would her father if he knew. She hasn't told him – or her mother – but I knew something was wrong when I found her at the bottom of our drive. I could see she'd been crying. She didn't want to tell me why at first and asked me to get her bike for her from the bike shop where she'd left it. Mum, he's nothing but a rotten pervert and you've *got* to divorce him,' he repeated.

Althea's heart rate had trebled during Daryl's outburst. She simply did not want to hear what her son was saying: she did not want to believe him and above all, she did not want to be made to face the fact that she had suspected for a long time, that Geoff had a dissolute side to his character. She said quietly:

'Geoff does have a name, Daryl, and you should use it if you are going to make these very serious allegations.' Now suddenly she did want to know more and keeping her voice as steady as she could, she asked bluntly: 'Are you trying to tell me Geoff raped Susie?'

To her concern, she saw tears brimming in her son's eyes.

'Did he?' she prompted in a quieter tone.

Daryl swallowed, brushing the threatening tears away with the back of his hand. The anger had gone and he sounded very young as he replied: 'No! But he tried to touch her up. He probably would have raped her if I hadn't come by. Mum . . .'

'Daryl, will you calm down and tell me quietly what this is all about? Are you referring to the fact that Geoff gave Susie a lift home this afternoon?'

Daryl looked surprised. 'So he's been home and told you, has he?'

'He came home early – and went out again just before you arrived,' she told him. 'He has gone to see Bob.'

'I bet he didn't tell you that he stopped at the Forester's Arms before he got here and gave Susie vodka to drink – vodka and Red Bull – which is really lethal. She had no idea there was vodka in it, she hadn't had Red Bull before. But that isn't all, Mum . . .'

He proceeded to tell her how Geoff had stopped at the

school and picked Susie up. She'd been really pleased to be getting a lift home, because her bike had a puncture and she had always had a bit of a 'thing' about Geoff and had never understood why he disliked him. 'If I hadn't stopped at the pub when I saw the Mercedes there with Susie's bike sticking out of the boot, he would probably have driven her off somewhere and raped her.'

'You can't know that, Daryl,' Althea said quietly.

'Yes I can!' he replied. 'When I went into the pub, there he was sitting next to Susie with his hand on her leg. They were in a dark corner and I didn't see them at first because the place was chock-a-block. When he saw me, he was obviously embarrassed and stood up saying they were about to leave. When I got to the bottom of the drive he'd dropped her outside the lodge.'

'Then if the pub was full of people, Geoff would have been quite ridiculously stupid to . . . to do anything nasty to Susie. There'd be dozens of witnesses and—'

Once again, Daryl interrupted. 'He was trying to get her drunk, Mum. She was holding a full glass of vodka and Red Bull and she told me she thought it was her second but she was a bit woozy by then and said it could have been her third. She said it tasted a bit like Coke . . . and that he'd been stroking her thigh and then he'd put an arm right round her shoulders and started to touch her breasts . . .'

Althea had known Susie White ever since she and Daryl had met in the sixth form. She was briefly acquainted with her parents, who she knew to be very strict with their only child. However improbable the story Susie had related to Daryl, she did not doubt its authenticity. A thought shot through her mind.

'Daryl, listen to me. Suppose Geoff *was* trying to get Susie drunk, that doesn't for a single moment mean that he intended to seduce her. He isn't like that, Daryl. He isn't interested in young girls – only in women. He has often told me that it is the older women who turn him on, and last night—' She broke off, unhappily aware that she was about to tell her teenage son that Geoff had, albeit unusually these days, made passionate love to her the previous night.

As she spoke, an ugly thought came into her mind. For some time now, Geoff had avoided love making, saying he was too tired or would have to be up early and needed an early night. It had crossed her mind ever more frequently that he, who in the early days of their marriage had been almost insatiable, was finding sex elsewhere. All the symptoms were there – his late arrivals home; a lipstick mark on a shirt; a woman telephoning who wanted to speak to him but gave no name; a hotel bill for a single room with breakfast and one extra breakfast. When she had queried this, he'd shrugged it off saying he had been out jogging and got back to the hotel hungry, so he'd ordered a second breakfast to be sent up.

Something about his story didn't ring true and albeit reluctantly she had done what she had never imagined she would have to do – employ a private investigator. She was still waiting for his report. Meanwhile she tried not to think about it as she reassured Daryl that even if he was right about Geoff fondling Susie, which of course was ridiculous, no way could he have taken it so far as to rape her.

Colour flared once more into Daryl's cheeks. 'Then why get her drunk? He was fondling her, she said so, and at the time she didn't want to get up and walk out because there were lots of people in the pub and she'd have been embarrassed; and anyway, her bike had a puncture so she would have had to walk home. You don't notice these things, Mum, but he's always fancied her, eyeing her up, paying her compliments. I thought he did it because he wanted to make me jealous but now I know it's not that. You've got to believe me, Mum. You've got to divorce him.'

Althea drew a deep breath in an attempt to steady her nerves. 'Darling, I'm not saying you and Susie are making all this up or, indeed, that it didn't happen just as she told you, but even if Geoff had meant to seduce her that doesn't make him a pervert, does it? He may have upset her by being too lovey-dovey and I totally agree he should not have given her alcohol when he knows very well she is below the age limit. But at the end of the day, he hasn't harmed her, has he? And there's no need for her to meet Geoff again and I shall tell him so.' She reached up and touched Daryl's cheek.

'Does that mean you aren't going to divorce him?' Daryl asked sharply, as he shrugged off her hand angrily. 'If you don't, I shall go and live with Dad. I'm perfectly capable of getting to school by myself so there's no *need* for me to go on living here. The only reason I stayed here was because of you; but not any more; not if *he* stays.'

Althea was appalled – not just by what Daryl had revealed about Geoff but about his threat to leave home. Ever since she and Geoff had somehow drifted apart, Daryl had been her raison d'être. There were days when she had no plans or occupations and she would look constantly at her watch marking how long it would be before he came up the drive on his bike. Sometimes Susie came with him but she liked the girl and, seeing how happy she made Daryl, she was more than prepared to 'share' him.

Aware that Daryl was waiting for her to speak, she said: 'You realize this has come as quite a nasty shock, Daryl, and I need time to think about it . . . to talk to Geoff.' She paused briefly, her eyes thoughtful as she added: 'Do you want to go back to Dad's tonight? I need to talk to Geoff on his own and you won't want . . .'

'No, I don't want to see him – ever again. He really, really frightened Susie and she can't tell her parents because her father would blow his top and her mother would be telling her she mustn't go back to school or something like that. I said I'd pick her up at the lodge after I'd talked to you, so I might as well go on to Dad's from there. Maybe her parents will let her stay the night at the farm.'

Seeing the look on Althea's face, it struck him suddenly that she had aged. His friends had always said how pretty his mother was; nearly young enough to be taken for an older sister. Now she looked more like fifty than forty. Impulsively he put his arm round her.

'I'm sorry, Mum. I suppose I should have told you less . . . well, not so suddenly but I was so angry and—'

'It's all right, darling! Of course you must go and comfort

Susie. I just hope there might have been a misunderstanding and that Geoff didn't mean . . .'

'You can't not mean it when you ply someone with alcohol and then start touching them like he did. I bet he tries to say he didn't do it but even if Susie had wanted to make up such a thing she wouldn't have been in the state she was, crying and shaking and saying it was all her own fault.'

They were now walking towards the house, Althea's flower basket in her hand. She stopped and looked at Daryl.

'Did Susie say that?' she asked. 'Had she been . . . well . . . egging Geoff on and making him think she wanted him to touch her? I know she has always had a kind of childish crush on him.'

'Mum, I know you don't want to think that he's the rotten lech I know he is. If you saw how upset Susie is, you'd know it wasn't a silly game she was playing.'

Althea caught his arm and looking up into her son's face, she said: 'When you stop to think about it, Daryl, there could never have been any possibility of what you're suggesting. For one thing, Geoff knew you biked home and would in all probability see his car – as indeed you did – and see him with Susie. Where would it have taken place? Now, I'll speak to Geoff this evening, you go and comfort Susie. I expect she would like to stay at Logan Hill Farm if you are going to be there. If her parents see she's been crying, they'll be sure to cross-question her. Susie told me once that they were hopelessly overprotective of her and still thought of her as a little girl. Is Susie still at the lodge?'

For the first time during their conversation, he smiled. 'Yes, I left her with Mrs Emery. I told her Susie had been knocked off her bike and that I was coming up here to ask you to drive her home.'

He'd thought of everything, Althea told herself. He was showing the maturity of a much older person – and ingenuity – too.

'I'll get the Audi out of the garage and drive you both to Logan Hill Farm. Shall I telephone her parents first and ask them if they will allow Susie to stay the night there?'

Daryl leaned down and kissed the top of her head. 'You are the best mother anyone could have,' he said, 'and Mum, whatever happens about . . . about Geoff, I'll never stop seeing you even if I don't live here any more.'

There were tears in Althea's eyes as she hurried away to telephone Susie's parents, who, having heard about the puncture, somewhat reluctantly gave their permission on the understanding that Susie did all her homework before anything else.

Susie was no longer crying when they stopped at the lodge, but when Althea said how sorry she was about what had happened she dissolved into tears again. It was as well the girl wasn't going home, Althea thought.

Fortuitously, Terence was not in the house when they arrived and Althea found him feeding the chickens behind the barn. He looked surprised to see her, but when he heard the reason for her arrival with the two children, his face gave no sign of his reaction. He said simply:

'Of course, they are both welcome for as long as necessary. Can I get you a cup of tea, or a drink, or something?'

Althea felt a rush of gratitude that Terence had not reacted as some other man might have done on learning of the allegations. Indeed, he might well have asked her why in God's name had she married him. As it was, he tucked his arm through hers and led her back to her car.

'Probably all just a storm in a teacup,' he muttered as he closed the door. 'Try not to worry.'

As she drove off she could see him making his way towards the house. She thought what an understanding person he was, but he had never been a man of many words and now she wondered if she was wrong to assume that because of that he had no strong feelings. It occurred to her that perhaps she was being very short-sighted not to realize that his reticence could be covering greater depths than she had supposed.

The telephone was ringing when she got home. It was six o'clock but Geoff had not returned. She hurried to answer the phone and was thrilled to hear Phoebe's voice.

'Is that you, Al? I tried to phone earlier but you must have been out. You got my message?'

Althea drew a deep breath of delight, and taking the handset she sank gratefully into the nearest armchair.

'Phoebe! How lovely to hear from you! And yes, I was out. If you've got a few minutes, I'll tell you the reason, but first I want to know how and where you are.'

'Skegness, of all places. I'm a governess again! In a play called *Once Too Often* – nothing very spectacular. Anyway, I'll be going down to London next week and wondered if we could meet up?'

Smiling delightedly, Althea said: 'It's so good to talk to you, Phebes, and yes, of course we'll meet. Actually, I'd love a day in London and it would be easier for you than coming down here, wouldn't it? I've got time on my hands whereas you seem to be keeping very busy.'

She could hear Phoebe's girlish laugh and was momentarily reminded of their teenage years.

'I'm not going to be busy once this play closes, so I'm going to take a holiday – a cruise, maybe. I've never been on one.'

'Nor I!' Althea said. 'Maybe I'll come with you! I think I'm going to need to get away for a bit.' She broke off. 'Phebes, have you really got time for a chat? And before you start arguing about the cost of a long call, Geoff claims most of our phone charges against his tax!'

They both laughed and then Phoebe told Althea to fetch her diary before they resumed the conversation.

'I'll make any date you say, Phoebe, so you choose. If it coincides with the dentist or the hairdresser or something, I'll postpone it. You know, I've missed you!'

'And I love you lots, too, Al!' Phoebe replied. 'Now fetch your diary and ring me back. I can't wait to hear all your news.'

'It isn't good news, I'm afraid. But I do need to talk to you privately and fortunately Geoff's not home yet. I'll only be a minute.'

Phoebe, who was the only person other than Cressy in whom she would confide, had never married – the proverbial fate of 'silly women like herself', she'd confessed, who had become the mistress of a married man. Neither she, Althea, nor Cressida had met him. They had presumed that because of the necessary secrecy Phoebe's affair demanded, she'd been afraid to tell Cressida as well as herself, too much about it knowing they would advise her not to go on waiting for a married man to leave his wife. Year after year he had always found some excuse not to do so.

Maybe darling Phoebe would find some rational explanation for Geoff's behaviour, she thought, as she walked back into the drawing room with her diary. Maybe Phoebe would laugh off the whole thing and tell her she and Daryl were making a mountain out of a molehill. Maybe Daryl had exaggerated the whole episode . . . not purposely, perhaps, but because he so disliked Geoff. It was only as she was talking to Phoebe that she suddenly realized that her heart wouldn't break if she split up with Geoff. What she would mind far more was the loss of her home. The law might allow her to continue living in the matrimonial home as long as Daryl lived with her, but only until he left school. If Geoff decided to sell the Grange, she could never raise enough money to buy his share in the property.

Phoebe heard her out and only then said what she could to reassure her.

'You know what girls are like these days, Al. At Susie's age, they're still finding out if they are attractive to the opposite sex. Geoff was probably just playing along and when he gets home, he'll say any allegations of impropriety are ridiculous; say Daryl and the girl are making a mountain out of a molehill.'

When Althea put down the phone, she tried to believe Phoebe was right. Maybe Geoff did 'play away', as he told her Bob Pearson did from time to time; maybe he did flirt a bit with Susie, touch her inappropriately; but with nothing else in mind.

Althea almost managed to convince herself that Geoff would simply laugh the whole thing off.

THIRTEEN

Despite himself, Daryl was beginning to feel a trifle impatient with Susie. Sitting beside him in the stopping train from Hurston Green to Brighton, she was constantly dabbing at her red-rimmed eyes and he was conscious of the stares of the people seated opposite them. He was certain they thought he and Susie had quarrelled and that was why she was dripping tears. He was glad when the couple got out at the next station and he was able to suggest as nicely as he could that she pulled herself together.

'After all, Sue, it isn't as if he actually *did* anything!' he said. 'I mean . . . well, he only sent you a letter . . .'

He got no further before she rounded on him, half angry, half crying.

'I know it was only a letter of apology, but when Dad found it he said he was going to kill him and he'll never, ever let me get married into your family and I'm not supposed to see you any more, and if he finds out I've been with you today . . .'

She now burst fully into tears and not knowing what else to do, Daryl put an arm awkwardly round her shoulders and lent her a dry handkerchief. When her sobs subsided, he said tentatively: 'We can still see each other at school; your dad can't stop that. Please don't go on crying, Sue. Aunt Phoebe says she'll help think of something! She's really, really nice, and although I know she hasn't got kids of her own, she's always been fantastic with me. I mean, Mum loves me, I know she does, but it hasn't always been easy with me having to live with a stepfather I hate.'

The gentle monotony of his voice seemed to calm Susie down. She had recovered quite quickly from the unpleasant episode in the pub. Other girls at school had had the same sort of thing done to them and they just joked about it. They said things like: 'Lay off, Granddad,' or 'I'll report you to the police!' The trouble was – and remained – that her father was so old-fashioned he would curtail all her privileges even if she wasn't responsible. He said the way she dressed was provocative and it was partly her fault if she got messed around. He didn't seem to appreciate that all the girls – even those with big boobs and bottoms – wore low-cut jeans and skimpy tops.

At first, he had known nothing about the pub episode and then, a week ago, Mr Lewis had stopped his car at the bike shed and shoved an envelope into her bag. Before she could say anything, he'd driven off and she just shoved it further down, meaning to burn it when she got home. As usual, she had flung her bag down by the back door and hurried into the kitchen to give her mother a hug and start on the tea that was invariably ready for her. It was only when she heard the back door bang and realized her father was home that she remembered the letter. She jumped up to go and get it but remained rooted to the spot as her father came in waving it in one hand, his face scarlet.

'Thought I wouldn't see this . . . this filthy piece of paper, did you?' he demanded. '*Really sorry if I upset you but you looked so pretty I couldn't resist a quick cuddle. Ever since Daryl brought you home, I've wished I had a daughter like you to spoil but I suppose with all these silly human rights regulations, I shouldn't have touched you . . .* So what did he do, Susannah? Answer me. *Couldn't resist a cuddle. Didn't mean to upset you . . .*' He was almost shouting as he read aloud: '*Tell Daryl to bring you up to the Grange so I can apologize properly.* WHAT FOR? What did the bastard do?'

Even now, Susie still trembled at the degree of her father's anger. He had ranted on for twenty minutes before her mother had managed to calm him, but even she was unable to dismiss the letter entirely. Mr Lewis wouldn't be apologizing if there been no reason for it, she agreed with her husband. The man did not have the best of reputations.

His reaction to Mr Lewis's letter was to gate Susie, forbidding her to leave the house after she returned from school. When he had calmed down a little, her mother was able to talk him into agreeing she should still be allowed to meet her girlfriends, though not Daryl. The only reason she was here on the train with Daryl today was because she had told her parents she was spending the day at the home of one of her schoolfriends.

It wasn't the incident with Daryl's stepfather which was still upsetting Susie. After all, as her friends had commented, it wasn't as if he'd raped her! It was her father's ban on her relationship with Daryl, which he'd never been all that keen about in the first place, saying that she was far too young to have a regular boyfriend.

The train was now drawing into Brighton station, and wiping her eyes, Susie followed Daryl on to the platform. They walked to the big, imposing Metropole Hotel on the seafront where Daryl's Aunt Phoebe was meeting them for tea. There were several big lounges where they could sit and talk in private, his aunt had explained, whereas her digs in Worthing would be less easy for the young ones to get to.

She was waiting for them in the foyer. Her thin somewhat pale face lit up with a smile as she recognized Daryl.

'Do I get a kiss?' she asked laughing as she stood on tiptoe to reach up to him. Turning to Susie, she tucked her arm through the young girl's and led them to the far end of one of the comfortable lounges.

'I've ordered a cream tea for us in the terrace lounge at four o'clock!' she said. 'Now take off your jackets and we'll get down to problems in a minute. First I want to hear more about your mum's fête. Did you get the good results that the fortune-teller forecast, Daryl?'

Warming to Phoebe's natural friendliness, Susie was soon vying with Daryl to describe the various activities that had taken place. It was Daryl who relayed the strange coincidences which occurred after the fortune-teller had predicted disaster awaiting his stepfather. Phoebe was intrigued.

'You know it was I who suggested your mum might like to have that woman at the fête,' she said to Daryl. 'I'd met the clairvoyant up in Skegness where I was stand-in for a member of the cast of a play they were showing. One of

the girls invited her round to our digs and we all had a
whale of a time having our fortunes told. She was a Gypsy
woman, wasn't she? Called herself Madame Kotoly or something like that.'

'Tokoly!' Daryl said laughing. 'I liked her. She said I'd
get six A-levels – what a hope! She seemed OK to me but
my stepfather said she was a charlatan. Mum said he didn't
want to believe she was really able to tell the future because
she'd forecast such nasty things for him!' His expression
changed suddenly as he drew a deep breath before saying:
'You know what a . . . a pig he is, Aunt Phoebe! Everyone
says how charming he is and women like him because he
says flattering things to them. Susie used to like him, too,
didn't you, Sue? But underneath – well, I've heard him be
perfectly horrible to Mum. It's the way he talks to her sometimes . . . as if . . . well, as if he didn't love her any more
the way he used to. And he hates me because she sticks up
for me. Anyway, I've gone to live with Dad now so I don't
have to put up with him. I do like being with Dad – we
get on fine; but I know Mum misses having me around.'

Beside him, Susie was fidgeting with her mobile phone and
Daryl realized that he had usurped the conversation. They were
here to ask Aunt Phoebe's advice about their future . . . about
Mr White's refusal to allow Susie to meet him after school.

Phoebe put a hand on Susie's and said gently: 'I do see
why you are so upset – especially when none of what took
place with Mr Lewis was your fault. But you are still under
age, Susie, and it would be wrong of me to suggest you
deliberately disobey your father.'

Seeing the tears welling into the young girl's eyes, she
took out a handkerchief from her handbag and gave it to
her.

'Have you thought that it's a couple of years before you
come of age and can do as you wish?' she said. 'And it
isn't as if you and Daryl can't see each other at school
every day: and you have your mobiles so you can text each
other all evening, can't you?' She smiled. 'I know it isn't
the same as actually being together but your father can't
reasonably forbid you to talk to each other.'

Daryl's face had brightened considerably. 'That's what I said. Sue, and I know a year is absolutely ages but maybe your father will come round a bit when he knows I'm never going to take you near the Grange again. It's silly anyway not letting me look after you. If I'd not been playing rugger the afternoon he took you to the pub, I'd have been biking home with you and you'd never have got in the car with . . . with him.'

What a very nice, level-headed boy Daryl was, Phoebe thought as the waiter arrived with a tray laden with plates of scones and cakes and bowls of cream and jam, which he put on the low coffee table in front of them. She had not envied Althea her big house and cars and expensive clothes and holidays, but she had always envied her her young son. From a mischievous youngster, he had grown into a handsome, delightful youth and she could well understand why this young girl was in love with him.

As far as she knew, Susie was hoping to gain enough top-grade A-levels to go to university to train as a vet. Daryl was now hoping to study farm management so it seemed likely their two worlds would become close when they were older. But meanwhile, they made a touching pair of first-time lovers and she understood Daryl's bitterness that his stepfather should have muddied the waters.

While the youngsters tucked into the food, she reflected how long ago it was since she had been a witness with Cressy at Althea's registry office marriage to Geoff. Before then she had been a frequent visitor to her and Terence at Logan Hill Farm; but then she had stopped going. Her acting career, she explained, took her all over the country, keeping her away from Sussex for weeks on end. Then there had been the miserable spells in hospital and the months of chemotherapy when she'd remained in her digs hiding her bald head and trying to come to terms with the fact that the previous year's treatment had not prevented a spread of the cancer.

Occasionally, she had chided herself for her isolationism; for not letting her two dearest friends know what was happening to her so they could lend their support. There were times when she had been so low, so depressed that she had nearly broken her vow of independence and telephoned Cressy or Al; when the urge was nearly overwhelming to expel some of the bitterness which was eating away at her ever since her long-time lover had walked out on her when he'd discovered she had cancer.

As always, she had curbed her moments of weakness, reminding herself that ultimately she had only herself to blame. She had always known but ignored the fact that there was never an excuse for a woman to become the mistress of a married man. Even if she herself did not lie to his wife, she was willing for her lover to do so. Even if he did not love his wife, time spent with his mistress was that much less time spent with the woman he'd married; gifts to her were presents he might have given his wife. But such realizations did not assuage the bitterness she felt at being abandoned the very day she'd told her lover her illness was terminal. If ever there was a time she needed his support, it was then when her courage was at its lowest ebb.

Looking now at Daryl and his pretty girlfriend, both smiling happily as they argued as to who would have the coffee and who the chocolate cake, she could accept the fact that she wasn't going to live long enough to see them married, or even off to their universities. Her oncologist had told her she had six to twelve months at most and her time was nearly up. She might not even be here for Christmas. Already she had played her last part on stage. Neither the cast nor the producer had known of her cancer and she had been able to conceal her steady loss of weight and growing exhaustion from them with bulky clothes and clever make-up. But that this present engagement was the last was something she preferred not to think about.

'Just be glad you have each other!' she told the two youngsters as they all prepared to leave. 'And Susie, don't be too hard on your father. These days the newspapers are full of dreadful stories about young girls like you being raped, killed, abducted. Like all fathers, he wants to protect you.'

Linking arms with each of them, she added: 'I expect

your father will have calmed down a little before long. It's not as if Mr Lewis is likely ever to approach you again now your family knows what happened. One has to assume he'd had too much to drink to behave like that with a school-girl such as yourself. I very much doubt he was conceited enough to believe you wanted him to fondle you. Daryl told me you had a crush on him, though?'

'Yes, I did!' Susie admitted. 'Because he was always so nice and polite and treated me like a grown-up whereas Dad and Mum treat me like a kid. But . . .' She shivered and Daryl quickly put an arm round her shoulders.

'Aunt Phoebe's right, Sue. Don't think about it. He won't dare do anything silly again, not now everyone knows. Maybe Mum will go and talk to your dad; make him see it wasn't such a big deal.'

'That's right, Daryl!' Phoebe said as she reached up to kiss him goodbye. 'And tell Mum I really will take time to come and have lunch with her soon. I'm off to London tomorrow so it won't be for a while, but when I get back . . .' The lie slid off her lips with ease. It was as if she was now playing the part of a busy, healthy career woman whose life was filled with activity.

She drove them both to the station and waved them goodbye. It was only as she turned her car round and headed back towards Worthing that she allowed herself to slump with exhaustion. The afternoon, simple though it had been, sapped what strength she had left. With fourteen miles to go, it would be at least another half-hour before she could let herself into her digs and lie down on her bed.

Trying not to let herself realize how relentlessly her body was weakening, Phoebe turned the car on to the coast road and headed back to the dingy, lonely room she called home.

FOURTEEN

Geoff sat at his desk in his London office, his expression mutinous as he opened the pile of letters his secretary had left for him. The first was from a Swedish client backing out on a deal he had thought was watertight. The second was a letter forwarded by his elderly aunt's solicitor, saying he had virtually ignored her, his only relative, so she had left her not inconsiderable wealth to the old people's home where she had lived the last years of her life. It was the more galling as only a few weeks ago he had decided too much time had passed since he last visited her, but more pressing events had taken precedence.

Putting the letter through the shredder, he determined that he would not go to the funeral nor would he send flowers. The third letter, in a round untidy handwriting, was from Scarlett informing him that she had changed her mind yet again; that she would have liked to come to London and have her own flat and boutique, but she didn't dare do so. Squid, it seemed, had found out about her intention to go to London and was terribly jealous. She had written:

> He went into a rage and said he'd kill us both and you'd better know he meant it. He's going home to see his family next month so I thought if I come down to London while he's away, he won't know where I am if I'm living in your flat, so he can't follow me and do anything nasty to either of us . . .

There was a lot more in the same vein. The threats he decided to ignore. Most of Scarlett's conversation included huge exaggerations of events. A chimney fire became 'a huge great big mass of flames pouring out of the windows spreading everywhere'; but it turned out there was only one fire engine needed which quickly put out the inferno using 'hundreds and thousands of litres of water'.

Geoff put the colourful sheets of notepaper through the shredder and told himself he should be feeling happy with the news; but for one thing, he had not yet found another shop with accommodation over it; and for a second, he was due to go to Dubai in ten days' time, so even if by some miracle another suitable flat was found he wouldn't be there to inspect it and sign the lease. He could suggest putting her in a suite in the Dorchester when Squid went back to Italy, but she'd hate being there on her own with nothing to do. Either she would go running back to Manchester or she'd go down to the bar and get picked up by one of the unattached men who would doubtless fancy her as much as he did!

He would have to make time to go up to Manchester and talk to her, he decided – before he went to Dubai. Perhaps he would take her a really expensive piece of jewellery, as she was always particularly accommodating when he brought her presents. He was not so naive as to imagine the girl loved him. He knew it was his money which attracted her. The boyfriend was a waiter in a second-rate restaurant and no match for him. If Althea ever found out he had been unfaithful to her, though, she would divorce him and take him to the cleaners. He would, he thought now as his secretary came in with a tray of coffee and biscuits, have to be a lot more careful about his meetings with Scarlett. He was pretty certain Althea had never hired a detective to follow him. Although he gave her a generous allowance, he doubted she could afford an investigator even if she wanted to do so. No, he was certain Althea knew nothing of his private life, of Scarlett, or indeed, the mistresses he had kept in the past.

Having drunk his coffee, he turned back to the pile of papers in his in-tray. There were several bills, which he transferred to his out-tray; an invitation to a charity ball at the Dorchester, a financial query from his accountant, and a driving licence renewal reminder which he also put in the tray for his secretary to deal with.

The last envelope, which had been forwarded from Brighton, held a typewritten letter. As he started to read it, he caught his breath.

Dear Mr Lewis,

I am writing to advise you that in a few days' time I shall be leaving England to return to my own country to visit friends. I am telling you this so that you do not think the following request is to receive money from you.

I am most urgently wishing to see you as, since our last meeting, I have been troubled again by even stronger presentiments regarding your future and I feel compelled to warn you of them. You cannot avoid your Destiny but if you are forewarned as to any disaster threatening you, you will at least be best prepared to deal with it.

Tomorrow, 13th September, I am meeting with our mutual friend, Miss Phoebe Denton. I wish to say goodbye to her as she has been a good friend to me. On the 15th I shall be departing from Gatwick so I can only offer you a little time on Sunday, 14th, when I shall be in Brighton during the afternoon. Is it possible we could meet there at your agency? I imagine it will be quite private on such a day.

Perhaps you or your secretary could leave a message for me with Miss Denton who has kindly given me her mobile number as I do not have one of my own, advising me if you wish to keep this appointment.

Yours very sincerely,
Kara Tokoly (Clairvoyant)

Geoff's mouth tightened as he screwed up the letter in his clenched fist. His first thought was that the woman would surely ask for money despite saying she wouldn't. However, one couldn't fault her for persistence. Even knowing he had not wanted to have his fortune told at the fête, she was still intent upon telling him what she called his Destiny. Destiny! he repeated to himself. And 'presentiments' about which she wanted to warn him! It was all complete rubbish – a clairvoyant who couldn't foresee whether he would make the appointment? He would not go to see her.

His secretary came in to collect the tray. She noted the thunderous look on her boss's face as she enquired if he wanted to dictate any letters. On an impulse, Geoff picked up Madame Tokoly's crumpled letter and smoothing it out showed it to her. Diane did not, as he had expected, ridicule the contents.

'I expect you think I'm a bit nutty,' she said apologetically, 'but I've never ruled out second sight and horoscopes and things like ESP. Animals are an example. They are far more sensitive than we are. Did you see in the newspaper a while ago that dogs could foretell impending death, and cancer, of all things? And we've all heard about the elephants who knew the tsunami was coming.'

'This woman is a Gypsy!' Geoff told her. 'Russian or Hungarian or whatever. She's in this country illegally and I could, if I wanted, report her.'

Diane nodded. 'But it wouldn't do much good, would it? I mean she says she is leaving the country of her own accord in three days' time. Did she get anything right when you last visited her?'

'I didn't visit her!' Geoff said sharply. 'The wretched Gypsy saw me going past her tent at our fête and literally dragged me inside. She sat down and read those Tarot cards and then I had to shuffle them and she starts moaning and goes into a trance – fake, probably.'

He gave Diane a sheepish grin. 'The odd thing was, she forecast a major disaster but for some obscure reason, she didn't want to tell me about it – anyway, not then – and coincidentally I had two near fatalities in the space of the following fortnight.'

Diane nodded. 'You mean that motorway pile-up.' She paused to think and then added: 'And that plane you were on which had an electrical fault. How weird!'

Then she smiled. 'I expect you're right and they were just coincidences.'

Geoff looked sheepish. 'There's a third and a fourth,

Diane. Have you forgotten that client who suddenly called off the deal without – in my humble opinion – any valid reason? Then this morning I heard from my aunt's solicitor that she has died and left all her money to an old people's home, for God's sake! I'm beginning to wonder if there are any more nasties coming my way.'

Diane put the files she was holding in Geoff's in-tray and said: 'As the Gypsy woman seems to think there are, why don't you go and see her and hear what she has up her sleeve? She said she doesn't want paying, so you've nothing but time to lose and, if she's really psychic, you might be able to avoid these impending disasters.' She gave a sudden smile. 'Cheer up, Mr Lewis! It's a beautiful day and you're playing golf this afternoon with Mr Albany. Had you forgotten?'

Geoff nodded, reassured to have his elderly secretary's opinion. She might have a face like a harridan, but she had a keen brain and a good heart. Moreover, she was nearly sixty and therefore happy with part-time work, only coming in when he needed her in his London office.

'Yes, I had forgotten Mr Albany,' he said as he put down his now empty coffee cup. 'Maybe I'll take your advice, Diane, and go and see what Madame Whatshername has to say.'

'Her name is Madame Kara Tokoly!' Diane reminded him. 'Shall I ring Miss Denton for you and say you'll see Madame Tokoly in the Brighton agency on Sunday between two and three? You're free until six o'clock when it's drinks in Headingborough with the Petersons ... you know, sir, the couple who want to buy that former Butlin's site for redevelopment?'

Geoff nodded. 'OK! Tell the woman to ring the front-door bell. The porter at Templeton House will let her into my office.'

The following Sunday, after an early lunch at his golf club, Geoff drove himself down the A23 with mixed feelings, in part apprehensive, partly castigating himself for being so naive as even to think of taking the Gypsy woman

seriously. Maybe Diane was right in suggesting he would
be better warned if he knew what disasters awaited him;
on the other hand, there was nothing he could have done
to prevent the accidents the clairvoyant had previously
predicted. Maybe he could have chosen a different day or
time to go up to Manchester and so avoid the motorway
crash which had so nearly killed him. Maybe he could have
chosen a different airline so he wouldn't have been on the
faulty plane. Maybe if he had been a bit less tight dealing
with the Swedish client, the man wouldn't have called off
the deal. Maybe had he employed a bona-fide electrician
in his office in Brighton instead of the cowboy who'd
happened to offer his services so cheaply there wouldn't
have been a fire. Fortunately, the insurance company had
paid up in full, despite the fact that it looked as if the fire
might have been his fault.

His mood a little happier at the memory, Geoff turned
off the A23 on to the road leading along Brighton seafront.
His estimated travel time had been excellent as his watch
indicated it was five minutes to two when he walked into
his office.

There was no sign as yet of Madame Tokoly and suddenly
he badly needed a drink. He was pouring a bottle of ginger
ale into a tumbler of whisky when Madame Tokoly startled
him with her sudden appearance in the doorway. She did
not hold out her hand but said briefly: 'I'm glad you're here,
Mr Lewis. I was afraid you might have changed your mind
and cancelled our appointment. Do please finish your drink.
It would be a pity to waste it.'

Feeling not a little ridiculous standing by his desk while
his visitor – having declined a drink – watched him drain
his glass, Geoff indicated that they should be seated.

'You seem to think I need warning of something, Madame
Tokoly!' he said, trying to keep the impatience out of his
voice. 'Perhaps you would be good enough to explain?'

Madame Tokoly's heavily painted mouth widened in a
strange fashion that was not quite a grimace as she replied:
'It is in the cards, Mr Lewis. They never lie. They speak
of the future. It is possible to misinterpret them, but . . .'

She paused, regarding him over the top of a pair of gold-rimmed spectacles. Suddenly feeling like a schoolboy facing his headmaster, Geoff became impatient.

'If you have anything to tell me, madam, I wish you would stop talking in riddles and do so. I have a busy schedule this afternoon and—'

'I do understand,' the woman interrupted quietly, 'and I apologize if you feel I am prevaricating. I had hoped to break this to you gently, but since you insist, I have to tell you that each time I have looked into the cards to advise me of your future, I have come upon the Death Card.'

'The *what*?' Geoff's voice was sharpened by a mixture of disbelief and anxiety. 'What are you talking about? What Death Card?'

'It's number thirteen of my Tarot cards, Mr Lewis. It symbolizes absolute endings and absolute beginnings among other things. But you cannot escape your Destiny – it is the Death Card, as any other astrologer will tell you.'

Geoff's face which had whitened was now flushed an angry red. He stood up and stared angrily down at his visitor.

'I've never heard such rubbish! I don't know why I am allowing you to waste my time with this ridiculous mumbo-jumbo. Death Card! For heaven's sake, we're all going to die sometime! You, me, everyone.' He strode round his desk and stood looking down at the Gypsy.

'Just tell me when, if you know so much . . . when am I supposed to die? Just tell me that!' he repeated.

Before Madame Tokoly could reply, there was a knock on the door and the hall porter peered round it.

'There's someone wants to see you, Mr Lewis. I said as how you had a visitor but . . . well, they're insisting. Shall I say they can see you?'

'No! Yes! No!' Ashen-faced, Geoffrey faced the half-open door, for one of the few times in his life unable to make up his mind.

PART TWO

FIFTEEN

At half-past seven on the evening of Tuesday the 16th of September, Inspector Govern decided he had done enough work and for once would go home early. He was on the point of leaving the car park when he saw the tall, lanky figure of his detective sergeant hurrying towards him. He rolled down the car window.

'What's up, Beck?' he asked as he came up to him. David Beck and he had worked together for the past seven years, and although Govern maintained his authority at work, off duty he treated the younger man more as a son.

'The Chief wants to see you, sir – about the Templeton House murder. He's been trying to get you on your mobile since four o'clock.'

'I thought DI Simmonds was handling it!' Govern said.

'Well, he was but he's gone down with this flu bug everyone seems to be catching. Anyway, the Chief says he knows it's late but he wants to see you tonight! He thinks the case is right up your street, the victim being the chap whose office had the fire we investigated on the ground floor of Templeton House a while back. We thought it was arson, remember? A Mr Geoffrey Lewis. Lives at Hurston Grange. Great big house with mullioned—'

'My memory is still in good order, thank you, Beck!' Inspector Govern interrupted tersely as he switched off the engine and began to extricate himself from the front seat of his BMW.

Beck looked sheepish. 'Sorry, sir! But I thought . . .'

'I'll do the thinking, Beck, you do what you're told!' Despite the words, the rebuke was light-hearted in tone. 'Do I take it Chief Inspector Murley is in his office and I'm to report to him there?' he asked as he closed the car door and turned towards the police station.

'Yes, sir! He's waiting for you.' As they walked together

into the large brick building, Beck added with a twinkle: 'He wondered if you forgot to switch on your mobile as the switchboard couldn't locate you!'

Govern laughed. His readiness to see a joke against himself was one of the reasons David Beck was so fond of his boss.

'OK, so my memory isn't infallible,' he said. 'I had forgotten. One up to you, David!'

The DCI greeted him with his usual curt nod. Detective Chief Inspector Murley was a somewhat military-looking man with a clipped moustache and straight back. He was tapping the top of his desk rhythmically as he barked out some facts.

'Sit down! Sit down, Govern! Glad your sergeant caught you in time. Told you Simmonds had rung in sick, did he?' Without waiting for a reply, he continued: 'Murder at Lewis & Gibbs Estate Agents on Sunday. DI Simmonds took the 999 call so I left him on the case although I remembered it was you who handled the suspected arson there in the summer. Up to yesterday, it looked pretty straightforward, but it's not quite so simple as we first thought.'

He cleared his throat. 'This Lewis chap was murdered on Sunday afternoon. SOCO went in and did their stuff, picked up dozens of prints but we've no matching ones on record. The office cleaner found the body on Monday, yesterday, morning. Porter cum caretaker said he'd seen a resident from one of the flats above the agency – the agency has the ground floor of Templeton House: upstairs is all residential – but you'd know that. It looked a strong lead because the chap the porter saw didn't have an alibi. But when Simmonds questioned the caretaker a second time this morning, he admitted that there had been quite a few strangers going in and out of the estate agents, which he'd thought a bit odd seeing as it was Sunday when it's closed; not to mention Mr Lewis being there in person. Here, take a look at these.'

He handed Govern the notes DI Simmonds had made before he signed off sick. The caretaker, a retired warrant officer, was also porter for the block of flats above Lewis

& Gibbs. Under more vigorous questioning, he remembered that one of the strangers looked foreign. He recalled the woman because he thought she might be an immigrant. He wasn't on duty, Sunday being his day off, but thought the owner of the agency, Mr Lewis, must have left the door to his office open and the woman had let herself in.

A second page of DI Simmonds's notes contained further comments from the porter. He'd gone back to his own flat in the basement so he hadn't seen the foreign woman leaving. He'd heard the door of the agency bang once or twice – springs needed replacing. It had come as a very nasty shock when the cleaner had come screaming down the passage next morning saying Mr Lewis was dead and there was blood everywhere! The porter's main concern from then on was that he would be blamed for not apprehending an intruder despite his being off duty on the Sunday.

Simmonds had then questioned the residents, one of whom, an elderly gentleman, had seen a woman leaving Mr Lewis's private office when he'd gone out to post a letter sometime after three o'clock. He was prepared to make a statement but didn't have an alibi for himself. The man gave a vague description of the woman he had purported to have seen: middle-aged, swarthy, about five foot five. He had not noticed what she was wearing but did remember large dangling gold earrings. She hadn't spoken to him or he to her. He thought she was carrying a large shopping bag – one of the kind the supermarkets sold to stop customers using plastic bags. The resident had then said he'd glimpsed a man leaving the agency about half-past three on his return from his walk but couldn't describe him.

Simmonds had put an asterisk by this last statement querying whether the resident had introduced this character in order to deflect suspicion from himself; one to be interviewed again.

Chief Inspector Murley had been watching Govern silently while he glanced through the notes. Now he said: 'Before he went off duty, Simmonds left those notes on my desk saying he thought it looked fairly certain the woman killed him. However, when they did the post-mortem yesterday, this was found in Lewis's shirt pocket.'

He handed Govern a small lined piece of paper on which was typed:

MT .2.A.2.15. 2.30 PW-2.45. TH..3 PM Sun

'Obviously a time schedule memo,' DCI Murley said, 'but Simmonds hadn't got around to identifying the initials. If those are people who had appointments with Lewis for some reason and they turned up on time, they are all suspects. See what you can do, Govern. I have a feeling this case is turning out to be quite a twister.'

Far from looking dismayed, Govern's face lit up. He hadn't had a homicide since the Cheyne Manor Golf Club murders, and if there was one thing he most enjoyed in his police work, it was pitting his wits against that of a murderer.

'Victim died sometime between two thirty and three thirty p.m. Sunday afternoon; three gunshot wounds, one fatal,' Chief Inspector Murley stated, 'but the doc has ruled out suicide. The victim wasn't found till six thirty next morning when the cleaner went in to do the room. There's an alert out to find the foreign woman but no sightings as yet. However we got this from an off-duty officer who thought it important enough to come in with it.'

The chief inspector handed Govern a copy of the *Argus*, folded back to the page of advertisements. Ringed with a marker pen was the following:

> Madame Kara Tokoly, clairvoyant, regrets that she will shortly be leaving the country. However, she will be available at 1–5 Templeton House, Brighton, on Sunday 14th September between 2 and 5 p.m. for final readings or horoscopes for clients requiring her expertise.

He looked up at Govern, peering closely at him over the top of gold-rimmed spectacles.

'There is an unknown number of people who might have read that advertisement. Think you can help, Govern? How much d'you know about the victim?'

'Well, sir, quite a bit as it happens. When there was that fire in Mr Lewis's estate agency in Brighton, the insurance people thought it was arson. We thought so too but there was no way to prove it, and they paid out.'

The chief inspector took off his spectacles and polished them with a large white handkerchief before glancing down at his notes again and saying:

'One of our sergeants went to Hurston Grange this morning to break the news to Lewis's wife – job I'm glad doesn't come my way these days. Said the wife hadn't reported him missing because he often stayed a night or two away on business. She looked shocked but not particularly heart-broken.' He released a photograph from the clipboard and handed it to Govern. 'Dare say you recognize him. Chaps on the scene said thirtyish, good-looking fellow – what can be seen of him as he was covered in blood; six foot or so, expensive chinos and Fred Perry shirt, Rolex watch. Signs of wealth tied in with the credit cards in his wallet. Match your chap, eh?'

Govern nodded. 'Yes, he had a number of different property companies; an office in London as well as in Headingborough, and here in Brighton and Preston Park, but he also had deals going both in Europe and the States. Bragged about them when I interviewed him over his Brighton office fire. His wife told me she rarely saw him as he was always dashing off somewhere or other, more often than not abroad. Anyway, as you say, sir, no lack of money.'

The chief inspector looked thoughtful. Indeed: the wallet had a stash of fifty-pound notes and there was a Rolex on his wrist. 'Odd thing – the woman had a definite appointment with him. The appointment was written in his desk diary. Seems a bit illogical to me for a murderer to make a public date to see him with the intention of killing him. She must have known she'd be a suspect. Still, there's no knowing what foreigners will do.' He gave a deep sigh. 'Madame Kara Tokoly! We've got an alert out for her at all sea and airports. No luck so far, but if she is guilty, she may be lying low for a bit.'

He sat back in his chair and for a moment said nothing as he stroked his moustache. Then he said thoughtfully: 'Fact is, Govern, she could be perfectly innocent. The porter said there are fifteen bedsits and two flats in the Templeton House block, so there are always people coming and going, not just residents but their friends, relations, doctor, electric-meter chap and so on. Any one of them could have nipped into Lewis's office, which he must have unlocked to let Madame Whatever in, and shot him. We need two things, Govern, the woman and a motive. One thing we do know, no one of her name is registered in this country. I want you to get on to this right away. You can have that sergeant you seem to favour. I've heard you put him up for promotion, didn't you?'

Govern smiled. 'Yes, I've recommended DS Beck several times in the past. He's a keen, dedicated policeman who, as you know, I've worked with for the past seven years. I can bounce ideas off him and get an intelligent answer. He'll be as keen as I am to take on this case. Do you know anything more, sir? Was there a weapon in the room?'

'We've not found one. The pathologist said the gun was possibly small-calibre, but they'll confirm when they check the bullets.'

He stood up and walked round his desk to face Inspector Govern, his somewhat stern countenance softened by a half smile. 'Know a lot about you, Govern. Turned down promotion a year or two ago, if my memory serves me right; because you like to be hands-on-the-job. Don't blame you. Admin is a challenge, I suppose, but it's no damn fun!'

Unsure how to reply to this remark, Govern said nothing. The chief inspector now resumed his official manner.

'Ask Simmonds's sergeant, young Peterson, to give you any new info the chap garnered before he checked out. You're officially on the case as of now. Report back to me when you've got something worthwhile to tell me.'

Aware that he was dismissed, Govern left the room and went in search of the young police sergeant who was manning the telephone in the computer room. When he had introduced himself, he pulled up a chair and unscrewing his fountain pen, started to take notes.

It seemed they had been trying all Monday to contact Mrs Smythe, the manageress, but the premises had been sealed off when the murder was discovered so neither she nor any of the staff had gone in.

According to his sergeant, DI Simmonds had appropriated the office address book and noted that the manageress, Mrs Smythe, lived in Eastbourne. Simmonds was going to interview her ASAP. When he told her Lewis had been killed, she wanted to go straight to the office but apart from forensics being there, the room was a pretty grisly sight, blood, brains etc., so he told her to stay at home. The woman sounded shocked. Doubtful suspect – she'd just been given a substantial rise!

He gave Govern the address book and also Lewis's diary. Flipping over the pages, Govern saw the two o'clock reservation for the mysterious 'Madame Tokoly'. In brackets beside the entry, someone had scrawled: *'(Sunday only as going abroad and in transit on Monday)'*. There was a mobile-phone number but when Simmonds had tried it, he was informed that it didn't exist.

'Sounds a bit fishy,' Govern said as he jotted down the number, 'although I have to say with eleven digits, it's not unusual for people to get one wrong.'

There was little else Sergeant Peterson could tell him other than that forensics had matched Lewis's fingerprints, but even when they had got around to eliminating his and those of his staff, probably dozens more had been left by the day-to-day stream of clients being interviewed or signing documents in his office.

'DI Simmonds hoped that Madame Tokoly's prints were among them, but if it was she who had shot Lewis, it stands to reason she would have eradicated them,' he concluded as Govern stood up to leave.

Thanking him for his time, Govern stuck his notes and the copy of the *Argus* into his briefcase and returned to his office. It was now 9 p.m. Despite the hour, Beck was waiting for him. He jumped up as his boss came in.

'Bought you a pizza, sir,' he said grinning. 'Got one for myself. I reckoned you'd be as famished as I was it being all of eight hours since we finished our lunch at our inimitable canteen! How did it go?'

Govern sat down at his desk and tried not to see the crumbs Beck had left on its polished surface when he'd consumed his own supper. He took the now cold pizza Beck had thoughtfully bought him, and after a couple of mouthfuls, he regaled his sergeant with such facts as he had.

'Too late to start now,' he concluded, 'but first thing tomorrow – and that means eight thirty, not nine o'clock, Sergeant – we'll be on the job. So far, it sounds really interesting. Remember Lewis? You took a dislike to him although he was trying to charm the daylight off us both. You thought he was showing off!'

Beck laughed. 'You agreed with me, sir. But his wife was nice, wasn't she? I don't know about the son – seemed an uncommunicative little bastard. I got the impression that he didn't care for his stepfather.'

'Kids seldom do get on with replacement parents,' Govern said through another mouthful of pizza, which was surprisingly good seeing it had all but solidified. He glanced at his watch and saw that it was now nearly half-past. 'Tell you what, Beck, I'll finish this and we'll go to the Greyhound and have ourselves a beer while I fill you in. You don't have to hurry home, do you?'

The sergeant was in the process of selling his flat and was living temporarily with a colleague in Preston Park.

'I've already told my flatmate I might be working late,' Beck said, adding pointedly: 'Will you be buying, sir?'

Govern sighed. 'I suppose you're going to tell me you spent all your spare cash on our pizzas! Oh, well, fair do's, I guess, if I pay for the beer.'

Ten minutes later, the two had left the police station and were on their way in Govern's BMW to their favourite pub, Mr Geoffrey Lewis's murder still very much on their minds.

Govern was back in his office by eight o'clock the following morning. By nine, he had interviewed the porter at Templeton House and obtained a list of all the tenants. These were to be checked at the police station. Beck, who had somewhat unusually arrived at eight fifteen instead of nine, was waiting for him.

'There's a constable on guard outside Lewis's office,' Govern said, 'so I told him to send the manageress round here as soon as she arrives. Get someone to take her finger-prints and check them against forensics' list.'

'Could *she* – Mrs Smythe, isn't it? – have killed Lewis?' Beck said frowning. 'Maybe he was about to sack her; or he was having an affair with her and dumped her, or—'

'The porter described her as an old-fashioned spinster with a sharp tongue!' Govern interrupted. 'Anyway, appar-ently she'd just been given a pay rise. And please, Sergeant Beck, will you stop speculating and listen to me. I know we've got out an alert for airports but a bit of individual enquiring by you might pay dividends. I want the clair-voyant found and if necessary eliminated from the enquiry. For the present, I can't think what possible reason she might have had for killing Lewis, or anyone else for that matter.'

Beck looked thoughtful. 'So we're looking for someone with an obvious motive,' he said. 'If not the Tokoly woman, a disgruntled previous member of staff, perhaps?'

'Could be a previous employee, but I think that's unlikely. You don't shoot someone just because they've given you the sack. These days you take them before a tribunal and claim massive damages. If we're playing the guessing game, I think it far more probable that a successful businessman such as we know Lewis to have been would have made several enemies on his way up the ladder. His family weren't wealthy, you know. He made his own successes. Clever enough to employ devoted unmarried females – the loyal-to-the-death type – rather than a Sloane or a dolly bird who'd either try to make time with the boss or else leave him for fresh pastures!'

Beck grinned. 'Maybe that Madame Tokoly is a dolly bird! Some of the foreign girls I've come across are real smashers! Polish, probably – the country's full of them!'

'That's wild and unnecessary speculation,' Govern reproved him. 'According to the porter she's middle-aged and dumpy! And now will you stop talking so we can get down to the hospital and see the pathologist? He did the post-mortem and may have some more facts for us.'

The grey-haired but obviously very competent pathologist had a good many facts and a few extra details Beck would prefer not to have heard. It seemed the unfortunate cleaner who had found the body had opened the office door and seen the prone figure of the murdered man on the far side of the room. He was lying on his back just as he had fallen, a tiny hole in his forehead where one of the bullets had penetrated his skull, shattering the back where it had exited. The contents encircled his head like a dark red halo.

'Seems the cleaning woman was too hysterical to make much sense at first,' Beck said to Govern as they left the hospital, 'but Doc reported the man's position as being even quite relaxed, and there was a quizzical rather than a fearful expression on his face.'

'Sounds as if Lewis wasn't expecting to be killed!' Govern muttered more to himself than to Beck.

'So the murderer was probably a friend or acquaintance who Lewis trusted,' Beck suggested.

'The Tokoly woman could have been an acquaintance,' Govern argued. 'The fact that he was shot the same afternoon as the clairvoyant visited him is certainly not proof that she killed him.' He withdrew the artist's impression of the suspect which DI Simmonds's sergeant had given him from his briefcase, and a list of the high-denomination notes found in the dead man's open wallet.

When they got back to the station Govern checked the messages on his desk and, with a sigh, addressed his waiting sergeant.

'Nothing yet from airports or seaports. Maybe we should start this end . . . question local taxi-drivers and see if one of them picked this woman up from Templeton House on Sunday. See to it, Beck, there's a good chap. After that, get over to Gatwick. Use that charm of yours to get the check-in girls or booking clerks to go through their lists again. I know Simmonds asked for the info yesterday, but one of them just might recall some detail they'd missed. We want passenger lists for all flights leaving Gatwick between five p.m. Sunday and twelve noon Monday. Give them a description as well as the woman's name. She must have looked odd enough for someone to have noticed her. And make sure the CCTV cameras were checked for the same period.'

When DS Beck returned that afternoon, he greeted his boss with the announcement that he had both good and bad news. Which, he asked, would Govern like first? Seeing the look of impatience on the older man's face, he decided this was not the time to be light-hearted.

'No passenger remotely resembling Madame Tokoly checked in at EasyJet, destination Budapest, last Sunday, or indeed on Monday,' he said. 'The good news is that I found a taxi-driver – quite a pretty girl as it happens – who said a Gypsy-looking middle-aged female hailed her at Brighton station between two-thirty and three on Sunday afternoon and asked to be taken to the airport. She charged her forty pounds and the woman paid her with two twenty notes and a fiver for a tip. She thought it a bit odd as the passenger could have got to Gatwick from Brighton by train for a fraction of the price but she was quite elderly and she had a very large suitcase so the driver presumed she thought it worth the extra money.'

Govern remained silent for a moment, tapping his pen against the side of his laptop as he considered Beck's information.

'So she did go to Gatwick! Obviously not to Budapest. We were wrong to assume that was her destination simply because the secretary said she'd put in her letter to Lewis that she was, quote, "going home".' He gave a long drawn-out sigh.

'Possibly Mrs Lewis will be able to tell us more about the woman. The manageress, Mrs Smythe, who I interviewed this morning while you were out, said she'd heard that a fortune-teller was at the Lewises' fête, but she never met her. The sooner we get out to Hurston Grange and interview the widow the better. And get someone to go round to Templeton House again and tell that elderly resident I'd like to see him. What's the chap's name?'

'Ingram, Laurence Ingram!' Beck said reading from his notebook. 'Shall I organize a car to pick him up?'

Govern sighed. 'Doesn't sound like a murderer to me! However, Lewis's very efficient manageress was a fount of information. Said Lewis bought the whole of Templeton block, so he is – or was – the landlord. Got that list of the other tenants, David?'

It was not very often that Govern used his sergeant's Christian name in office hours, but sometimes, when, as now, his mind was working furiously to sort out a mass of possible clues to the murder he wished to solve, he would use the familiar form of address. Although he never let the younger man know it, DS David Beck was, after all these years of working together, like the son he had never had.

SIXTEEN

The weather had suddenly turned cold and blustery as Inspector Govern and his sergeant drove over the South Downs to Hurston Green. Detective Sergeant Beck was, as usual, in a talkative mood.

'Sergeant Peterson said Mrs Lewis had taken the news of her husband's death quite calmly, which he thought was somehow suspicious, but women from her sort of background don't always show their feelings all that much, do they? I mean, they don't have hysterics or faint or anything!'

Govern, who preferred to drive himself, slowed down a fraction as he negotiated a Z bend.

'I agree lots don't, but some do. Remember that wing commander's death in Miller's Lane? His wife went completely to pieces when they fished him out of the lake!'

Beck nodded.

'Well, Peterson said Mrs Lewis was no more than matter-of-fact when she went down to Brighton mortuary to identify her husband; showed no emotion at all.' Govern turned the car into the road leading to Headingborough and thence to Hurston Green.

'I shall keep an open mind, and suggest you do the same,' he said. Nevertheless, he was finding it difficult to believe that Geoffrey Lewis's wife would have gone down to Brighton to his office to shoot him. Why not at home, although that would have marked her as the most likely suspect? From his visits to the house when he had been making enquiries about the office fire he had registered the degree of opulence. There had to be a motive for murder and one thing was certain, Mrs Althea Lewis would have been silly to have killed the goose that was laying copious golden eggs. At that time, she had been helpful, hospitable, pleasant, and he'd thought her all in all an attractive woman.

Forcing himself now to keep an open mind, as he had

instructed his sergeant to do, he parked his BMW in front of the beautiful old half-timbered Elizabethan house, and with Beck beside him, pulled the big cast-iron doorbell.

The door was opened by a middle-aged woman he knew to be the cleaner, Mrs Clark, who said her employer had told her they were expected and to enquire whether they would like coffee. Govern had already instructed Beck he must find a way to question Mrs Clark, who would in all likelihood know something of the Lewis family's relationships. Beck now suggested that it would be very pleasant if he could have his coffee in the kitchen because Inspector Govern wished to interview Mrs Lewis on his own.

Mrs Clark was delighted to fall in with the idea. The sergeant was a really nice-looking young man with slightly curly brown hair and hazel eyes just like her eldest son. He would be company while she had her coffee break, she said.

'The coffee's ready in the percolator, sir,' she told Govern as she beckoned the sergeant to follow her. 'I'll bring it straight in.'

Althea Lewis was waiting for the inspector in the drawing room. A fire was burning in the grate and two of the standard lamps were on, so despite the grey day, the room looked and felt warm and welcoming. Seated beside the fire was another woman, who stood up as Althea introduced her.

'You may have seen some of my friend Cressida's paintings, Cressida Cruse,' she told Govern. 'I would like her to stay if you have no objection, Inspector, but—'

'Of course not,' Govern broke in quickly. Experience had told him that it was much harder for a possible suspect to lie if a third person was present who might show surprise or even correct an erroneous statement.

There was a pause as the housekeeper brought in a tray of coffee cups and put it on the table beside the sofa. Althea pointed Govern to an armchair near the fire.

'I know it's only September but it's bitterly cold out!' she said sitting beside Cressida. She poured out a cup of coffee and handed it to him. 'I suppose we shall all get used to these vagaries in the weather they say are due to global warming. Do you know, Inspector, my son Daryl's birthday was two days ago and I can remember him having birthday parties in the garden when he was little.' She turned to face Cressida. 'Remember, Cressy, you used to referee the sports—'

She broke off, turning apologetically to Govern. 'I'm digressing, aren't I? You've come to ask questions about Geoffrey.'

Noting that Althea had been able to mention Lewis's name without a tremor in her voice, he proceeded to offer his condolences. Her face remained impassive. The other woman looked quite distressed.

'It's been the most awful shock,' she said. 'Poor Geoffrey! Do you have any idea who could have . . . have killed him?'

Certainly not you, Govern thought but did not say as he took a sip of coffee. But Lewis's wife . . .? She remained a possibility.

'Can I ask where you both were on Sunday?' he said, adding: 'It's just a formality so we can eliminate as many people as possible who knew Mr Lewis. Then perhaps we can start looking for his assassin.' Murderer was not a word he used with relatives.

'I was in my cottage . . . I live at the end of Glebe Lane, Inspector,' Cressida said at once. 'I'm afraid I don't have an alibi. I was painting in my studio and people tend not to interrupt me if they call and I'm not downstairs, so no one saw me.'

'I understand, Miss Cruse,' Govern said. 'Have you known the family for some time?'

Both Althea and Cressida spoke together as they explained their schoolgirl friendship, which had been a trio including a Phoebe Denton.

'She's an actress, you know,' Cressida elaborated. 'She said she was going up to London last Sunday because she was going to audition for a part in some play or other and wanted to be in town early Monday morning.'

'Thanks for the information, Miss Cruse,' Govern said, 'I'm sure I can eliminate her, too. I can see her some other time.' He turned his attention back to Althea.

'May I enquire where you were on Sunday afternoon, Mrs Lewis?' he asked.

Althea returned his gaze, her tone of voice expressionless as she said: 'I was here, Inspector. Geoff . . . my husband and I were to have gone out to lunch – we usually do on a Sunday when he's home. Saves cooking, you see, and I don't have Mrs Clark to wash up! But . . .' Her voice dropped a level as she said in a quiet, controlled tone: 'We had a bit of an argument on Saturday and Geoff stormed out of the house saying his golf club was a more congenial place than home!'

It was pretty obvious to Govern now that the marital relationship between the Lewises had been far from good. It explained Mrs Lewis's calm acceptance of the news of her husband's death and the unemotional way in which she spoke of him. But to have shot him? It was possible, presumably. It wouldn't be the first time marital discord was grounds for murder. Hopefully Beck would have got some inside information from the daily help, Mrs Clark. Domestic servants frequently heard a lot more than they were supposed to.

'So you were here all Sunday afternoon, Mrs Lewis?' Govern persisted.

'More or less! I did nip over to Logan Hill Farm to give my son a rugger shirt he wanted. Daryl's currently living with my ex – his father.' Her voice trailed away and Govern noticed the look of unconcern had given way to unease. Drawing on his phenomenal memory, he said:

'I did meet your son when I was last here. He showed me the sports trophy he'd won this summer.' Daryl had fetched it voluntarily from his bedroom to show it off, obviously proud of his achievement. 'So he lives with his father now?'

Althea's face took on a look of distress and her mouth tightened. 'Yes, he wasn't getting on all that well with my husband. They . . . well, I suppose a lot of teenage kids, especially boys, come up against their parents, don't they, especially step-parents? And Terence, my ex, is always happy to have him around.'

Making a mental note to check up on both Mrs Lewis's former husband and her son, he put down his coffee cup and took out his notebook.

'Just a formality, Mrs Lewis, but can you tell me what time that would have been?'

'About three . . . four o'clock, I suppose,' Althea replied vaguely. 'I didn't notice the time. Terence may remember.'

Brighton was only fifteen miles away, Govern told himself. She could have driven down there, shot her husband, and been back by three o'clock. But what was the motive? Discord between the son and his stepfather was not a good enough excuse for murder. Was the boy's dislike of his stepfather sufficiently strong for *him* to have shot Lewis? He must check on him later . . . see if he had a foolproof alibi.

Quite suddenly, Cressida spoke. Her cheeks were flushed and she looked thoroughly disturbed as she burst out: 'Al, you should tell the Inspector what a bastard Geoff is . . . was,' she corrected herself. Then afraid she had spoken out of turn, she said, 'I don't mean to tell tales, Al, but he *ought* to know what kind of man Geoff was.' Looking thoroughly unhappy, she clearly steeled herself to continue. 'I know it's awful that he's been murdered but despite all his outward charm, he must have had quite a few enemies. I know one shouldn't speak ill of the dead but . . .'

Unexpectedly, tears filled Althea's eyes but did not fall.

'I don't mind, Cressy, honestly,' she broke in. She looked down at her hands, which were twisted together on her lap. 'I was very much in love with Geoff when I married him,' she told Govern. 'I knew he was younger than me but it didn't seem to matter to either of us – the difference. But . . .' she cleared her throat, 'but he was a workaholic and we sort of drifted apart. I . . . I suppose I knew somewhere in the back of my mind that he was probably being unfaithful to me, but . . . I suppose I didn't really want to know. Then—'

She broke off, her composure now vanished as her face creased with bitterness and her eyes filled with angry tears.

'The usual story, Inspector!' she said. 'Hotel bills, telephone numbers . . . I never checked up on him but he must have got complacent as he left his mobile phone behind one day. I put a private detective on to him and learned he was planning to set up his mistress with a flat and a business in London.'

'So when was this, Mrs Lewis?' Govern asked.

There was a moment's hesitation before Althea said: 'Last week. I was going to have it out with Geoff at the weekend but after our row he didn't come home on Saturday night and rang me to say he'd be going to the office in Brighton on the Sunday. He said he'd be home later that evening but . . .'

So there was a motive for murder and every opportunity to carry it out, Govern thought, his nerve ends starting to tingle as they so often did when he sensed he was on to something.

'You told me you were here on your own on Sunday and only left the house once to take some sports clothes to your son at Logan Hill Farm? Just for the record, can you be more precise about the time?'

Althea frowned. 'As I said, I'm not sure. I mean, I think it was about three-ish. I don't know. I was a bit upset you see and I was thinking about how I was going to deal with our marriage and . . . well, Terence or my son Daryl would be able to confirm when I arrived at the farm.'

'Of course! I will be interviewing them in due course. I have one last question, Mrs Lewis – did you know that your husband had arranged to meet someone at his agency on Sunday?'

It was a moment or two before Althea replied. Her tone was bitter when she said: 'Other than to entertain his clients, Geoff never let me have anything to do with his work. I would have like to . . . well, have a career or at least a job, but he wanted me to be the proverbial housewife – ready and waiting at home for the master to return for a hot meal, his slippers and, if he wasn't too tired, his marital rights!'

Cressida was now looking distressed and she put an arm comfortingly around Althea's shoulders.

'Al, he wasn't all bad . . . I mean, he was very generous to you. He did . . . well, in the early days he was crazy about you, and you—'

'Cress, I don't think Inspector Govern will be in the least interested in my relationship with Geoff,' she said, gently removing her shoulder so Cressida's arm fell to her side. 'The facts are quite simple, I did love Geoff, he betrayed me and I'm not the least sorry he's dead.'

Ignoring the shocked expression on Cressida's face, she turned to the Inspector.

'Can I offer you something more before you leave?' she asked. 'Another coffee, perhaps, or . . .'

'No, thank you, Mrs Lewis.' Govern put his notebook in his pocket and stood up. 'There is just one other matter, however. Your husband had an appointment at his Brighton agency – to meet a Madame Tokoly. His London secretary emailed his office to that effect, and we know for a fact that she was there.'

Both Althea and Cressida looked at one another in astonishment. Gradually, a faint smile softened Althea's face.

'So Geoff did take her warnings seriously after all!' she commented. She looked at Govern. 'The woman was at our fête,' she explained, 'and told his fortune . . . or I suppose I should say the reverse of good news. Apparently she was using Tarot cards and warned him something nasty was going to happen . . . something to do with him drawing the Death Card, whatever that is. She forecast trouble but didn't say what trouble. Geoff pooh-poohed the whole thing . . . or so we all thought. Frankly, Inspector, I'm not a believer in second sight and all that stuff! I would have thought Geoff was the last person. His . . . his death is only a coincidence.'

'I'm sure you're right,' Govern said untruthfully. 'I will keep in touch with you, Mrs Lewis.' He turned to nod to Cressida. 'And thank you both for your patience. These routine enquiries can be very tedious, I know, but my job is to find your husband's killer. Meanwhile, would you be able to tell me how your husband got in touch with this fortune-teller?'

'Oh, it was Phoebe who told me about Madame Tokoly!' Cressida said. 'She'd met her through some of her stage friends. I don't think she knew her very well but Al and I thought it would be a fun thing to do, didn't we, Al?'

Althea nodded. 'If you want to ask Phoebe about her, I'll give you her mobile number,' she said, and calling it up on her own mobile, she gave it to the inspector.

Neither of the two women made any attempt to detain him, and having collected his sergeant from the kitchen, they returned to his car and drove off in the direction of Logan Hill Farm.

Beck had little to tell him about the Lewises from their daily help. It seemed Geoffrey Lewis went out of his way to flatter Mrs Clark, who would fall over backwards to please him. Mrs Lewis she described as more formal but very fair. The only rows she had ever overheard were about the boy, Daryl. His mother wouldn't hear a word against him and his stepfather hadn't a good word to say for him, calling him 'an ungrateful little toad' because the money he freely spent on him failed to buy his affection. She had witnessed the occasional blow-up, Mrs Clark had said, when Daryl had gone storming upstairs to his room swearing he wished Mr Lewis was dead! But that was only boys' talk, Mrs Clark said, Daryl 'being hot-tempered and that!' His mother always calmed him down.

'Sounds par for today's teenager,' Govern said, 'but I'll check his alibi.'

Logan Hill Farm appeared deserted when Detective Inspector Govern and his sergeant drove up to the farmhouse. The yard was reasonably tidy. Several young bantams scratched among the cobbles but the path leading to the farm-house door was neatly swept, a pile of logs heaped tidily on one side, a new-looking green water butt on the other. There was no sign of Terence Hutchins or his son but Govern could see a tractor working in a nearby field. He decided to blow his horn in an attempt to get the driver's attention.

A few minutes later, the tractor turned into the yard and the tall, broad-shouldered figure of Terence Hutchins in an old many-pocketed waxed jacket, corduroy trousers and wellingtons climbed down.

'What can I do for you gentlemen?' he enquired. 'I presume it is something urgent for you to interrupt my ploughing?'

Govern introduced himself and Beck and apologized for the interruption before saying: 'It's about Mr Geoffrey Lewis!' he said, watching the man's expression as he spoke.

'Lewis! What about him?' Terence's voice was suddenly sharp, his not unhandsome face hardening.

'As I expect you already know, Mr Hutchins, he was found dead in his office in Brighton on Monday,' Govern told him carefully. The look on the man's face remained unchanged.

'Can't say I'm sorry!' he said laconically. 'Presumably you are aware, Inspector, that Lewis robbed me of my wife? Who killed him?'

'That's what we are trying to find out,' Govern replied. 'We know he was shot but we don't have the weapon as yet.'

Terence looked thoughtful as he kicked a clod of earth off one of his boots with the toe of the other.

'Better come indoors,' he said. 'Not that I can be of much help.'

He led the way into the farmhouse and indicated several chairs drawn up to a scrubbed wooden table in a typical large kitchen warmed by a modern-looking Aga.

'Coffee?' he asked, but when Govern declined, he sat down at the table opposite them.

'Presumably you've spoken to Al . . . Mrs Lewis? Is she OK?'

'Shocked, naturally!' Govern replied, mentally noting that this tall, quiet man was almost certainly still carrying a torch for his former wife. Was he capable of committing murder for her? It seemed unlikely, although it was quite often the strong, silent types in whom emotions ran deepest; resentments sometimes building like a rumbling volcano and needing only a trigger to erupt.

But what trigger, if such it was?

'I presume you can provide an alibi for last Sunday?' he asked casually. 'This is just a formality – we have to eliminate as many of Mr Lewis's family and acquaintances as possible. At the moment, we don't know the motive for the killing, you see.'

The bitter expression on Terence's face grew even more marked.

'I can give you a few!' he said. 'Lewis was ruthless. He didn't care who he trod on to get where he wanted to be – rich, powerful. Take Ingram – Laurence Ingram. Used to own Hurston Grange, his family home. Lewis knew Ingram was on the point of bankruptcy and literally stole the estate from the old boy knowing that he could get planning permission to make a fortune out of the land. All but broke Ingram's heart. There was a time I thought it might all be too much for him – he was old and ill. But as far as I know he's still alive. Lives in a retirement flat in Hove, or maybe Brighton.'

Beck was scribbling in his notebook as Terence Hutchins continued: 'As for my movements, Inspector, I was here most of the day. I did go out after lunch . . . I was interested in a second-hand baler a farmer just outside Ditchling was selling. It wasn't what I wanted so . . . so I came home.'

Or nipped over the Downs into Brighton? Govern asked himself. Over Ditchling Beacon, Hutchins could have been there and back in an hour. Could this man be a killer and if so, why wait eight years to revenge yourself on the man who stole your wife?

It wasn't until he was driving back to Brighton that Beck suddenly broke into the thoughtful silence that had befallen them both.

'Suppose Hutchins had found out about Lewis being unfaithful to his former missus; suppose he suddenly realized that it was one thing to surrender your wife to a man who was going to make her happier than you could but quite another to learn he was ruining her life. Maybe it just brought all the old resentments to the fore and he nipped into Brighton and finished Lewis off.'

It was on the tip of Govern's tongue to ridicule Beck's theory but he didn't dismiss it entirely. As he knew very well, murder was by no means always committed on the spur of the moment. Often, the desire to kill was latent and was all the more virulent when finally it surfaced. It happened, for example, with children who had been abused by their parents in childhood and years later, their hatred of their abuser erupted into murder.

'I'm not ruling Hutchins out!' he told Beck. 'Tell Peterson to get his alibi checked and the exact time he arrived and left the Ditchling farmer. And tomorrow morning, I want reports of the interviews of both Lewis's manageress and his secretary in my office, and the London engagement diary. Then in an hour's time, we'll go and meet this Ingram fellow.'

'What Ingram fellow?' Beck asked innocently.

Govern sighed. 'You should pay more attention, David!' he said as they crested the hill and in the far distance the grey waters of the English Channel came into sight. 'Ingram was the name of the previous owner of Lewis's mansion, Hurston Grange, remember? But other than the fellow's obvious motive for disliking Lewis, his name is also on the list the Templeton House porter gave us of first- and second-floor residents. Here's a suspect with a motive and who's living literally on the spot . . . nips downstairs, bumps off Lewis, and back upstairs for the second half of the football game!'

'Sounds too easy,' Beck said grinning, 'and didn't Mr Hutchins say Ingram was old and frail?'

'So what! It doesn't take strength to hold, point and fire a gun. The shooter wasn't that steady-handed anyway; it took three shots to kill the victim.'

Govern did not as a rule allow his personal likes and dislikes to surface when he was on a case; but now as he pulled to a halt outside the police station, he found himself hoping that the old man Lewis was purported to have exploited had a sound alibi for Sunday afternoon. He did not like it when someone old and frail turned out to be a murderer.

SEVENTEEN

'Miss Phoebe Denton to see you, sir!' Beck informed Inspector Govern as he showed her into his office. Govern stood up and, shaking Phoebe's hand, offered her the chair on the far side of his desk.

'It was good of you to call in, Miss Denton!' Govern said as he, too, sat down.

Phoebe returned his smile. 'Althea – Mrs Lewis – telephoned me and told me you wanted to talk to me, Inspector, so as I was not working and back home again, here I am!'

'Very good of you,' Govern said again, his keen eye observing the middle-aged woman opposite him. She must have been a very pretty girl, he thought; but unlike her two schoolfriends, Mrs Lewis and the artist, Cressida Cruse, the years had not dealt kindly with her. There were dark hollows under her eyes which were an unusual but still striking grey-green, and her cheekbones stood out prominently. In fact, he decided, the woman looked ill.

'I understood from Mrs Lewis when I spoke to her this morning that you introduced the clairvoyant, Madame Tokoly, to the family. We are naturally very interested in her as she was the last person seen in the late Mr Lewis's office.'

Phoebe shook her head. 'I know, Al told me. It's almost unbelievable that Geoff – Mr Lewis – would have anything to do with someone like that. I mean, he was a businessman, a very successful one, and not exactly given to whimsies. Frankly, I find it very hard to believe he drove into Brighton on a Sunday just to have his fortune told!'

She smiled at the thought and once again, Govern was struck by what must have been her youthful beauty.

'As far as the clairvoyant is concerned,' Phoebe continued, 'I'm afraid I can't tell you much about the woman, Inspector, but for what it's worth, I've found this.'

She handed across the desk a coloured postcard on one side of which were the signs of the Zodiac and on the other in black type was the name, 'MADAME KARA TOKOLY'. Under the name was a list of her varied accomplishments – '*Tarot Card and Psychic Readings. Numerology and Astrology. Your future revealed by renowned clairvoyant.* This was followed in red print by: '*For private appointment, please telephone between 5 & 8 p.m.*' There followed an eleven-digit mobile number which, Phoebe said, had clearly been misprinted because when she had tried to ring it, it was declared unobtainable.

Inspector Govern took the card from her and gave it to his sergeant.

'Check with the phone company,' he told him, 'just in case they were printed in the wrong order.' As Beck left the room, he turned his attention back to Phoebe.

'Mrs Lewis said she thought you had only met the clair-voyant once, when you were in Newcastle?' he said. 'Is that correct?'

Phoebe nodded. 'One of the girls in the play we were doing had heard her telling fortunes at a twenty-first birthday party and suggested we all club together and have her tell our fortune one Sunday when we weren't performing. As a matter of fact, she was quite uncanny. One of the girls had just lost her mother and the clairvoyant told her she had a message for the daughter about her cat who'd been ill. She told Betty her mother wanted to be reassured that Betty was giving the cat its medicine twice a day! There was absolutely no way she could have known about the cat. Even if she made a habit of reading the death notices, the chances of her remembering Betty's mother's name must virtually have been nil, especially as the mother had married twice so she and Betty didn't even share the same surname. It was quite impressive.'

She smiled at the inspector. 'Well, even if you are a sceptic about such things, one can't ignore them entirely, can one? Anyway, she handed out these cards and I was using mine as a bookmark so I still had it last summer when I heard my friends the Lewises were giving their usual charity fête in July. So I asked our friend Cressy – Cressida Cruse, the artist – if she'd like me to try and get hold of her. That's when I tried the number on the card and I'd given up the idea when out of the blue Madame Tokoly telephoned me. She'd seen my name on the cast list of a play I was in and wanted to know if I or any of my friends would like her to give a reading. So of course, it was a lucky coincidence that she was available for the fête, and even more lucky really because when I told her the funds raised at the fête this year were going to a breast-cancer charity, she said she wouldn't charge a fee. Geoff and Al were delighted. I'd hoped to go to the fête but I wasn't very well but Cressy said the fortune-telling had been a great success and raised several hundred pounds.'

Inspector Govern had listened to Phoebe's account in silence. When she ceased talking, he said: 'You are aware that Mr Lewis's death was not a natural one; that he died of gunshot wounds, Miss Denton? And that the clairvoyant was seen in his office on Sunday afternoon?'

'Yes, I know!' Phoebe said. 'Cressy rang and told me. She said it wasn't an accident, but no one seemed to know what exactly had happened. It wasn't . . . suicide, was it? I mean, I wouldn't have thought Geoff would . . .'

'No, Miss Denton, Mr Lewis was shot by a third party.'

Phoebe looked puzzled. 'You mean by the fortune-teller?'

Govern shook his head. 'We don't know that, Miss Denton – only that the clairvoyant was there during the afternoon. But there were others, which is one of the reasons I'm pleased you could come today. I understand from Mrs Lewis that you and Miss Cruse and she have been friends since your schooldays; you must therefore have known Mr Lewis very well. Is there anyone you can think of who might possibly have wanted to kill him?'

Phoebe shrugged, her expression now sardonic as she said: 'I can think of quite a few people who didn't like Geoff but not who might dislike him enough to kill him! All I can say is that there were two distinct sides to Geoffrey Lewis. He could be utterly charming, generous, amusing, entertaining. Women loved him. Al – Althea – loved him enough to leave her husband in order to marry him. He wasn't faithful to her, of course. I think Al knew it but didn't want to know, if you understand what I mean. But Al wouldn't *kill* him, for heaven's sake! There'd be no point, would there, when she could simply divorce him if she wanted him out of her life.'

'So is there anyone else?' Govern prompted, pleased to have someone as outspoken and articulate as Miss Phoebe Denton to give him background information.

Phoebe was now smiling. 'Young Daryl, Geoffrey's stepson. He *hated* Geoffrey, with a capital H. Then there was the incident of Daryl's girlfriend – Geoff took the child to a pub and gave her too much to drink and then started to fondle her. Daryl was beside himself and threatened to kill Geoff but of course he didn't mean it seriously. You can strike Daryl off your list of suspects, Inspector.'

'So who can we put on it, Miss Denton?' Govern asked with a smile. 'Not Mrs Lewis; not Master Lewis. How about the estranged husband?'

'Terence? No motive, Inspector. If he'd ever thought of killing Geoff, surely it would have been when Althea left him. That was years ago.' Her voice softened. 'He's a lovely man . . . Do you know, I thought I was in love with him once, but he only had eyes for Al, which is not surprising. She was a very beautiful girl.'

'Are you sure you wouldn't like some coffee, Miss Denton? Or tea? You are being most helpful and I'd like to ask you a few more questions if you are not too tired.'

She certainly looked exhausted, Govern thought as she leaned back in her chair. According to Beck, who had done a quick search on the Internet about the actress when she'd called in at the station that afternoon, there had been a spell the previous year when Miss Denton had been 'resting', which could mean simply that she had not had any engagements but could equally mean she'd been ill. Observing her when Beck had shown her into his office his keen eye had noticed that there was no sign of the silky blonde hair that had framed her heart-shaped face in the theatre advertising posters Beck had printed out. In fact, there was very little sign of any hair at all beneath the smart bright orange hat. Was it possible, he asked himself, that this still relatively young attractive woman facing him was a cancer patient who had lost her hair during chemotherapy?

He put the thought from him since it had nothing whatever to do with the murder he was investigating.

'You spoke just now of Mr Lewis's inappropriate behaviour with his stepson's girlfriend?' he prompted.

Phoebe quickly corrected him. 'Yes, there was a bit of a hoo-hah about Susie. Her father – that's Peter White – is something of a despot and when he learned about it he blew his top, as they say. But although I have only met the man once or twice, I can't believe he'd take the law into his own hands. He's an ex-policeman, you know.'

'That's news to me, Miss Denton. Thank you for the information. I take it you are familiar with many of the other residents in Hurston Green? The Lewises' neighbours?'

A constable now came in with a tray of tea and Phoebe took a cup and asked Inspector Govern to excuse her while she swallowed one of her pills.

'Dreadful things, aren't they!' she said vaguely. 'My mother said she had never taken a single pill other than the occasional aspirin in the whole of her life – and she lived to seventy! But I am digressing. Yes, I suppose I do know most of Al's friends, but as a matter of fact, they didn't have that many. Geoff was away on business during the week, and at the weekends he liked to play golf or relax at home. When they did entertain, it was always a lavish "do" – forty or so people, Geoff's clients usually, champagne, all the trimmings. In the summer they had the fête and they did have couples up to play tennis, but I don't recall any really close friends, other than Cressy, of course. She lives in the village, so she is a lot closer to Al than I am as I move around the country.'

'And were you moving around the country, as you put it, Miss Denton, last Sunday? For the record, of course. You live in Worthing, I understand.'

Phoebe put down her empty teacup and met the inspector's

gaze, her grey-green eyes unblinking as she told him she had gone to sit in one of the shelters on the Brighton front overlooking the sea.

'You may think that a little odd, Inspector,' she said with a smile, 'but when I was a child, we lived in Hove and my father liked to fish off the end of the pier. After he died, Mother liked to take me to the same shelter where we used to sit and watch him. She said it was where his spirit would be if there were such things as spirits. So now I go there from time to time in case my mother's spirit is hovering around there. Do you believe in an afterlife, Inspector?'

Govern sighed. 'I'd like to, but my life is spent searching for facts, which are sadly lacking when it comes to the occult. Maybe this Madame Tokoly could give you a more definitive answer, Miss Denton. Our problem is to find her.'

Phoebe nodded. 'She was always a bit elusive. The girls and I were of the opinion she was an illegal immigrant; that was why she kept moving around. As far as I know, she didn't have a permanent address anywhere. Do you think she might have gone back to her own country? I think she said she came from Poland, or maybe it was Hungary.'

'We're looking into that possibility,' Govern said. 'You probably saw her more than anyone else, would you consider her capable of violence? Hatred? Homicide?'

Phoebe laughed. 'That old woman? Never! Her whole life seemed wrapped up in the mumbo-jumbo she went in for – séances and card-reading and communicating with the spirit world; that sort of thing. She seemed to me to be a troubled soul . . . as if she was tormented by these weird presentiments about people and believed the spirits wanted her to warn them so they could avoid disaster.'

'Well, she didn't succeed in warning Mr Lewis about his imminent disaster!' Beck said, having heard Phoebe's comments as he returned to the room. Seeing his boss's scowl, he resumed a more serious expression and apologized to Phoebe for sounding frivolous.

'Please don't apologize!' she said. 'As far as I'm concerned, Mr Lewis's death, murder or otherwise, is of total unconcern to me. Frankly, I didn't like the guy!'

After Beck had shown Phoebe out to her car and returned to the office, the inspector asked him if there had been any progress with the telephone number, but there was none. The number remained unobtainable.

'Which doesn't really surprise me!' Govern said. 'It's pretty clear the woman wished to remain sub rosa, whether because she was an illegal immigrant or for some other reason we known nothing about. For all we know, she could have been handling or smuggling drugs and the clairvoyant business was just a cover! On the other hand, she was by all accounts pretty conspicuous – togged up like a Gypsy by the sound of it. That would be a very silly way to behave if you were involved in clandestine activities.'

'I don't think she had anything to do with the murder,' Beck said taking an uneaten biscuit off Phoebe's tea tray and eating it. 'After all, according to the porter, she made no attempt to hide from him either on the way in or out. She even spoke to him when she arrived asking if Mr Lewis was in his office. That wouldn't make sense if she was about to bump him off.'

'A conclusion I had reached yesterday when we interviewed the porter, but don't let me discourage you from using your brains, young man. I think what we both need now is a nice, friendly talk to the old gentleman who lives above Lewis & Gibbs Estate Agents. It's high time we heard what he has to say, so get your jacket on, Sergeant, and put that last biscuit down. We're on our way to Templeton House and I don't want you arriving with crumbs all over your lapels!'

In the car, Beck reported that there had still been no information forthcoming from Gatwick Airport and they had widened the enquiry to Heathrow and Stansted.

'And notify Interpol!' Govern said. 'If the woman did kill him and escaped to Europe, we can't let the trail go cold. Although frankly, I don't think she killed Lewis. They were virtual strangers, so what motive would she have had?'

'Maybe he tried to rape her!' Beck said, grinning. 'If he was chatting up a teenage girl, why not an older woman?'

Inspector Govern turned into the parking space outside the block of flats and switched off the engine.

'There are times, David, when you are either being extremely silly or else being unnecessarily frivolous. You heard what Miss Denton said, he was attractive to women. He was not very likely to have wasted his time on a cranky old female who, from all accounts, looked more like a bag lady than a page-three model.'

Beck got out of the car and went round to the driver's side to open the door for his boss.

'Maybe we should look for a mistress,' he suggested. 'Miss Denton said Lewis was unfaithful to his wife. We should have asked her if she knew who with. If the woman was married and her husband found out, he might have shot Lewis in a fit of jealousy!'

'Yes, and pigs might fly, David!' Govern said as he walked towards the front door to the right of which were the large glass windows of Lewis & Gibbs Estate Agents. 'However, if we get nowhere with our elderly gentleman today, you can pop in and see Miss Denton in Worthing and satisfy yourself about Lewis's mistress.'

Beck grinned. 'Or mistresses!' he suggested. 'I'll bet you fifty quid he had at least one, if not two!'

Govern halted outside the door and turned to face his sergeant.

'You know perfectly well I never bet on the outcome of a murder case,' he said. 'As for the possibility of a mistress, I'm open to any facts you can unearth. Now stop talking about Lewis and concentrate on the man we've come to see.'

'Mr Laurence Ingram, Flat 4!' Beck said quickly.

'I'm well aware of it!' Govern said irritably. 'You may hold the opinion, Beck, that my memory is failing now I'm in my dotage, but I assure you I am in no need of your assistance.'

'Yes, sir!' Beck answered grinning. 'I'll do my best to remember not to remind you if I think you've forgotten something, like where you left your car keys.'

'Enough!' Govern interrupted, but there was a glint of laughter in his eyes. Apart from anything else, his memory wasn't all that good and Beck's was like that of an elephant. It was what made him such a good sergeant.

There was no time for further banter as the front door opened and they were confronted by the stooped figure of the elderly porter of Templeton House.

'Mr Ingram's been waiting for you, sir,' he said to Govern. 'You're to go up to his flat, Number 4, first on the right as you reach the landing.'

Thanking him, Govern nodded to Beck and the two of them made their way upstairs.

EIGHTEEN

Govern's first impression of Mr Laurence Ingram was of a twentieth-century English gentleman. His thin, bony frame was immaculately attired in a navy blue cardigan, check shirt and camel-coloured moleskin trousers. There was a paisley silk cravat knotted at his throat. His surprisingly abundant white hair was parted at one side and brushed back from his forehead. Faded blue eyes stared back at the inspector from a white, gaunt face and his hands shook a little as he greeted the two policemen. Govern instantly judged the man to be in his late seventies or early eighties.

'Please do sit down, Inspector, Sergeant!' he said, indicating a somewhat threadbare chintz-covered settee by the unlit fire. 'I'm afraid I don't have any coffee but I could offer you tea – or a glass of sherry, perhaps?'

Govern declined both and when Ingram himself was seated, he repeated the remarks he had made earlier on the telephone.

'We are investigating the murder of Mr Geoffrey Lewis, sir, and hope you might be able to assist us. According to your hall porter, you were one of the last people to see him.'

Ingram nodded, a derisive expression creasing his aristocratic features.

'I don't know about me being the last but I certainly saw him on the Sunday. I was watching the seagulls out of my window when I saw Lewis's fancy Mercedes draw up outside. As a rule, the man never came to the agency on Sundays when it was closed, so I was curious to see what he was up to.' He gave a look that was almost one of apology as he added: 'I don't have much to occupy me on a Sunday, you see, as I am not a television enthusiast and my eyesight is going, so I find it a strain to read.'

He paused momentarily before saying: 'I'd been going to write to Lewis . . . about the rent. He'd put it up again, d'you see, and that was the second time this year.' His voice hardened. 'We're mostly old people in this block. People like Margaret Endersley, a widow in her eighties, can't afford these increases any more than I can. We're on fixed pensions, you see. Frankly, I think Lewis is – I mean was – charging far too high a rent in the first place, but that's about par for the course where he was concerned.'

As he paused once again, Govern noted the change in Mr Ingram's tone when he referred to Lewis's management. Obviously there had been no love lost between landlord and tenant. He waited for the old man to continue.

'When I saw Lewis arriving here on Sunday, it occurred to me that I could go and speak to him in person; that it might be more expedient than writing a letter.'

Govern's instincts sharpened. Was this going to turn out to be a confession?

'So you went downstairs to see him, sir?' he prompted.

Ingram nodded. 'Yes! But he had somebody with him, a foreigner I think, she was so oddly attired, so I said I would go down again later. When I did so I saw him lying there on the floor. I left immediately. I knew he was dead; I thought he might have shot himself but your constable told me someone killed him.'

'But not you, sir?' Govern said, a half smile making his question appear more casual than accusing.

It was a moment or two before Ingram replied. Then he said: 'In point of fact it could have been me. That's why I didn't report it, though I knew I should. God knows there have been enough times in my life when I wanted to wipe the fellow off the face of this earth. I met a chap like him in the war, you know, devious, greedy, amoral. He was an officer in my regiment and when he was found one day with his throat cut, all the evidence pointed to the fact that he hadn't been killed by the enemy. Fortunately the killer's comrades all covered up for him. That officer was a nasty bit of work and Lewis reminded me of him!'

He looked from Inspector Govern to his sergeant, his

face contorted as if he was struggling for words. Then he got up stiffly and went across the room to a desk from the drawer of which he produced a photograph album. He found the page he wanted and handed the opened book to Govern.

'You may know that Hurston Grange was my family home. Ingrams lived there for generations. After my father died, I had a job to find the death duties – as inheritance tax used to be called!' he added wryly. 'That's my wife there on the terrace with a flower basket on her arm. She developed multiple sclerosis and for the last two years before she died, I had to employ full-time carers for her. I'd given her my word I wouldn't put her in a home, you see.'

He took the album back from Govern and replaced it in the desk drawer. Seated once more, he continued:

'The house needed an increasing number of repairs and – well, the end of the story is I got heavily into debt. My accountant suggested I sell some of the land, if possible as building land rather than as agricultural as it could raise sufficient money to put my finances back on the level. I did apply to the council but I was turned down – green belt, you see. So then I had no choice but to sell the whole of my estate. That was when Lewis got word of my need to sell up and came along with a very good offer. It was enough to clear my debts and give me a little income so I could afford to rent one of the flats here at Templeton House. At the time I was very grateful to Lewis for clearing up the mess I'd been in.'

He broke off, his face contorted; his hands clasped together so tightly his knuckle bones showed through the paper-thin skin.

'I'd been here about six months when I found out Lewis had obtained planning permission to build on a ten-acre field fronting the road into the village. God knows how he got it. A friend who was on the town council told me he'd seen Lewis entertaining one of the planning officers at the Headingborough Country Club. That's the sort of place where a sandwich will cost you the best part of a fiver. Another friend told me Lewis had proposed this planning chap for the golf club; membership there was very selective but Lewis had got himself on to the committee so he could pretty well put anyone up he wanted.'

His expression had become one of extreme bitterness as he said bitingly: 'Eighteen months later, the first row of houses was built on that site and sold and with another half dozen to follow, Lewis made himself a nice little fortune. I realized then why he had originally made me such a generous offer for the house and grounds; he'd already found out he could swing the planning permission for my land. Nothing I could do about it, but you'll understand why I felt no regrets when I saw his body and knew he was dead. There was many a time when I'd thought of killing him myself. Once I even worked out a way to do it – invite him to do some rough shooting on my land and then aim my gun "accidentally" in his direction.'

He gave a hollow laugh. 'Of course, it wasn't my land any more, or my shoot. As I get older, I find myself forgetting that the Grange isn't my home.'

It was a moment or two after he had stopped speaking before Beck broke the silence. He pointed to a glass case above the mantelpiece in which was a velvet-lined box containing two pistols.

'You a collector, sir?' he asked.

Ingram's face became suddenly animated.

'Not a collector. Those are a pair of flintlock duelling pistols, which belonged to my great-great-grandfather. They were a present to him from Brigadier-General Sir Henry Calder, whose life he saved in the Battle for St Lucia in 1780.'

'Well, you don't need a gun licence for those antiques!' Beck said admiringly.

Laurence Ingram smiled. 'No, but I see you are interested in guns, Sergeant, so you might like to see my Purdeys. They're under lock and key, of course, and I do have a licence for them!'

He went out to the hall and returned with one of his Purdey shotguns, which he handed to Beck while giving his gun licence to Govern to scrutinize.

'I think I would have to be starving before I parted with that pair,' he said, 'not that I get any shooting these days. I did pawn them once when my wife was ill but when the Grange was sold I managed to redeem them. Their worth had gone up in that short while from around eighty thousand to a hundred thousand pounds.' He gave a wry smile.

'Sounds a lot, doesn't it, Sergeant, but it was by no means enough to pay all the debts and the repairs needed to the Grange. I used to shoot several times a month between September and January, but of course I don't any longer. I keep the guns as much for sentimental reasons as for financial fall-back for a rainy day.'

'I feel quite privileged just to be holding this,' Beck said.

Inspector Govern now broke into the conversation. 'I see this permit includes a pistol, sir? Do you have that handy?'

Beck's interest sharpened immediately. Although no weapon had been found in Lewis's office, forensics were in no doubt he had been shot by a .38 calibre hand gun.

'It's in the drawer of my bedside table,' Ingram said. 'I keep it there in case of burglars.'

While he was out of the room, Govern said quietly: 'We'll take it with us. I very much hope I'm wrong, but it's just possible—'

He broke off as Ingram returned to the room carrying the hand gun. As if he'd heard what Govern had been saying, he gave it to him.

'You can check the ballistics,' he said with a wry smile, 'but I can assure you I didn't shoot Lewis, much as I might have wished to.'

Before Inspector Govern and his sergeant left the building, they stopped for a further talk to the hall porter. He went by the very ordinary name of John Smith and was clearly delighted to be consulted about the murder for a second time. He looked at the two detectives with interest.

'Don't expect you've cornered the culprit yet, Inspector!' he said laconically. 'I know Mr Ingram was around on Sunday but he's a gentleman of the old order. Not like Mr Lewis. Worse than a sergeant-major, *he* was, barking out orders, Smith do this, Smith do that without so much as a please and certainly never a thank you. I only stay here because of my flat. I have the basement, you see; used to be the kitchens when Templeton House was a hotel. Nice and warm my flat is. He only pays me a pittance but I have my pension and I get tips from time to time. Not from Mr Lewis, though.'

'Yes, well, I understand how you feel,' Govern said, 'but however unpleasant a character Mr Lewis may have been, he was entitled to his life, and he forfeited it. So we do need to find out who killed him. You told the constable a dark-haired foreign-looking man came to the agency about teatime on Sunday. Would you be able to identify him? Give an artist enough detail to do a sketch?'

The porter shook his head. 'It's as I keep telling everyone, I'm on my day off on a Sunday. I only saw the Gypsy woman by chance as I'd heard Lewis go into his office and thought I'd better make sure it was him and not burglars. So I passed her as I was about to go back downstairs and she asked me if he was in. I did see Mr Ingram later when I went out to post a letter – shocking cost of a stamp these days! Then when I came back I caught a glimpse of the dark-haired man coming out of the front door. I didn't think to mention him last time you was here as I'd assumed he was a relative of one of the residents. Then I thought as how I know most of their regulars and he wasn't one of them. He was in a hurry to get out of the door and barged past me. I didn't see his face so I can't say as how I'd recognize him as I wouldn't be able.'

There was little more he could tell Govern other than that the mystery man was quite tall, middle-aged and wearing grey trousers and a rather military looking jacket.

'Could be our other possible suspect – the girl's father,' Beck said as he and Govern drove back to the police station. 'Even an ex-policeman might get wound up enough to lose control and shoot someone he considered a threat to his precious daughter.'

'But unlikely!' Govern replied. 'It's not as if Lewis had actually harmed the girl. However, we'll drive out to Hurston Green again and have a word with him. White, his name was, Peter White!'

'You've got a good memory, sir!' Beck said, his eyes glinting with laughter.

'And you're going to get more than you bargained for if you don't show a little more respect!' Govern replied with false severity. 'Now give Ingram's pistol to ballistics and then get busy on the other airports. I still have the feeling that somehow or other, Madame Tokoly, clairvoyant par excellence, is the key to solving this murder.'

Seeing Beck's puzzled expression, he patted him on the shoulder.

'Time you learned a little French, David!' he said. 'You never know, it might come in handy one day!'

He was still smiling to himself as they parked the car in the station forecourt and went back indoors. It was not until he was seated once more at his desk that Govern realized he had nothing much to smile about. The two of them had been out for most of the day and were no nearer finding out who had killed Mr Geoffrey Lewis than they had been when his body was first found. For the present, he ruled out the porter, Mrs and Master Lewis although they had yet to interview the boy, Miss Cruse, Miss Denton and the elderly devoted local manageress, Mrs Smythe. Beck had been up to London and brought back a statement from Lewis's London secretary, Diane Turner, describing her as elderly, plain and an admirer of her employer. It stood to reason that Lewis had almost certainly treated well the two women who managed his day-to-day engagements.

The only information that had been forthcoming from Miss Turner was that she had made the appointment with Madame Tokoly for her boss following his receipt of the woman's letter announcing her impending departure from the country. In fact, she admitted, she had more or less talked him into meeting the clairvoyant as it sounded 'fun'. She was more than a little upset to think she was responsible for his seeing the woman. The day had not turned out to be much fun for the unfortunate man whose Death Card had surfaced, Beck had commented.

Death Card! Govern wrote on a pad of paper in front of him. Was there a clue in those somewhat grisly words? He had never been to a fortune-teller in his life nor was likely to do so but now he found himself wondering how he would feel if he cut a pack of cards and drew one called the Death Card. In a way, he was well accustomed to sudden un-expected death; it was his job to find the perpetrators, but it had never occurred to him to consider that he, too, might suddenly die. It would certainly not be very pleasant to be told by a clairvoyant that the cards were foretelling your imminent demise!

He told himself not to be so morbid – something almost unheard of in his make-up – and get on with the job of finding Lewis's killer. No matter how much the dead man was disliked, he was still entitled to receive the same justice as anyone else. His murderer had to be found.

'Where to now, sir?' Beck asked the following afternoon as they drove along the seafront.

'Hurston Green again. I want to be able to eliminate the ex-policeman – White, wasn't it? Peter White! And if possible, I'll have a word with the boy, Daryl, first, when he gets back from school. I may be wrong but I have an idea I saw him when we went to Logan Hill Farm to inter-view his father. I thought I saw a curtain move in one of the downstairs windows.'

'You mean he deliberately avoided meeting us?' Beck said.

'No, I'm not saying that – simply that I'd like to get his alibi for Sunday afternoon so we can eliminate him. He did have a motive for killing his stepfather, who by all accounts he thoroughly disliked. Suppose he'd found out Lewis had been cheating on his mother? Wanted to avenge her? Suppose he didn't trust Lewis not to try to seduce his girl-friend again? I grant that sounds a bit far-fetched but it's happened before as well you know, David. Remember those teenage twins and the Cheyne Manor Golf Club murder? They were the most unlikely suspects!'

Beck sighed. As always, his boss was not only extremely astute but he relied, too, on his instinct, and nine times out of ten, his theories helped solve a seemingly unresolvable case.

Once again when they drove up to Logan Hill Farm there was no sign of the owner. This time, however, the back door opened even before they could knock and the tall, thin figure of the boy stood facing them.

'If you're looking for Dad, he's gone into Hurston Green to get something from the vet,' he said. 'He didn't say how long he'd be!'

'That's OK. Daryl, isn't it? Actually it was you I wanted to see. May we come in? This is my sergeant, Detective Sergeant Beck, and I'm Detective Inspector Govern.'

Without a word, the boy led them into the large kitchen and indicated they should sit down at the table. Only then did he speak.

'I suppose you've come about my stepfather's murder,' he said.

Govern nodded. 'Yes, I do have some questions to ask. I would have done so when we were last here, but you chose not to put in an appearance.'

Daryl looked sheepish. 'I didn't think you knew I was here! School was closed for the day so I was working at home,' he admitted. 'Actually, I was watching the Arsenal–Liverpool game and . . . well, I didn't want to miss it. Sorry!'

Govern did not tell the boy that his sergeant was also a football fanatic and would sympathize entirely with Daryl's excuse. However, it could be just that – an excuse not to have to face unwelcome questions about his stepfather's death.

'Where were you on Sunday afternoon?' he asked and was instantly alerted by the colour which rushed into Daryl's face as he stammered:

'Oh, around somewhere. Helping Dad, I expect.'

Govern knew instinctively this was a lie. 'You realize I can ask your father to confirm that, and I don't think he would do so. In your own interest, Daryl, I suggest you tell me the truth. If you weren't in Brighton on Sunday after-noon, we can eliminate you from our enquiries.'

Daryl reached across the table and started fidgeting with the salt cellar, which had been left in the centre. He did not look at Govern as he said: 'I went into Hurston . . . on my bike. Dad saw me leave so you can ask him.'

Govern ignored the boy's last remark and said in a casual tone: 'So you were in Hurston Green on Sunday afternoon when presumably you met up with friends who will confirm the fact?'

Daryl's face now turned an angry red. 'If you're trying to make out I was in Brighton and killed my stepfather, then you'll have to think again. I didn't do it!'

Govern's instinct told him the boy was speaking the truth but he could not be sure.

'Look, Daryl, I am not suggesting you killed your step-father, but it is part of my duty, since we don't know who the murderer was, to eliminate all possible suspects; and I'm sure you are honest enough to admit that Mr Lewis was not your favourite person.'

Daryl's expression now changed. 'You're dead right!' he said. 'I shouldn't think he was anyone's favourite person. He hated me and he'd get at me just to upset Mum. He was horrid to her and I'd bet anything he wasn't faithful to her. He even—'

He broke off aware that he was about to reveal how his stepfather had behaved with Susie. Guessing this was the case, Govern said quietly:

'We do know he took your girlfriend to a pub and chatted her up.'

'Touched her up!' Daryl broke in furiously.

'But no real harm done?' Govern suggested. Daryl turned to look at him, his expression now bitter.

'Yes there was!' He was almost shouting. 'Susie's father found out and now he's forbidden us to meet after school and we were going to go biking in the Lake District and camp out next summer and now we won't be able to go—' He broke off, his voice shaking as if he was on the verge of tears.

'Maybe Mr White will lift the ban now that Mr Lewis is dead!' Govern suggested. Daryl shook his head.

'I said that to Susie on Sunday when we—' He broke off and sat back in his chair no longer defiant but abject.

'I'm not about to tell Susie's father that you two were together on Sunday, if that's what's concerning you, Daryl,' Govern said. 'I only need to know you have an alibi for the afternoon when Mr Lewis was killed.'

Daryl's stance stiffened as he leaned forward to say: 'Yes, I was with Susie and she'd tell you we were together all afternoon – we went to the cinema in Headingborough – but if she had to make a statement or something and her father . . .'

'Don't worry, Daryl!' Govern was completely satisfied now that the boy had nothing to do with his stepfather's death. 'You can ask Susie to drop me a line at Brighton Police Station confirming what you have told me. I promise you it will be treated entirely confidentially.'

'That's cool! Thanks very much, Inspector. I . . .' He grinned sheepishly. 'I'm sorry you had to come here twice. I mean, I was watching the football but that wasn't why I didn't put in an appearance. I guessed it was about my stepfather's death and I might be asked where I was on Sunday and I didn't want Dad to know. He and Mr White are sort of friends – they go shooting together, you see, and Dad says he understands Susie's father losing his rag about what happened and not wanting Susie to have anything to do with Mr Lewis's family. Sue used to spend quite a lot of time at the Grange with me, playing tennis, swimming – that sort of thing. Dad thinks it'll all blow over, which is what Aunt Phoebe said when we told her.'

Govern was no longer in any doubt now about the boy's innocence, but he was not so certain about Mr White. His behaviour seemed on the face of it to be extreme. Daryl was not Lewis's son and was now living away from his stepfather's house. To ban the youngsters meeting out of school was unreasonable when nothing had actually happened to the girl. It seemed incredible that Lewis had not taken into account that the daughter would in all probability tell her parents what he'd been up to and they'd report him for inappropriate behaviour.

'Perhaps that is exactly what White meant to do when he heard about Lewis's behaviour with his daughter,' he said to Beck as they drove away from Logan Hill Farm and headed down the lane towards the village. 'But instead of reporting Lewis with no more than such flimsy evidence, he decided to take matters into his own hands.'

'But not to the extent of *killing* Lewis!' Beck argued. 'And White is an ex-policeman, don't forget, sir. A man with his background isn't easily going to break the law.'

Govern eased the car down the one-way street leading into the town centre and parked it in a vacant spot outside an Indian restaurant.

'Supper first, I think, David, and then we'll go and see what your policeman has to say for himself. I take in what you say but it wouldn't be the first time one of us has gone off the rails, when sufficiently provoked.'

Beck grinned as he got out of the car and went round to open the door for his boss. 'Can't see you suddenly going berserk in your old age, sir!' he said.

Govern shook his head. 'Anything is possible where human nature is concerned, Beck, my boy! You should know that by now. Remember the old girl with the batty sister who lived in Miller's Lane? You would have bet your very life she wasn't responsible for all those murders. No, everyone is a possibility, Beck, even you – given enough incentive.'

Once in the restaurant with large glasses of cold beer and a curry steaming in front of them, Govern pursued the subject.

'Imagine you have a much-loved child – a dog, even – and you are out in the country shooting pigeons when a car comes tearing down the lane and runs over your child, seriously injuring it. The driver doesn't stop but you take his car number. Later that day, you see his car outside a pub and you go inside and hear him boasting about how he never bothers about speed restrictions and it's bad luck if anyone gets in his way. You have just been told that your child has died. You still have your shotgun in your car and he comes out of the pub obviously the worse for wear and you tell him he's killed your child. He shrugs his shoulders and says that's your worry, not his. Now, the gun is in your hands, loaded but broken. Don't you think you might snap it shut and fire it at him? Don't you think that at that moment all you want to do is to blast him off the face of the earth?'

Beck nodded. 'OK, I take your argument, but that's not premeditated murder. If we are considering White as Mr Lewis's killer, he would have had to go down to Brighton with the express purpose of bumping him off. In other words, in cold blood.'

Govern pushed the bowl of mango chutney in front of Beck saying: 'Do you know, David, at times like this, I'm encouraged to put you forward for promotion again.' Still smiling, he added: 'You are quite right, of course, but I shall still want to know where Mr Peter White was on Sunday afternoon and if there was some other reason, of which we are presently unaware, that he might have thrown caution and his police training to the winds and decided to shoot the man.'

Beck nodded his head in agreement. 'Everything we've found out so far, sir, leads one to think there are a great many people who will not be shedding tears at Lewis's funeral.'

'Maybe not, but someone somewhere may have loved the bloke,' Govern said thoughtfully.

'His mistress? A lover?' Beck suggested. 'But if they loved him, why bump him off?'

'How should I know?' Govern replied. 'But Lewis was by all accounts being unfaithful to his wife and she has the private detective's report to prove it. That female is next on our visiting list once we have seen and eliminated ex-police constable White. Now eat your supper, David, and stop asking questions so I can eat mine. OK?'

'Yes, sir!' Beck said, and helped himself liberally to the mango chutney.

NINETEEN

'How much longer do you think it will be, Inspector – before we can have the funeral, I mean?'

Govern looked at Althea's pale drawn face and thought how much she had aged in these last few days.

'I came to tell you that we can now release your husband's body so you may make arrangements for the cremation as soon as you wish,' he said. As he followed her into the drawing room, Althea corrected him.

'Geoffrey specified in his will that he was to be buried, not cremated,' she told him, her voice steady as she added: 'He used to say whenever the subject came up that absolutely no way was he going to be incinerated!'

A log fire was burning cheerfully in the wrought-iron basket and despite the early morning hour a standard lamp lent a soft glow to the room. Govern had not really had the time or the interest to look around him on his previous visit to the Lewises' house, but now, remembering Laurence Ingram's nostalgic references to his family home, he understood why the old man had felt so bitter at losing it. Would Mrs Lewis leave her home once the funeral was over? he wondered. No doubt about the fact that her husband would have left her very well provided for – unless, of course, he had left all his money to the mistress he and Beck were now trying to locate!

Chiding himself for a thought more attributable to Beck than to himself, he explained: 'I'm afraid we're no nearer finding the person who shot your husband: we have been able to eliminate several suspects but so far we have been unable to locate the clairvoyant. There were others seen going into Mr Lewis's office that afternoon so it seems unlikely Madame Tokoly was the killer; but she forecast disaster of some kind, which does seem to indicate that she knew more than we know.'

Althea shook her head. 'None of it makes any sense to me,' she said. 'I know Geoff must have had enemies, but Cressy and I have been through every one of his papers and there isn't a single threatening letter, only . . .'

'Only what, Mrs Lewis? Any information you can give me may help.'

'Well, there was a nasty letter from Mr White, Susie's father, warning Geoff not even to speak to his daughter again.'

'I have eliminated him, Mrs Lewis,' Govern said. 'He told me that he and his wife had been to Wakehurst Place, where there was a plant sale. They had purchased quite a few plants and had tea in the cafeteria so they could provide a satisfactory alibi.'

Althea sighed. 'I suppose being an ex-policeman, Peter White wasn't the most likely suspect, was he, Inspector? Even though Geoff frightened young Susie, he didn't actually harm her, so for her father to rush off and shoot Geoffrey would have been a bit extreme to say the least.' She drew a deep breath. 'I suppose poor old Laurence Ingram couldn't have gone a bit mad?'

'Mr Ingram did have a weapon as well as a motive for the murder, but the pistol was the wrong calibre. No, Mrs Lewis, I think we may have to look further afield and I wondered if you would be so kind as to let me see that report you received from the private detective you hired which you told me about last time I was here?'

Althea drew in her breath. 'You think Geoffrey's girl-friend . . . mistress . . . could be involved?' she asked. 'I gather he lavished gifts and money on her so I would not have expected her to kill the goose that was laying the golden eggs!'

Reminded sharply that Beck had once made the same remark about Lewis's wife, Govern was pleased to be able to put forward a different angle.

'I was wondering whether the lady was by any chance married?' he said. 'A jealous husband . . . or boyfriend. Perhaps . . .'

'She isn't married but there was – is – a boyfriend!

I didn't read the details about him too carefully as it was the woman I was interested in. My husband was going to set her up in a flat in London with a boutique below . . . to keep her occupied when he wasn't there, I presume.'

She was unable to keep the bitterness from her voice and to ease the moment, Govern suggested she go and find the detective's report. When she returned with a large envelope which she handed to him, she was once more in control of her emotions.

'I haven't offered you anything to drink,' she apologized. She gave a sudden unexpected smile as she added: 'Cressy is dropping in for coffee later and Mrs Clark has made one of her mouth-watering walnut cakes. Can I tempt you to try a piece?'

Her smile had instantly transformed her face so that it was possible suddenly to see for the second time what a stunningly pretty girl she must have been. Govern now told her that he had to meet his sergeant in half an hour at the police station when Sergeant Peterson was reporting on such information as had come in regarding the whereabouts of Madame Tokoly. So far, he told Althea as he stood up to leave, Interpol had none and the airports had proved equally sterile. The search had widened on the Internet channels with such details and limited description as they had of the woman. No one had been able to produce a photograph but with Miss Denton's and Miss Cruse's assistance, an artist had come up with a reasonable likeness. With the clairvoyant's flamboyant clothes and headscarf, the picture was quite arresting and Govern was hoping the officers manning the telephone line at the station would by now have had some replies of sightings. Promising to keep in close touch, he said he would relay any progress of significance he was making.

'Please don't feel you shouldn't talk about Geoff's mistress to me, Inspector,' she said as she walked with him to the front door. 'It won't distress me, I can assure you.' She pointed to the envelope, her expression cynical as she added: 'I can't believe there's anything more to find out; it's all detailed there including the boyfriend. She calls herself Scarlett but she was christened Tracey. Presumably that wasn't glamorous enough for her. Her adopted surname is Lauren – after Sophia Lauren, presumably!'

Seeing the slightly derisive smile on Althea's face, Govern too allowed himself to smile. He held out his hand and shook Althea's with real liking. Her life had been turned upside down and whatever had been the unhappy state of her marriage, her husband's sudden, violent death must have been a horrible shock. He admired her spirit and attitude, which was justifiably bitter but not revengeful.

'Please let me know when and where the funeral will take place,' he said. 'If you have no objection, I should like to be there.'

Althea opened the front door and suddenly liking the good-looking, grey-haired detective inspector, she told him she would be pleased to have his support at the interment and suggested he bring his sergeant with him.

'I don't suppose there will be many of us at the funeral,' she said, her voice bitter once more as she added: 'Geoff's so-called friends have disappeared into the woodwork ever since the word "murder" appeared on the scene. In fact, the only people who have sounded perfectly genuine in their condolences are Geoff's London secretary and his Brighton manageress. But of course, he knew very well how devoted those two spinsters were and treated them like the treasures they were.' She drew a deep sigh, smiled and apologized for detaining him.

'I'll see you at the funeral, Inspector!' she said and stood watching as he got into his car and disappeared down the drive.

Inspector Govern returned to the police station, where he spent the next half-hour perusing the investigator's report. The man had summed up with a conclusion that the girl, Scarlett, was only really interested in Mr Lewis because of his wealth and was no threat to Mr Lewis's marriage. As for the boyfriend, a third-rate waiter of Italian origins, he was all talk but without the backbone for action. Mr Lewis was far from being the first of Scarlett's admirers and in the past it suited him to turn a blind eye as he hadn't thought they threatened his relationship with the girl. However, he had discovered she'd attracted the attention of an older man (Mr Geoffrey Lewis) who wanted to set her up in London as his mistress. This was going too far, Sylvester had declared, and he meant to put a stop to it – pronto!

According to the investigator, Sylvester hadn't stated how he intended going about it, but one thing was certain – Scarlett was staying in Manchester with him.

So here was a possible suspect, Govern thought as he made his way next door where Beck was seated with a sheath of papers piled in front of him. He looked up as Govern entered the room.

'Reported sightings of Madame Tokoly!' he said pointing to the overflowing in-tray and grinning. 'Some have to be seen to be believed. Look at this one: "I saw a woman looking like the picture when I was coming back from Calais on the ferry last Christmas . . ." And here's another: "I'm fairly certain I saw the Gypsy going into one of the toilet cubicles in Harrods, but I'm not sure when it was as I shop there several times a week . . ." And another: "I stood next to the woman in the drawing in the underground on Thursday but I didn't see where she got off as the train was crowded. I thought she looked like a foreign immigrant or one of those flower-power people there used to be a lot of in the sixties. She definitely had gold earrings . . ."'

'As indeed do a possible ten per cent of the female population!' Govern said, sighing. 'Get someone else on to the job, Beck. You and I are off to Manchester.' He waved the envelope Althea had given him. 'Seems the boyfriend of our victim's mistress was well aware what was going on and knew who Lewis was. I've had a quick look through the detective's report Mrs Lewis gave me. The boyfriend's name is Sylvester Piccione, Italian. The chap had found out that Miss Scarlett Lauren was two-timing him and intended to put a stop to it.'

'Hot-blooded Latin, madly jealous? Sounds interesting!' Beck said, heaping the papers in front of him into two piles, 'Rubbish' and 'Further checks', and followed Govern out to the car park. 'Train or car, sir?' he asked. 'Manchester must be all of two hundred miles.'

'Train,' Govern said at once. 'We can take a taxi from the station to the hotel in Manchester where our Miss Scarlett Lauren is employed. If my plan works, we'll invite her to have dinner with us and bring along the boyfriend. We will be commercial travellers who've pulled off a good deal and have money to burn. You, my boy, will have to charm the young lady!'

Beck grinned as he climbed in behind the steering wheel. He really loved driving his boss's BMW even if it was only a mile or so to the train station; and it was not very often that the Inspector did not wish to drive himself. What had started out as a boring day, he thought as he exited the car park, was turning out to be quite an interesting one. He would enjoy flirting with Lewis's former mistress, who presumably was something of a babe.

By four o'clock they were in the hotel they'd discovered Lewis always stayed in when he was in Manchester on business. Having booked in and left their luggage in their rooms, they went back downstairs and located the boutique. As expected, they found Scarlett, looking very with it in a tiny white miniskirt, knee-high white leather boots and a pink low-necked shirt, which revealed half of her breasts. She greeted them with a genuine smile of pleasure.

'Not one person has been in here all afternoon,' she said in her Midlands-accented voice, 'so I'm all yours! What can I do for you, gentlemen?'

As arranged, Beck stepped forward, returning her smile.

'We've both come without razors, believe it or not!' he said. 'I don't suppose a ladies' boutique would stock such a thing but we thought we'd try.'

Scarlett twirled a tendril of hair with one finger and said: 'Well, sir, you happen to be in luck. It isn't the first time I've been asked for one so I keep a few for gentlemen like you who don't use electrics.'

As she went to get them from a drawer beneath her cash desk, she gave Beck another flirtatious smile.

'You've only just caught me!' she said. 'I close at six

and it's been so boring I thought I might shut up shop a bit earlier.' She handed Beck the razors and turned to stare at Inspector Govern.

'You both staying in the hotel?' she asked. 'It's usually pretty full but there aren't a lot of guests at the moment. This job's so boring when there aren't any people about.'

Inspector Govern now spoke up. 'Sounds like we're not going to have much company, then.' He paused, looking from Beck back to Scarlett. 'I suppose if you really are closing the place you wouldn't consider joining us for a drink at the bar?'

Catching on, Beck added: 'Yes, please do! We've only had each other to talk to all day and it would be really nice to have someone else, especially someone as pretty as you to look at!'

Scarlett seemed pleased with the compliment but shook her head.

'I'd love to but I can't. I'm meeting my boyfriend in ten minutes and – ' she giggled – 'he wouldn't be a bit pleased to find me in the bar with two good-looking fellows like yourselves.'

Only with difficulty did Govern conceal his delight at this piece of information. 'Tell you what,' he said, 'why don't we include your boyfriend in the party? I mean, conversation is always easier if there are four not three.'

Scarlett looked more than a little surprised. 'D'you really mean that?' she asked. Most of the men who chatted her up – and there were always a few every week – were expecting, or hoping, for a lot more than her conversation. It was quite flattering to have these two well-dressed, obviously educated southerners so keen to have her company they were willing to include Sylvester. She could do with a change from *his* company. Ever since he had found out about Geoff, he'd been furiously jealous, then surly, then abusive, calling her a 'cheating little tart'. It wasn't as if he'd discovered she spent the night with Geoff from time to time. She'd always told him those nights had been 'sleep-overs' with one of her hypothetical girlfriends. It was when that horrid little London chap had come sneaking round their place asking questions about the flat and boutique Geoff had wanted to get her that she'd been obliged to confess to Squid that she'd had what she called 'a wealthy admirer'. Squid had been quite insanely jealous, even though she'd sworn she never meant to accept Geoff's offer; that she had only been playing him along, and that Sylvester was the only man she loved.

'Best not invite my boyfriend!' she said. 'Ever since he found out . . . well, that there was another fellow here in the hotel who used to chat me up, he's been trying to make me give up my job here, and I'm not going to. He's ever so jealous! I'll text him and say I've got to stay open a while longer.'

As she led them towards the hotel bar, Govern and his sergeant looked at one another with surprised satisfaction. The young woman's verbosity was exactly what they needed. When they were seated at a quiet table with their drinks in front of them, Govern said casually:

'Did you see in the paper about that man who got shot last Sunday? They said he often used to come to Manchester on business. What was his name, David? Very wealthy chap!'

Beck looked vague. 'Do you mean the estate agent? Lewin, wasn't it? Or was it Lewis?'

Ignoring Scarlett's sharp intake of breath, Govern said casually: 'That's right! Geoffrey Lewis. Tall, good-looking chap.' Noting the look on Scarlett's pretty face, he realized she had been unaware of Lewis's death and she was now looking at each of them, her expression shocked as she asked:

'Was he . . . was he . . . is he . . . dead?' she stammered.

When Govern affirmed the fact, Scarlett downed the remains of her drink and nodded when Beck offered to get her a second one.

'Bloody hell!' she said, and a moment later: 'But why? I mean who topped him? OK, so he was a bit of a lech, but . . . well, he was always very nice to me.'

'Oh, you knew him?' Govern asked innocently as Beck returned with the drinks. 'Guess what, David, Scarlett actually knew that chap in Brighton who was shot.'

'Did you really?' Beck commented. 'What a coincidence! Did you know him well?'

The colour returning to her cheeks, Scarlett now began to take pleasure in the interest these two pleasant companions were showing in her association with Geoff. Now that she was over the first shock she was beginning to feel a certain amount of relief that she wouldn't have to think up any more excuses for not going to London. No need to tell them about *that* little plan of Geoff's.

'He used to stay here in the hotel when he was up on business,' she said. 'He always looked in on the boutique and sometimes I used to stay after work – same as I'm doing today – and he'd buy me a drink. He was always very . . . well, friendly like . . . well, like he fancied me.'

Govern saw his chance to widen the discussion. 'Wasn't your boyfriend jealous?' he asked. 'Most men with a girl-friend as attractive as you wouldn't want them drinking alone with another man.'

Scarlett rose quickly to the bait. Smiling mischievously at Govern, she said: 'Sylvester – that's my boyfriend – didn't know . . . I mean, that I wasn't staying with a girl-friend like I said. We live together, you see. He works week-days like me, but being a waiter, he works evenings, too. So it's weekends we have most time together.'

Once again, Govern saw his chance to establish the Italian's whereabouts on the day Lewis was killed.

'Do you mean he gets *every* weekend off?' he asked.

'The restaurant where he works is closed Saturdays and Sundays,' Scarlett explained. 'The owner's funny about that but Squid, my boyfriend, says he makes enough money in the week and he wants time with his family.'

'Lucky chap!' Govern commented. 'So what do you do with yourselves at weekends?'

'Saturdays we shop in the morning and watch football after lunch; and Sundays, well . . . we get up late, you know!' She gave a little giggle. 'Then we go to the gym. I like it there, especially the pool, and Squid's a fitness fanatic.'

'You mean *every* weekend?' Govern prompted.

Scarlett nodded. 'Sometimes on Saturdays if it's a match

he doesn't much want to watch, we go to the ice rink. Squid's ever such a good skater! And I've got a smashing outfit – it's a lovely jade green with white fur round the neck . . . well . . .' She broke off giggling as she outlined a bare inch above her breasts.

'Bet you look really smart in that!' Beck said, and following Govern's lead, he added: 'Do you really work out *every* Sunday?'

Scarlett nodded emphatically. 'Too true! The only time I can remember Squid ever missing a gym was when he got flu last year. I don't mind. It's fun there and – ' she gave a wicked little smile –'the instructor's ever so keen to help me!'

'Which I can quite believe!' Beck said genuinely.

They had a third round of drinks and made no demur when Scarlett said she really must leave them. Only as she rose to go did she make a further reference to Geoffrey Lewis's death.

'I can't wait to tell Squid about Mr Lewis,' she said. 'He'll be over the moon, although I shouldn't say that, should I? Just think, while we were having ourselves a good time at the gym, someone went and shot him! Do you know who it was?'

'I don't think they've found that out yet – at least, there's not been anything in the papers!' Beck said as he followed Scarlett out to the foyer. 'We shall have to look out for you next time we come to Manchester. Maybe you and Sylvester will come and have a meal with us?'

'Cool!' Scarlett replied with a beaming smile. 'Next time, maybe you won't have your father with you and we can leave Squid at home!'

'Cool!' Beck replied, hardly able to contain his impatience to get back to his boss and address him as 'Papa'.

TWENTY

It was a bitterly cold November afternoon and the rain was driving across the porch as the funeral procession emerged from the doorway of Hurston Green church. One by one the mourners struggled to open their umbrellas, but the pall-bearers had no recourse but to bow their heads as they made their way slowly across the sodden grass towards the newly dug grave.

A gust of wind blew the solitary wreath from the top of the coffin and sent the circlet of chrysanthemums bowling across the old moss-covered gravestones into the base of a dripping yew tree. The men's black shoes squelched in the wet turf and the women tried not to stumble as their high heels dug deep into the earth, unbalancing them. Suddenly, the vicar's cassock blew over his head, startling him so that he dropped his prayer book. The two churchwardens hurried over to help him, one to retrieve the holy book and the other to readjust his cassock.

'I don't imagine many of the mourners are actually mourning this final chapter of Geoffrey Lewis's life,' Detective Inspector Govern said in a low voice to his companion. 'Presumably most of them are his employees or his work contacts.' The widow, Mrs Althea Lewis, was present, he presumed from a sense of duty, and Miss Cressida Cruse as an act of friendship. Mrs Clark the housekeeper was, perhaps, genuinely sad to say farewell to her late master as, quite possibly, were Lewis's two elderly female employees, one in a dark grey overcoat, the other in funereal black. His glance went to the couple behind the two women. With Althea's list of names of those intending to be present, he judged the middle-aged man and woman to be the Pearsons. The secretary of Lewis's golf club was among the few mourners. There was no sign of Laurence Ingram nor the Whites, which was not unexpected, but he was surprised that the boy, Daryl, was not among the small column of figures following the pall-bearers. Surprisingly, however, his father was.

'Why would Mr Hutchins come here today?' Beck, who had also recognized him, muttered in a low tone. 'Glad to see the last of the man who stole his wife?'

'More to support his ex-wife is my guess!' Govern said. He was watching as Terence hurried to Althea's side when her large golf umbrella suddenly blew inside out, and held his own over hers and Cressida's heads.

As the mourners stood in a circle around the sodden, fake emerald-green grass carpet covering the earth that had been extricated from the grave, they were silent as the six men carrying the coffin lowered it thankfully to the ground on top of the ropes with which they were about to lower it into the gaping hole. Each of them was attempting to wipe the streams of rain from his face. The vicar, his cassock now billowing around him, stepped forward and motioned them to proceed, his voice barely audible over the wind as he intoned:

'Man that is born of a woman hath but a short time to live and is full of misery . . .' His words were more guessed at than heard by Beck, who said in an aside to Govern: 'Hardly think Lewis's life was "full of misery"!'

Before Govern could reply, the pall-bearers started to lower the coffin into the grave. It was then, shockingly, a loud splash could be heard and a shower of the rainwater, which had been gathering all night, sprayed from the hole on to the grass covering the pall-bearers and the vicar's feet.

The vicar glanced anxiously at his shoes as he continued to intone: 'We therefore commit his body to the ground: earth to earth, ashes to ashes, dust to dust.'

Althea stepped forward and holding out her arm, dropped a single chrysanthemum on to the coffin. Simultaneously, the rain suddenly stopped and a burst of sunshine lit up the scene.

As the mourners made their way back to the cars parked in the road outside the church, the gravedigger removed the turf carpet and started to shovel the mound of earth on to the coffin. Govern and Beck had almost reached the BMW when Beck said: 'Sorry, sir, but I think I must have left my mobile on the pew in the church. I took it out of my pocket to make sure it was switched off and I can't have put it back. I'll nip back and get it.'

Govern look ruefully at the sky which had now darkened once more and a few drops of rain fell on his outstretched hand.

'I suppose I'd better come with you,' he said. 'It's going to pour again at any minute and since you forgot to bring yours, we have only *my* umbrella!'

Taking the rebuke as deserved, Beck hurried up the path and disappeared into the church. Govern stood watching the cars disappearing down the road when his eye was caught by a taxi pulling to a halt outside the lych-gate. It was now teeming with rain and he quickly took cover beneath the porch. Curious to see who this late arrival might be, he drew back into the shadows. Even through the rain, he was able to see that the newcomer was a woman, wearing, of all things, a black old-fashioned floor-length coat and a black hat from the brim of which hung a black veil covering her face. She was bent almost double as very slowly, with the aid of a walking stick, seemingly oblivious to the rain, she made her way towards the new grave. The gravedigger moved tactfully to one side as she approached.

Govern now urged Beck to follow him and, on the pretext that they were visiting a grave in the vicinity of Lewis's, they continued to observe the newcomer. She was standing quite still, staring down into the half-filled grave and, as far as could be judged, was saying a prayer for the deceased. But suddenly, without warning, she reached into the soft black leather handbag she was carrying, took an object from it and threw it into the grave. Without turning to see if anyone was watching her, she leaned forward and with her walking stick agitated the loose soil onto the coffin. Only then did she look round, her movements so stiff and slow Govern and Beck were able to turn their heads quickly back to the unknown gravestone they were supposedly inspecting.

Reassured that the two men were not interested in her activities, the latecomer took one long last look into the grave and then, moving slowly and with seeming difficulty, she made her way slowly back to the waiting taxi. The moment it moved off, Govern hurried to the graveside and stared down at the earth covering the coffin. Then he beckoned to the gravedigger and produced his identity card.

'That woman threw something into the grave and covered it up,' he said. 'Will you please find it and give it to me – as quickly as you can!' He turned to Beck. 'Go and get the car started, Beck and bring it up to the entrance.'

The tone of his boss's voice was such that Beck knew this was not the time to start asking questions. He hurried to carry out Govern's instructions. Within minutes, Govern had joined him by the car. He was holding his black city-type umbrella in one hand and in the other a small object around which he had tied a large, clean white handkerchief.

'Where to, sir?' Beck asked.

Govern frowned. 'Unfortunately I'm none too sure. That woman was in a Brighton taxi – I noticed the unmistakeable logo on the side. You know the one – two swifts chasing each other across a blue sky? If we're very lucky, we might catch up with it before we get to Brighton. I don't imagine it would be travelling very fast – that woman looked either very old or very ill.'

'Failing which I can find out from Swift's Car Hire who it was who booked a taxi to Hurston Green,' Beck said cheerfully. 'It's not very likely that the passenger hailed the driver on the street, so he must have an address where he picked her up. Can I ask what you're holding so carefully, sir?'

'Well, don't turn to look at it when I tell you, David,' Govern said, his quiet tone not quite concealing the underlying excitement. 'A gun – a .38 calibre revolver. Whoever that woman is, she's our murderer – or should I say murderess. Forensic will confirm it. And I'll hazard a guess that she isn't a young woman but a very elderly one.'

'You mean because she was wearing those old-fashioned mourning clothes?' Beck asked.

'Yes! It must be nearly a hundred years since women went to funerals attired like that. Let's suppose she is in her nineties – it would explain the clothes as well as her frailty, but do women of that age go round shooting people? No, they don't! Yet this one, if it was she who owned the gun she threw into the grave, chose not to attend the actual funeral – just as if she didn't want to be recognized.'

'Maybe she was Lewis's illegitimate grandmother!' Beck suggested with a grin. 'I mean suppose her daughter, Lewis's mother, had an illegitimate son who she was so ashamed of she wanted to kill him.'

'For pity's sake, David, stop making such idiotic suggestions. Anyone would think you'd been reading one of those twopenny-halfpenny women's novelettes. And don't try and pass the van, Beck. You may be driving my car but it's still a police car while we're on duty!'

As the inspector had feared, they were unable to overtake the hired taxi and as they turned off Dyke Road into West Street, Govern redirected Beck to the back street where Swifts Car Hire firm was located. Once there, a quick glance at the noticeboard established that the driver who had been sent on the Hurston Green trip had not yet returned to base.

'We can try and locate him on the radio, Inspector,' the girl at the desk suggested. 'But reception is very bad round here – a lot of interference, but I will try if you like.' She looked up at the board. 'Says he was to collect the caller from Aven Osp, so that's probably where he's taken his passenger back.'

Govern and Beck looked at one another before repeating in unison: 'Aven Osp?'

The girl behind the desk stifled a giggle. 'That's Bill's shorthand,' she said. 'Never does pronounce his h's so that's how he spells Haven Hospice. That's where he was to pick his passenger up.'

For a moment, Govern did not speak. The very last place he had expected his suspect to be was at a hospice. Was the woman one of the staff? On the other hand, the figure at the graveyard had looked unnaturally frail.

'Montgomery Street!' the girl said knowledgeably.

'Overlooks the sea about a quarter of a mile along Kings Cliff, but you're welcome to wait till Bill gets back.'

Govern declined the offer and, thanking the girl for her assistance, hurried back with Beck to his car.

'Haven Hospice!' he ordered unnecessarily. 'Believe it or not, my boy, I think we are going to find our murderer there.'

'As good a place to hide out as any, I suppose,' Beck replied. 'Maybe she's one of those nurses you read about who get a kick out of bumping off the elderly.'

'If that were the case, she wouldn't have to look for victims elsewhere!' Govern replied brusquely. 'What possible reason could a nurse have for eliminating Mr Geoffrey Lewis?'

'Well, maybe he'd found out somehow that she'd over-dosed his grandmother!' Beck replied as he negotiated a roundabout.

'Yes, and maybe you're secretly writing the next Harry Potter!' Govern said sharply. 'And take a sharp left here, Beck. I think that building on the corner may be the hospice.'

As always when Govern sensed he was close to his quarry, his heart beat a fraction faster and unaware that he was doing so, he started playing with the gold signet ring on his little finger. Seeing the familiar sign, Beck held his breath as they waited for the nurse who opened the door to them to reply to Govern's request to see the person who had just returned in a taxi.

'I'm sorry,' she replied at once, 'but we don't allow visitors after four o'clock – unless they are family.' She got no further before Govern produced his identity card.

'I'm afraid on this occasion I have to insist upon seeing the lady,' he said firmly. 'It is a police matter!'

As he spoke, a more mature-looking woman came up to the group and in a voice which brooked no argument, said firmly: 'In this instance, Inspector, the law will not be able to take precedence. The patient you wish to see is very ill. She collapsed on her return half an hour ago. The doctor is with her and she is barely conscious. May

I suggest you return tomorrow morning? Hopefully she will have recovered sufficiently for you to see her then, although I can't promise it. She is *very* ill!'

It was one of the few times in his life that Beck had ever seen his boss looking uncertain. After a full minute, Govern spoke.

'Very well, Sister! It is Sister I am speaking to? I'm sorry your patient is ill but I do have to speak to her on a very serious matter; so serious I shall have to send round a constable to sit outside your patient's door.'

The sister's expression was now one of extreme irony. 'I don't think you understand, Inspector, that our patients are all terminally ill. To put it bluntly, all our patients come here to die. I can assure you, your witness – if such she is – would be unable to disappear however much she might wish to do so.'

Govern looked undisturbed by the reproach. 'She managed to hire a taxi to take her all the way to Hurston Green today!' he said. 'And she is not a witness but a very real murder suspect.'

The woman looked momentarily shocked and then said: 'The doctor told Miss Jakes this morning that on no account should she leave the hospice,' she said, 'but she was determined to go to her friend's funeral. As she said to Dr Phillips, it didn't matter if the trip did kill her since she was going to die shortly anyway.'

Govern sighed. 'I'm sorry to hear that, but it is my job to carry out these enquiries even if it may seem cruel for me to do so. I hope you understand that, Sister. However, I will wait until tomorrow morning to see your patient. What did you say her name is, by the way?'

'Marianne Jakes! Miss. She's a retired schoolteacher; taught drama, I believe, or perhaps it was art. Which reminds me, Staff-nurse, did anyone deliver that bag of clothes Miss Jakes wanted taking to one of the charity shops? She was so insistent when she left this morning that it would be done but we've all been so busy – two deaths, you see, and a new patient arriving this evening.'

'I'm sorry but the bag is still in the hall,' the nurse said.

'I'd drop it in on my way home but the charity shops will have shut long before seven.'

'We'll do it!' Govern said quickly. 'It's no trouble. I insist!'

'Very well, Inspector. Miss Jakes will be happy to hear they've gone, if she recovers her faculties, that is.'

Five minutes later, the BMW was parked outside the aquarium in view of the Palace Pier and Govern took the plastic bag from the back seat and proceeded to untie the string securing the contents.

At first, it seemed as if the mysterious Miss Jakes had done no more than discard a lot of old, if colourful garments; but further down, in a voluminous scarlet Indian cloth skirt, Beck noticed what he feared at first was an animal, but as, he cautiously dragged it clear of the scarf encircling it, they were both able to see that it was a wig. Even further down in the pile was a black box sealed with Sellotape. The lid was all but covered by writing in black ink saying 'PRIVATE – TO BE INCINERATED AFTER MY DEATH'.

'Obviously this got into the charity bag by mistake,' Govern commented dryly, and ordered Beck to open it. On doing so, Beck described the contents as an elaborate mixture of beauty products.

'No, not beauty aids – theatrical aids!' Govern said, his hands searching feverishly for what he was now certain he would find – a little tooled-leather jewel box containing two large gold drop earrings; and a box containing a pack of cards.

As Govern removed the pack from their box, Beck gasped.

'Tarot cards!' he said, his voice hoarse with excitement. 'It's her, isn't it, sir? It's the Gypsy, Madame Tokoly. These are her things.'

For a moment, Govern did not speak. Then he said quietly: 'No, David, not Madame Tokoly's but the woman who masqueraded as the clairvoyant. See, these are her disguises, her clothes, her wig, her make-up and even . . .' He opened a tinier plastic box at the bottom of the black box. 'Even contact lenses to change her eye colour.'

'No wonder there were no sightings of her!' Beck

commented. 'So all this belongs to Marianne Jakes, the schoolteacher!'

'No!' Govern said sharply. 'Not the schoolteacher, Beck, but the drama teacher. Remember the sister – or was it the nurse – saying she taught drama? That's who we should have been looking for all this time – someone clever enough to disguise herself so well that no one would recognize her, least of all her victim. Now all we have to do to wrap this case up is find out why Miss Marianne Jakes wanted Geoffrey Lewis dead.'

Beck, who was now holding the box on his lap, took a deep breath.

'I don't think we need to look far, sir,' he said. 'I think we may find out all we want to know from these,' and he held out a bundle of letters, a faded photograph of a man and woman embracing on a holiday beach; a theatre programme across which was written in black felt pen: '*15th June – Miracle Day, my 18th birthday*' and in capital letters: '*I'VE FALLEN IN LOVE!*' Lastly, there was a large journal, which Govern put in his briefcase to read later that evening.

'I'll hazard a guess we have all the answers here, David,' he said quietly. 'If Miss Jakes's first love was Geoffrey Lewis and he married someone else, a woman scorned is always a possible suspect for murder. Back to base now, David, and get this lot into safe-keeping.'

Replacing the box and the clothes carefully back inside the bag, Beck put it on the back seat, knowing that when he handed it in at the station every item would be labelled as evidence to be used in the future trial.

'When we get back,' Govern said, 'you are to find out what you can about our teacher, alias Madame Tokoly. Tomorrow morning, eight-thirty sharp, we go to the Haven Hospice and hopefully get a confession from Miss Marianne Jakes.'

TWENTY-ONE

Only rarely had Detective Sergeant Beck ever seen his boss's face register his emotions but now he looked deeply shocked as the matron notified him Miss Jakes had died at four o'clock that morning.

'I had one of the nurses ring you at the police station about half-past eight,' she told him, 'but she was informed you had already left. Perhaps you and your sergeant would like to come to the visitors' room and I will answer such questions you may have as best I can.'

Silently, they followed the matron into the pleasantly furnished comfortable visitors' room where, despite the early hour of the morning, a vase of fresh-looking flowers had been placed on the mantelpiece.

Having seated herself opposite the two men, the matron said: 'I see you were not anticipating Miss Jakes's death to occur so soon; but she was very, very ill. She had cancer, you see. When you saw her yesterday, she was quite heavily dosed with painkillers – the maximum the doctor would prescribe; but she was determined to go to the funeral. I wanted someone to go with her but we couldn't spare one of the nurses and sadly, she did not seem to have any relatives or friends. It's always sad when there's no one but a nurse at the bedside when a patient is dying.'

Govern had now regained his voice. 'I'm sorry to have to say this, Matron, but it seems certain the late Miss Jakes was involved in a murder we are investigating, so you see this is a very serious matter and I do have to acquire such information about her as I can.'

It was now the matron's turn to look shocked, but she said: 'Of course, Inspector, although I have to say we all found Miss Jakes a very sweet, gentle person – reserved, of course, but very brave. She never complained, however poorly she was. How can I help?'

'For a start,' Govern replied, 'do you have Miss Jakes's home address?'

The woman hesitated, her expression agitated as she seemed unwilling to speak. Finally she said: 'I gave Miss Jakes my solemn promise that I would not reveal what she told me. She even made me swear it on her Bible. But I suppose in this instance . . .' She paused before finally blurting out:

'Her real name wasn't Marianne Jakes. It's Phoebe Denton. She was an actress who was quite well known down here so she didn't want any of her fans to see her when the chemotherapy caused the loss of all her hair. That was last spring, when she first came to see us. She did have an operation but the cancer returned and eventually there was nothing more the doctors could do for her. They gave her six months. She was living by herself in a flat in Worthing but inevitably she became too ill to stay there on her own. She was in hospital for a while and then when she knew the end was near, she came to us.'

As neither Govern nor Beck spoke, she added: 'I see death here nearly every day, Inspector, and our aim at this hospice is to make it as painless as possible for the patients as well as for their loved ones; but it is always sad when a patient has no one but a member of our staff with them. Miss Jakes would not allow me to notify anyone at all, so of course we obeyed her last wishes.'

Govern decided that it was not the right moment to tell this caring member of staff that the patient she pitied was without doubt a murderess. Not only had the forensics department matched the bullets to the revolver, but Phoebe Denton had written what amounted to a confession in her journal. He had read the sad tale of her life late into the evening, and it struck him quite forcibly now that death itself was not always unwelcome or sad. The unhappy woman would not have to face a murder trial – a likelihood she had realized when she'd left it to the last few weeks of her life to kill Geoffrey Lewis. He was reminded of the elderly woman who had killed three of her neighbours in Miller's Lane but died of a heart attack before she could be taken to court.

Since the matron had little more she could tell him and he had in his possession all the evidence he needed, Govern decided to return to the station to write up his report. It would take him some time, and when he had finished, he would make up his mind whether or not it was an appropriate time to go and tell the dead man's widow that one of her best friends had killed her husband.

Unexpectedly Detective Sergeant Beck had a lump in his throat as later that day he read the journal and perused the contents of the box containing what amounted to the story of Phoebe Denton's life. At the start of her career as an actress, at the age of eighteen, she'd had no more than a sentence to speak as a parlour maid. She had never fallen in love until ten years later, not only had it been her birthday but what she described as '*an astonishingly handsome man*' was waiting for her at the stage door wanting to take her out to dinner. Geoffrey Lewis, her first and (she had then believed) everlasting love.

'*For the next five years he was my lover!*' she had written.

Although it was late afternoon when Beck read that sentence in the dead woman's journal, he was compelled to read on, ignoring the paperwork waiting for him, to discover why she had ultimately killed the man she loved.

It seemed that although unmarried, Lewis told her he would not allow her to commit herself to marriage until she was much older. She'd been too deeply in love to bother about the delay. Her ambition to become a stage star now took second place whenever Geoffrey promised a whole week instead of the occasional weekend or night together. Then she would not even attempt to audition for the part in a play that would mean her missing the all too precious time with her lover. They shared idyllic holidays abroad, which left her devastated when they returned home and he disappeared once more 'on business'.

Far too inexperienced in those early years in the ways of the world, she never suspected that Geoff was frequently unfaithful to her. Even when her more worldly actress friends warned her not to trust so casual a lover, she closed her mind to any doubts or warnings they implied. He said he loved her to the exclusion of any other woman and she believed him.

If there was any cloud shadowing her happiness, it was that he refused to allow her to introduce him to her two best friends, Althea and Cressida, who were like family to her.

As far as Phoebe had been aware, Geoffrey had no further knowledge of them than their names and occupations. Suddenly, without a hint of warning, he dropped the bombshell that he was going to marry Althea; Al, who was already married to the young farmer who was her own first admirer, Terence Hutchins. She had been as ignorant of the fact that Geoff and Al had been seeing one another as Al was of the fact that she and Geoff were lovers. She had kept her promise to Geoff never to tell anyone about their relationship because, he'd explained vaguely, people might put pressure on them to get married and that would be far from ideal while they were both trying to get established in their careers.

It wasn't a valid reason but Phoebe, as she admitted in her journal, was too deeply infatuated to refuse Geoff any request or even to question why he made them. She wrote:

> I absolutely ADORED him. I was so naive. I even wanted to kill myself when he told me about Al. He said he wasn't in love with her – I was the only person he loved – but he needed Al as a hostess to run his house and entertain his important business friends. If I couldn't accept it, we would have to end our relationship.

What an utterly despicable character! Beck thought as he turned the page. If anyone deserved to die, Geoffrey Lewis did!

> Of course, Al had no idea about Geoff and me. I decided it wouldn't be fair to her for us to go on meeting, so I told him I didn't want to see him any more. He was more angry with me than sad! Every night I cried myself to sleep and tried to forget Geoff, going on tour as

often as I could. After he and Al were married, it wasn't always easy to find excuses not to accept Al's invitations to the Grange although I did meet her in London quite often. Once or twice when she or Cressy happened to say Geoff was abroad, I did go and visit them and darling Daryl. On two occasions, Geoff was there after all but he pretended we didn't know each other. I got away as soon as I could and went to see Terence. He told me he was still in love with Al and always would be so he would never marry again. I know how he feels – I could never love anyone but Geoff and although in a way I hate him now, I do still want to be with him quite desperately . . .

At this point in her life, Phoebe had discarded the unfinished journal and did not take up the story of her life until the following year when she began to write in it again. On the 15th of June in red ink was scrawled in capital letters:

MY BIRTHDAY AND THE MOST WONDERFUL SURPRISE I HAVE EVER HAD – GEOFF ARRIVED AT THE FLAT WITH A HUGE BUNCH OF RED ROSES AND A BOTTLE OF CHAMPAGNE. He'd never stopped loving me, he said, and he didn't want to go on any longer without me. He was devoted to Al but their sex life was almost non-existent as she didn't enjoy it and so they wouldn't be depriving Al of anything if they made love. On the contrary, if he could stop making demands on Al, she'd be a lot happier. I hope this is true! Geoff said if I was agreeable, we could go on seeing each other as we had before and because he knew I would never do or say anything to hurt Al, there would be no risk of her discovering he'd been unfaithful – something which might happen all to easily if I denied him as he was a man with a strong sexual appetite and another woman might not be so trustworthy as me and ruin Al's marriage.

'How can women fall for that ridiculous sort of coercion?'
Beck asked Govern when he came over to his desk. 'Phoebe
Denton was no longer an innocent girl. She must have
learned a bit about life from other actresses she met.
Couldn't she have seen his arguments were simply a way
of drawing her back into the net?'

'Obviously not!' Govern replied. He leafed through the
journal Beck returned to him and found, after a few blank
pages, across one page had been scrawled: '*IT'S ALL OVER.
I'M NEVER GOING TO SEE HIM AGAIN.*' On the next
page she accused Geoff of breaking her heart. Cressida had
told her Geoff had a girl in Manchester who he was planning to establish in a flat in London. '*HOW COULD HE!
HOW COULD HE! HOW COULD HE!*' was scrawled over
the page.

'So it's the old adage of there being no such fury as that
of a woman scorned,' Beck misquoted.

'Not quite!' Govern replied thoughtfully. 'Although that
probably did have some influence on what prompted her
to kill him. Read that very last page, David. I find it very
sad.'

Beck took the journal back from him and commenced to
read:

> 20th May. My nice oncologist told me today – as
> gently as he could – that neither the chemo nor the
> radiation or drugs have stopped the spread of the
> cancer. When I insisted on an answer, he said I might
> have until the end of the year at most. I suppose deep
> down inside I knew I wasn't going to get better, but
> being human, I hoped. I'm not all that frightened of
> death itself but I am scared of dying. I wish I had
> Cressy or Al with me. I know they would come but I
> dare not have them here as I can't be sure what I might
> say when the morphine kicks in. I never EVER want
> Al to know about Geoff and me. Besides, I have written
> to Geoff and told him how ill I am and asked him to
> come and see me. I just hope he won't be too shocked
> to see how thin and haggard I look. I know I'm being

silly but I would so, so love to have him hold me in his arms just once more before I die. I still love him, despite everything, and I pray he has just a little love left for me. Please, Geoff! Please come!

'But he never did!' Govern said. 'You know, David, people talk and write about broken hearts and mostly it's a load of rubbish, but I think Geoffrey Lewis did break Phoebe Denton's heart.'

'Do you think he lacked the will or the courage to go and see her, sir?' Beck asked. Govern shrugged.

'Both, probably. And it wasn't only the disappointment and his failure to turn up that I believe sent her over the edge of reason; it was that she finally had to face the fact that the man she had loved faithfully and solely for all her adult life was not worth one single hair of her head.'

'So she decided to kill him!'

Govern nodded. 'But not immediately. She must have realized she lacked the physical strength to do other than shoot him. She had her father's service revolver for that. But how to do it Lewis without her friend Althea finding out about her years of deception? She knew she could not escape discovery even if it happened after her death. She didn't want Althea to know the truth; so she thought up the idea of disguising herself as the clairvoyant, Madame Tokoly, illegal immigrant with no known address.'

'Which would have been easy for her as an actress,' Beck broke in. 'Wardrobes of costumes to choose from; wigs, although she probably had one of her own when she lost her hair with the chemotherapy.'

'That may have been the catalyst which prompted the idea of a disguise,' Govern agreed. 'Cosmetics – skilfully applied to make her appear different, older. And the contact lenses to change her own blue eyes to brown.'

'What about the voice?' Beck said. 'Surely one of her friends would have recognized her voice.'

'You don't have to be a particularly good actor to speak with a foreign accent, or a dialect. No, David, Miss Denton was able quite easily to pass herself off as Madame Tokoly.'

'But why the dire warnings to Lewis of pending disaster at the fête?' Beck said thoughtfully. 'Was she just wanting to frighten or torment him?'

Govern drew a deep sigh. 'It took me a while to find an answer to that,' he admitted. 'I think that was merely the trap. Don't forget, Lewis had declined to see her, but if she was to shoot him, she had to lure him to a place where she could carry out the act. She took a chance which paid off when she sent that last warning to his London office. He might so easily have put it in the shredder; but our Phoebe knew him; knew he was a man who always wanted positive answers to everything; knew he wouldn't be able to ignore the implied threat to his life. And her plan worked perfectly. She waited until she knew she'd not much longer to live, told the staff at the hospice that she had papers to see to at her flat and went there to change into her Tokoly get-up. Used her own car to get to Templeton House, shoot Lewis and go back to change her clothes once more then returned to the hospice.'

'It all adds up!' Beck agreed. 'She'd have brought her Gypsy outfit back to the hospice with her in case she needed it again for the funeral to which she must have made up her mind to go – a final goodbye.'

Govern nodded. 'And knowing there was a hue and cry to find Madame Tokoly, she chose old-fashioned widow's weeds in preference to Gypsy clothes for her visit to the funeral. It was her bad luck we saw her there and traced her back to the hospice.'

'Would she have got away with it, sir? I mean if we hadn't seen her throw the gun into the grave?'

'I doubt it, David!' Govern replied. 'The Tarot cards and clothes would have been dispersed by the charity shop they were supposed to go to, but they would have kept the journal and handed it in to the police, so there was something other than the clothes which could have connected Phoebe Denton to the fictitious clairvoyant. The journal, if true, proves beyond all doubt that Phoebe Denton had a very strong motive for killing Lewis.'

'How much will come out at the inquest – Lewis's inquest,

I mean?' Beck asked. 'Obviously it can't be "murder by persons unknown". It seems a shame his widow has to find out he'd been two-timing her with her best friend. And this Phoebe woman tried so hard to protect her from that knowledge.'

Govern was now looking thoughtful. 'There won't be a trial for Miss Denton now she's dead and there won't be an inquest as she died from natural causes,' he said, 'but she will be named at Lewis's inquest. That is unavoidable. However, there will be no need for details of their relationship to be established since we have what amounts to a straight confession of guilt.'

'So despite all Miss Denton's attempts to keep her on/off affair with Lewis a secret, Mrs Lewis will know about it. She's bound to put two and two together when she learns Miss Denton killed her husband.'

Govern frowned. 'I'm really sorry about that. In fact, you have given me an idea, David. I'm going to photocopy those journal entries and take them to show Mrs Lewis beforehand so it isn't too much of a shock at the inquest. I have a feeling she won't feel quite so bitter about her friend's betrayal when she reads them.'

'Bit unorthodox, isn't it, sir? I mean, is it OK to show evidence belonging to the police to a member of the public?'

A slow smile spread across Govern's face. He pointed to the journal.

'Just pop along to the photocopier, David, and make sure no one else reads the copies. You and I are the only people who will have read the journal's contents. While you are doing that, I shall telephone Mrs Lewis and tell her we are coming to see her with some news.'

An hour later, he and Beck were seated in the drawing room of Hurston Grange opposite Althea, who was sitting on the sofa with Cressida, who had her arm round her shoulders. Althea had the photocopies on her lap and was handing each page after reading it to Cressy. Once or twice, she gave a little gasp, and once Cressida murmured: 'Oh, no! Poor, poor Phebes!'

When the last page had been read, Althea replaced them one by one in a neat pile and handed them back. There were tears in her eyes as she looked up at the inspector and asked: 'Do these have to become public? It's not that I mind. I stopped loving my husband a long time ago. It's Phoebe; she wouldn't want her life story splashed over the media. I can just imagine it: FAKE CLAIRVOYANT GIVES TYCOON THE DEATH CARD BEFORE SHOOTING HIM DEAD!'

Beside her, Cressy muttered: 'Don't, Al! That's awful.' She looked across at the inspector thinking what a very kind man he had turned out to be – even warning her that he would be coming to see Al with bad news so she could be on hand to comfort her. Al, however, was remarkably calm.

'You may think it strange, Inspector Govern, but I don't blame Phoebe. Geoff was so good looking, so charming. I can quite see how easily Phebes was seduced by him. Eight years ago he seduced me – persuaded me to leave Terence. That must have been so awful for her. Her parents were dead and in a way, Cressy and I were her family; but she couldn't come to us for comfort.'

'We often wondered why she never found another boyfriend,' Cressida said. 'Al and I guessed she'd been having an affair – we thought with a married man. It's obvious now why she never let us meet him.'

Althea drew a deep sigh and shook her head.

'I suppose I should hate her for betraying me . . . I mean when she took Geoff back after he was married to me; but somehow I don't. I think she loved him far more than I ever did, and by then, I'm pretty certain he'd had other affairs – not to mention one-night stands. Geoff always wanted what wasn't his. I think he'd got away with it for so long that he started to become careless. That's when I hired that investigator to find out about that girl in Manchester who was his mistress. Despite her he even messed around with my son's school-age girlfriend. No, I'm not bitter about those . . .' She pointed to the photocopies Govern was holding. 'I don't blame Phoebe for killing Geoff. She was dying and he knew it but even then